THE VOYAGE OF CLARA BOWMAN

CHRONICLE OF THE SEEKERS: BOOK 1

MAKAYLA NIELSON
&
TRENNA MCMULLIN

I

Dedicated to:

Cadence, for being the opposite of useless
&
Elizabeth, for her passion

Contents

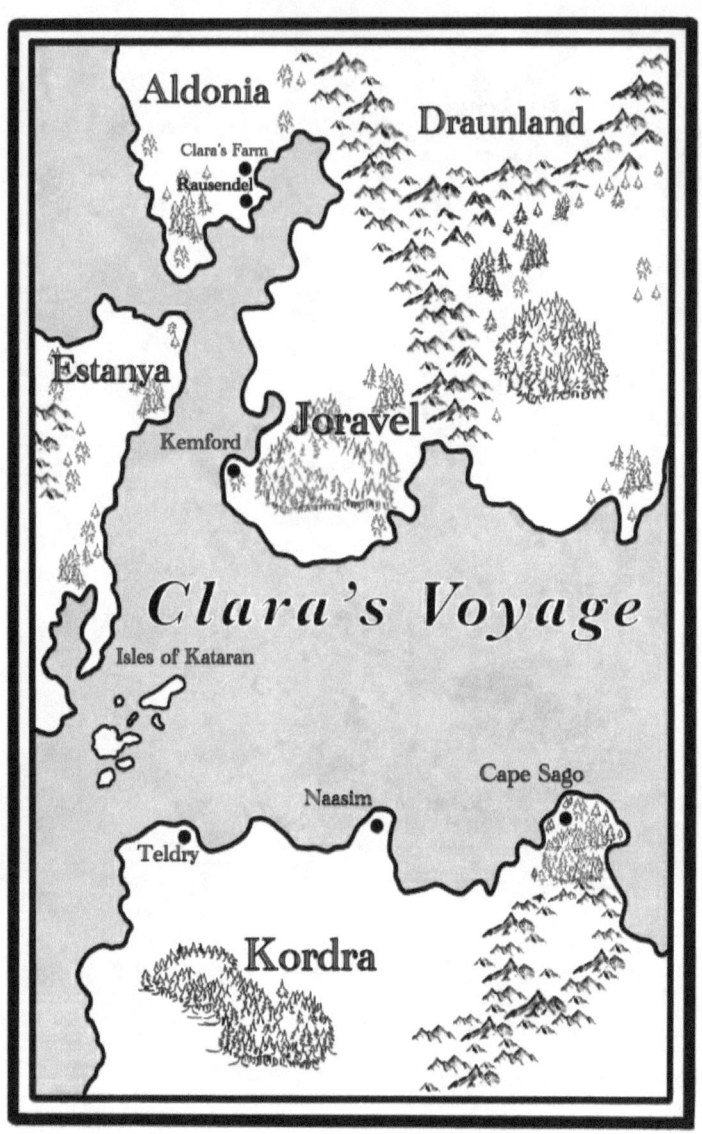

PROLOGUE

Somewhere in the jungle, Cape Sago,
38th year of the reign of King Aldus VII

A man lay prostrate in the bottom of a shallow canoe, feverish and muttering to himself. His two companions sat silently, one at his feet, one at his head. How long had he been here? His head ached and chills racked his body. He clutched his journal to his chest with shaking hands as he stared at the jungle canopy gliding by, eyes flickering back and forth. A trailing vine reached for their boat, and he cried out, thrashing.

"Lay still, doctor," the oarsman—a burly man with deeply tanned skin and copper hair shot through with gray —murmured. Despite his attempts to be soothing, his voice was tinged with fear.

The other passenger, a lanky teenage boy, huddled on the other side of the boat. The oarsman spoke again, and the sick man focused on the low, reassuring tones of the man's native tongue, struggling to decipher it. Anything to keep his mind off the pain.

"Time will heal this, Saanji. We have our lives. That is something to be grateful for. Let the dead rest."

The boy stared at him, rocking slowly back and forth, making the canoe wobble frightfully. His lips moved silently, forming the same word over and over.

On the shore, something green flickered through the leaves, a low buzzing momentarily overriding the other jungle sounds. The pain in his head increased, and the sick man cried out again. The oarsman began to mutter under his breath.

"The water protects us. The jungle enfolds us. We have trespassed beyond our privilege, and paid the price in blood. Grant us safe passage, so we may seek restitution beyond these borders." The cadence of his voice matched the stroke of his oars.

The vines retreated back into the trees as the oarsman repeated the chant. The sunlight made the leaves appear to glow. The sick man sighed and closed his eyes, clutching the book tighter, taking comfort in the familiar worn leather.

"Cursed," the boy whispered, voice shaking. "This place is cursed."

CHAPTER 1

❖

Persecution

C lara Bowman tilted her head back to feel the crisp autumn breeze, closing her eyes and taking a steadying breath. There was a slight tang of salt in the air, carried from the harbor miles away. There was also, unfortunately, the clatter of carts and cacophony of voices. She opened her eyes reluctantly and confronted the sounds.

Rausendel marketplace was bustling with people. The harvest had just come in and the stalls were overflowing with produce like winter squash and late season chard.

Clara gripped her skirts tightly with one hand as she edged her way past a group of men haggling over the price of a bushel of apples, then covered her nose as she passed a pen full of well-fed hogs ready to butcher and cure.

"Can we hurry and get this taken care of, Frederick?" she asked her cousin, a stocky, dark-haired boy a few years older than her own eighteen years.

"Don't like being around so many people, cuz?" he teased, pulling her to the side as a group of porters carrying heavy boxes on their shoulders plowed through the crowd.

She straightened her apron and tucked a lock of curly brown hair back behind her ear. Frederick tipped his hat to a group of women at a fabric stall on their right, and was rewarded with cold stares. Some of them even turned rather pointedly away.

"I'm not partial to being treated like I have the plague," she mumbled.

"It's not as bad as all that," Frederick said as they passed a jewelry stall. The shopkeeper stepped up beside his wares and watched them closely, not even bothering to hide his suspicion.

"Right," Clara murmured, casting her gaze downward to avoid the man's stare.

Frederick kept his eyes forward. "Regardless, you can't let it bother you. We have a right to believe what we want."

"Not for much longer if the rumors are true."

Frederick pursed his lips. Clara knew he agreed with her, even if he was trying to put on a brave face.

Up until last month Frederick had been courting a pretty girl who worked at the flower shop, then out of the blue she had cut all contact with him, saying her father had forbidden her from fraternizing with a Separatist. His story wasn't unusual either, they'd all lost friendships lately. She hadn't heard from the Hendersons in a month, and she used to watch their kids for an afternoon or two every week. "What is it about believing there's somewhere better out there that scares people so bad?" Clara wondered aloud.

Frederick shrugged. Clara hated feeling this way, but the marketplace made her nervous. Normally she saw the world as a wonderful, happy place. She knew it wasn't all sunshine and roses, but why dwell on the bad things if they just made you miserable?

They passed another fruit stall and she smiled. It had been a good harvest this year. The plums were big and juicy

4

looking. Maybe if they had enough left over after getting the necessities, she'd come back and purchase some. Plum jam was her favorite.

She glanced up and caught the gaze of the girl working there. The girl smiled back, then noticed Clara's amulet and her face took on a stony expression. Clara's smile faded and she looked down again. Even her normally sunny disposition couldn't withstand the constant barrage of judgment she felt from the people here. Between that and the worries about the law they were considering far away in the capital, she was struggling to keep her spirits up.

"This is it." Frederick stopped in front of a stall with a low brown tent pitched behind it. "You stay out here while I take care of payment and make arrangements for delivery. Then we can get the things Aunt Kate sent you for."

Clara nodded, standing beside the awning while her cousin said a few words to the boy out front and then went around back with the owner to secure the latest shipment of grain. They purchased regular lots from this merchant in order to help feed the poor families in her father's little congregation. It was far cheaper to purchase in bulk and store over the winter than to get a little at a time as people actually needed it.

The minutes passed and Clara pulled her shawl more tightly around her shoulders. Though the sun was hot overhead, the breeze carried with it the crisp hint of cooler weather to come. As she waited, she glanced idly at the nearby stalls, mentally running through the list of items her mother had asked her to get. If she could get them all from places nearby, they could be done sooner and get out of the market and away from the suspicious looks and murmured insults.

Separatists. That's what others called them, but they didn't want to be separate from the rest of the Church of the Divine. If forced to name themselves, they'd have chosen the term "Seekers". Her people believed this land they lived in was merely a stopping point—somewhere they'd been blessed to settle temporarily but not meant to linger in. Somewhere out there was a more perfect place for them, a valley where all life had originated, where the land could produce everything they needed to flourish and thrive. The Archdeacon called this blasphemy, he labeled them malcontents and encouraged others to shun them for implying that life here wasn't good enough. He'd even gotten the king on his side, and now Parliament was considering a law to ban their beliefs.

It was maddening. Part of her couldn't fathom how anyone could justify such a law, but the concerned whispers her father traded with the other men in their congregation seemed to indicate it was not only possible, but likely.

Frederick came back around the side of the tent, his lips drawn in a tight line and a stormcloud in his eyes.

"What is it?" Clara asked, "Is there something wrong with the grain?"

"Nothing wrong with the grain, just a whole lot wrong with the grain merchant!" Frederick muttered. "Issak wants twice what we paid him last time. Claims it costs more to deal with us, since it drives other customers away."

Clara shook her head. "Still think it's not as bad as all that?"

Frederick sighed. "I had to decrease our order. We can't afford to pay that much for grain, we're stretching our budget as it is with the repairs to the wagon and the extra help some families have needed... Come on, let's see if we can buy your things and get home."

Clara nodded, laying her hand on his arm and giving it a comforting squeeze. "We'll make things work somehow. Father can't be angry with you over this—and he's dealt with Issak for years. Maybe he can talk some sense into him."

They headed back down the line of stalls until they reached the textile merchant they'd passed earlier. Clara bargained with the owner for a bolt of muslin, arguing desperately when the woman named a price so high it might as well have been silk. She finally got the woman to accept a price that she could afford, though it was far higher than she had expected to pay. It looked like she wasn't going to be getting those plums.

"At this rate, I'll be lucky to get half the things we need," Clara muttered, looking at her list.

Frederick sighed and ran his finger beneath each item. "I'll go see if I can get the salt—Jode the butcher is sympathetic to us, he might be willing to purchase an extra bag with his own order and sell it to me at a reasonable cost."

Clara nodded as he moved off and continued to make her way down the line of stalls, arguing with shop owners and either paying exorbitant prices or deciding she would have to do without. In the middle of one such argument, she looked up and caught a man at the next booth watching her.

He was too well-dressed to be an average market-goer, in polished black boots, tan trousers, and a long, double-breasted suit jacket. The man he was in conversation with treated him with deference as well, nodding and motioning to his wares in the way that shopkeepers do when they know you have money. Clara looked down almost immediately, but she must've been distracted longer than she thought, because the shopkeeper she'd been arguing with was tapping her fingers impatiently on the block of wax they'd been haggling over.

"My family needs this and we can't afford to pay that kind of money," Clara pleaded, "Last year it was less than half that!"

"Circumstances change," the woman said harshly, "take it or leave it, but stop wasting my time." She moved away to straighten up some other products, keeping an eye on Clara.

Clara felt someone come up beside her. She glanced over and then lowered her gaze. It was the man who'd been watching her.

"Tough market today?" he asked, keeping his eyes on her. Clara pressed her lips together and nodded once, flushing from embarrassment. His voice had the slightest lilt to it, a foreign accent too faint to place. He was obviously a merchant, and a successful one at that. He'd be well-traveled, respected, rich—someone like him couldn't possibly understand what her day had been like.

"You know, you might find it easier if you tucked that necklace out of sight. People here don't seem to be too happy with Separatists right now."

Clara glanced up at him, aghast. "I shouldn't have to hide who I am to get people to treat me with a little common courtesy," she said vehemently, then cringed inside, realizing that speaking like that to someone like him was not a good idea.

"Maybe," he responded blithely, picking up some items from the display and creating a neat little stack of fancy-smelling soaps and other expensive toiletries. "But it seems silly to let your pride get in the way of buying what you need."

Clara nearly gasped, but managed to restrain the impulse. Was he calling her prideful? What an arrogant, odious, condescending pig! She opened her mouth to give him a piece of her mind, then thought better of it and snapped her mouth shut, settling on balling her hands into fists.

The man caught the shopkeeper's eye and motioned to the items he'd been selecting. She bustled over, added up the total and began wrapping the items in brown paper. He motioned to the block of wax in front of Clara as well, and the woman wrapped it up without so much as a second glance at her.

Of all the nerve! First he insulted her and now he was stealing her wax! She couldn't even bring herself to protest, afraid all the anger and frustration she'd been feeling would make her say something she would regret. So instead she stood frozen, biting her lip.

The man gave the shopkeeper a handful of coins and took his packages. "What is it anyway, some sort of star? I've always wondered." It took Clara a second to realize he was talking to her again.

"It's a compass rose," she said through clenched teeth.

"Fascinating," the man said, "I hope it's worth all the trouble it's giving you." He held out the package with the block of wax, and she took it from him instinctively, hardly realizing what she was doing.

A tall, slender man came up behind them with a ledger. "Wax?" the man asked, his pen hovering over the paper.

"No need to mark it down, it was a personal item." Then he just walked away.

The scribe gave Clara a curious glance and then hurried to follow, his voice trailing into the distance. "You know very well that personal items still have to be accounted for..."

Clara stared after them, then looked down at the package in her hands. Conflicting emotions warred within her. On one hand, she had another item from her list without having to pay for it. On the other, she couldn't help feeling he'd only given it to her to prove something, and by taking it she was somehow admitting he was right. She was about to call after him and insist he take the package back, or at least accept payment for it, when Frederick returned, out of breath and looking grim.

"What is it?" she asked, tucking the wax into her basket with the rest of their purchases and abandoning the thought of chasing the man down.

"A town crier just arrived, people are gathering in the square for his announcement."

Clara felt her heart rate quicken. This was it. Apparently the Aldonian Parliament had made a decision. They both walked briskly to the edge of the market. A fancy carriage was parked next to the low wooden stage used for public meetings, announcements, and entertainment. A man in official uniform was climbing onto it just as they reached the back of the crowd.

"Hear ye, hear ye, it is thenceforth declared on this the seventh day of the month of harvest during the twelfth year of the reign of King Aldus the Tenth..." Clara tuned out the official drivel that always preceded such announcements, twisting the corner of her apron tighter with each pointless syllable.

Just get to it already, what did they decide?

"...that anyone preaching, teaching, or otherwise indicating through their words and/or actions that this land upon which we have established our sovereignty is in any way deficient or lacking in holiness shall be brought before the court to prove his or her loyalty to the church and state, and in the event a suitable declaration of allegiance is not obtained, shall be henceforth punished according to the established laws for treason. Any native business, individual, or entity found to be assisting in the dissemination of these lies, whether by allowing said lies to be spoken in their establishment or similar form of tacit approval, shall be subject to five years imprisonment or the equivalent fine thereof."

Clara stiffened as shock ran through her. She clutched her amulet in one hand, simultaneously hiding it and seeking comfort. There'd been rumors of course, but even she hadn't expected that the law would be this

10

harsh. How could they live this way? Hiding in plain sight, afraid to say anything that might give away their beliefs? Frederick tugged on her sleeve, breaking her thoughts from their downward spiral.

"Come on, we'd better go tell your father." Frederick's voice was pitched low, an undercurrent of fear running through it, though Clara could tell he was trying to mask it.

She nodded numbly, tucking the amulet into her blouse and hurrying after him, keeping her eyes down so she didn't have to see the self-righteous expressions on the people they passed.

CHAPTER 2

Decisions

Frederick and Clara burst through the farmhouse door and Frederick went straight to the cellar where Clara's father, Warren, was taking inventory of their stores of food for the winter. Clara stayed by the door.

"Where's he off to in such a hurry?" Her mother, Kate, glanced up from the carrots she was chopping and blew a strand of hair away from her eyes.

"Mama, it was just awful." Clara set down her packages and walked across the room to lean her head on the woman's shoulder. Kate stroked Clara's hair for a moment before taking a step back, turning the girl to face her, and holding her at arm's length.

"What happened?" Kate's eyes went to Clara's neckline. She gently tugged upward on the chain around Clara's neck until the compass was once again visible. "Why is your compass hidden?"

Clara looked down at her feet, shame welling in the pit of her stomach. "I know I shouldn't have hidden it, but I didn't know what else to do..." She trailed off and looked up at her mother. "There was a man in the market... he made me question myself, talking about how life would be easier if I tucked my compass away—"

"This is what frightened you?" Her mother's eyes were sincere, full of concern.

"No." Clara looked away, fingers crumpling the corner of her apron. "The rumors about the law changing? They were true. To believe in the Holy Land is treason."

Her mother stiffened and she drew in a sharp breath. "Your father and I worried something like this would happen, but we thought we had more time."

"What are we going to—"

"I will discuss it with your father. For now, go tend to the chickens." Kate gently pushed her daughter toward the door.

"You don't need to protect me from this. I can help, we can make a plan and—"

"I'll see you at supper." Kate turned on her heel and scurried down to the cellar after Frederick.

Clara stood in the doorway alone, head spinning. Her parents never allowed her to participate in these conversations, to have a say in her own life. They meant well, and as their only daughter she knew they wanted to protect her. But at times it felt like they'd traded her agency for their own peace of mind.

What are we going to do?

She put away the few items she'd purchased at the market, straining to make out the words being spoken downstairs. Frederick's deep, animated tone mingled with Father's calm, soothing one. She didn't hear her mother.

It was too difficult to decipher anything coherent, so she stepped outside to do as her mother had asked.

The scene before her was far too serene for the circumstances. Chickens bobbed and clucked in their enclosure, oblivious to the change that had occurred. The large garden on the other side of the coop still held the vines and stalks that had supplied her family with a bounteous harvest of squash, tomatoes, and tubers to see them through the winter. They'd need to clear those before the snows came, to make the space ready for spring. Beyond that lay the rolling fields where their little flock of sheep gamboled and grazed contentedly.

On their little farm it seemed as if none of Parliament's decisions could touch them. They never had before, not really. There were stringent rules for Separatists in public places—where they could buy goods, times they could be out, where they could worship—but never before had the law dictated what they could believe.

Clara scoffed.

Good thing Parliament can't read my mind.

Clara replenished the chickens' water and freshened the nest boxes. She was tempted to go back to the house, but knew better than to put herself in a conversation when she wasn't wanted. Even if she could help.

She left the coop, the evening becoming chillier than she was dressed for, and tramped through the damp yard to a tall, sturdy oak tree. She pulled herself into the low-hanging branches and climbed until she reached her favorite spot where she could nestle herself into a fork, lean back against the trunk, and watch the clouds float across the sky through the leaves.

How she wished she could be one of those clouds, floating above the farm and the marketplace and all the people who decided the circumstances of her life. If she was one of them, she could see the world, see other lands, maybe even the land they'd been promised.

Orange and scarlet painted the evening sky before Frederick came to fetch her as he left to return to his own home.

Clara ran back to the house, her dress tripping her as she went. She stopped abruptly at the door, smoothing her hair and trying to pull the wrinkles from her apron to no avail. She turned the doorknob slowly and pushed the door open, finding her parents sitting across the kitchen table from each other, their hands clasped, their heads bowed in prayer. Their empty food dishes sat on the table beside them.

She joined them, quietly slipping into the seat next to her mother and placing her hand atop theirs. A sense of peace settled over her. A few moments later, her parents' hands unclasped and they opened their eyes.

Her father smiled sadly at her and her mother stood and walked to the counter, grabbing a plate of food. She brought it back to the table and placed it in front of Clara.

"Thank you." Clara took a bite of roasted carrot, aware of her own chewing in the silence. When neither of her parents spoke, she swallowed and asked, "What are we going to do?"

"You don't need to worry about that now. It's been a long day." Her mother placed a hand on Clara's shoulder.

"We've made a plan and we'll tell you about it in the morning. Everything will be all right. Finish your dinner and get to bed now."

———————◆———————

Clara pushed the front door open with her back, trying not to jostle the basket of eggs looped through her arm. Her cheeks were flushed from the cold morning air and the heat from the fire felt heavenly against her skin.

"Good morning, Mama." Clara kissed her mother on the cheek. She felt much more like her normal self this morning, without the dread of going to the market hanging over her and the long-reaching hands of Parliament far from her. "I know I'm late bringing in the eggs, but the way the sun broke through the trees this morning was so delightful! I had to sit and admire how it reflected off the leaves and—"

"Clara," her mother said. Clara's smile faded as she noticed the checkered blanket draped over her mother's arm.

Her father came from a back room carrying a picnic basket.

"We're going to the meadow? Is it really that bad?" Clara set the eggs on the kitchen table and her father wrapped his arm around her shoulders.

"I'm afraid so, my doll."

Clara nodded and let her parents lead her out the door, through the yard, and to the edge of their property where thin beech trees crowded together. Her father led the way along a well-worn path that wove its way through them, holding branches to the side as Clara and her mother passed.

A true gentleman, she thought—though it could have been an echo of a sentiment she'd heard her mother say many times.

Though the path to the meadow was beautiful and one she knew well, it wasn't a stroll she liked to take. The meadow held no fond memories for her.

It was where her parents had taken her when her dog ran away, the place they'd gone when Papa lost his job at the mill, when relatives had passed away...

And now.

The home was a sacred place of peace and safety. The cares of the world couldn't always be kept out of it, but Clara's parents tried. During the worst storms of life, the moments they knew would cut her deepest, they didn't want to tarnish their little farmhouse. Hence, the meadow.

Her mother spread out the blanket and motioned for Clara to sit next to her. Her father joined them on the ground, sitting across from the two within arm's reach. He sighed, then looked at Clara with serious, pain-filled eyes.

"We can no longer stay here."

"What!" She didn't know what she'd been expecting, but this was far, far worse than anything she'd considered.

"We can't live somewhere our beliefs are considered treason. We will not abandon our God, so we must abandon

16

our home instead."

"But that's not fair!" Clara burst, earning a warning look from her mother. Her father held up a hand and Clara pursed her lips, letting him continue.

"Our best option is to flee to Draunland."

"They hate us there too," Clara mumbled.

"Maybe so, but their laws are not as strict."

"For the moment." Her mother looked to her father. A sadness passed between them that Clara had never seen. They didn't want this.

"There has to be something else we can do," Clara pleaded. The farm was all she'd ever known. What of the years they'd spent improving the soil, or the berry bushes they'd planted in the spring? They'd never even gotten a harvest from them. And the sheep, would they sell them for a pittance to an unfriendly buyer? They couldn't take them along, could they?

"Think of it as an adventure, Clara." Her father's voice was gentle, but firm. "Maybe that will make it more palatable."

"Being forced from one oppressive country to another is not an adventure," Clara scoffed, "at least here we have a home!"

Her mother shot her another sharp look, then her gaze softened, and she reached across to take Clara's hand. Tears came unbidden to Clara's eyes and she blinked them away. *How can this be the only option?*

"Until The Divine One makes His will known, we must do what we can to keep our people safe. To keep you safe." Her father looked toward the horizon. "We need to speak with the other families, find out what their plans are. Maybe we can all travel together and have safety in numbers. But in the meantime, we need to raise money for the journey."

"Raise money?" Clara asked. "How? We just spent it all on supplies for winter!"

"We have plenty of things we can sell," her mother said, her eyes full of sympathy. "We won't be able to take it all with us anyway. When we return home I'll need your help going through the attic and finding the things we can bear to part with."

CHAPTER 3

Journal

After walking back from the meadow, Clara ran inside and headed straight for the attic. She wanted to be alone, and the only way to ensure that was to do what her parents had asked.

She stomped up the narrow stairway, two steps at a time, hiking her dress up around her knees. She pushed the attic door open with a huff and was greeted with stagnant air and a plume of dust.

When was the last time someone came up here?

Clara stood in the middle of the room. It was the only place she could stand at her full height, as the ceiling slanted to either side. Around her, worn furniture pieces from her childhood mingled with out-of-season linens and clothing packed in boxes, which lined the walls in neat rows.

Waving her hand in front of her face to clear the dust away, she knelt down and began pulling blankets from the crate closest to her, separating them into piles to keep or sell. When she was done with the crate, there was much more in the keep pile.

Her shoulders slumped. Every one of the blankets

had been handmade by the women of her family. She held up a loose-knit, faded baby blanket for a moment, weaving her fingers through the holes before letting it fall onto her lap.

How could her family give these precious memories away? They didn't have young children around any more, but Clara had always assumed these heirlooms would be passed down so her children could enjoy them and feel tethered to their heritage.

She folded the blanket and placed it back in the keep pile. There had to be something easier she could start with.

Standing up, she surveyed the room.It would be easy to part with the extra bedding on the old, lumpy straw bed in the corner. She yanked the cases from the pillows. One of them fell to the floor, half under the bed, and with a sigh she bent down to pick it up.

Her hand scraped something rough, and she knelt to get a better look under the bedframe. Wooden boxes she'd never seen before filled the space. She pulled them out one by one and opened them up. Some had old documents that she set aside for her father, and some had hats or shoes, items that were easy to sort into the "sell" pile. She was making good progress until she opened a box full of old journals.

Clara hauled the box up onto the bed and sat down, her back against the wall. She pulled her knees to her chest as she opened the journals to read the inscriptions inside. She had never been much of a reader, but something about the journals made her curious.

She skimmed a few passages, reading moments in the lives of her ancestors. The joy of new children added to the family, the sorrow of losing elders, the faith they showed throughout their lives, and the hope of the Holy Land. Many of the significant stories had been passed down through the years and Clara recognized them.

Sighing, she closed the journal and ran her hand

over the cover. The stories of her family all bled together, creating a painting that Clara felt needed more color. Her family had put all of their energy, time, commitment, and love into future generations. It was a heritage she hoped to continue, in her own way and in her own time. She didn't doubt their lives were full of purpose—taking care of their families and homes, consumed with duty and tradition. It was not the kind of adventure she'd often daydreamed about, but it was admirable in its own way.

They were ordinary people trying their best to get by. Their journals were reminders of why Parliament's law was so unjust. The people who had taken the time to write the words on those pages were not criminals.

Clara didn't want to read any more. She couldn't help but feel like she'd failed them somehow. There had to be a better answer than leaving their home and giving in to tyrants.

She dropped the journal she was holding back into the box and heard the clanking of metal. Curious, she dug around, tossing diaries she'd already flipped through onto the bed. At the bottom of the box was a leather-bound journal with a metal lock on it.

Brow furrowed, Clara turned the journal over in her hands. She yanked on the lock, but it held firm.

"There has to be a key somewhere," she mumbled. Setting the journal back on the bed, she dug through the box once more, tossing the other journals aside, until it was empty. No key.

Picking up the journal again, she tapped it against her lips, thinking.

"I could try to pick the lock…" she looked about the room half-heartedly. She didn't know what she would need to even begin doing that. "Or—"

Clara stood and set the journal by the foot of the bed, positioning the lock so it stuck out from the book as much as possible. She lifted the bed frame so the leg was a few inches above the lock, arms straining as she tried to get it placed just right before dropping it. The heavy wooden bedframe smashed against the lock. She repeated the process for good measure, then picked up the journal, the pieces of now twisted metal breaking apart and landing on the ground with a satisfying clank.

"Clara?" Her mother called up the stairs. "Are you all right?"

"Yes, just a clumsy moment!" Clara beamed. She jumped onto the bed and lay on her stomach with the journal in front of her.

She opened it to the first page and read the name "Henry J. Karrow". Her interest piqued. This had to be her mother's grandfather, since her maiden name was Karrow and her father's first name was Gerald, not Henry.

If Clara remembered her mother's stories correctly, Henry had been a botanist and explorer.

This journal might actually be interesting.

She flipped through the first few pages, taking a moment to examine a rough map of a sea voyage, then skimming past drawings of plants and detailed explanations of their anatomical structures. Just when she was about to give up and toss it with all the others, she came to a drawing that made her pause.

Vines trailed around an ancient looking archway, mostly crumbled away and covered in runes she didn't recognize.

"Cape Sago, Day 17, We came across the largest specimen of creeping verdantia I have ever encountered. I examined it closely and determined it is likely also the oldest such specimen ever recorded, with over five hundred bifurcations in the main stem line."

Clara smirked at the thought of her great-grandfather making the expedition wait while he counted forks in a vine. She skipped the rest of his notes on the plant and went on to the next entry that caught her eye.

"Cape Sago, Day 23, The further into the jungle we get the more perplexed I am by the sheer variety of plants we've encountered. Not just in species and phenotype, but also in age of the specimens. The flora in this region grow at incredible rates, with some plants regenerating mere hours after our passing. This should mean that most of the specimens are young, but intermingled with the newest budding tendril ferns are stalks of churnberry and ivescent spikebranch with base rings indicating eight centuries of growth!

"Cape Sago, Day 24, Found more creeping verdantia today. This one was wrapped around a tree so wide ten men couldn't fit their arms around it. I couldn't count the age of the vine, since it spiraled up too far to see, but it has to be twice as old as the one on the archway. The plants seem to be getting bigger and older the further inland we go."

Clara's heart raced.

Plants that grow in hours, mixed with plants almost a thousand years old...

She flipped past the next few pages, looking for something to indicate how far her ancestor had traveled, and what else he may have found.

Is it possible?

"Cape Sago, Day 31, We're running out of provisions, and had to attempt to hunt. The animals here are just as strange as the plants, however, and seem to be incredibly cunning. They've evaded our snares and proven difficult to shoot. We may have to turn back prematurely or risk starvation. On a happy turn, I took a soil sample and initial analysis indicates a complex composition that may be the key to why plants grow to such incredible sizes."

"Come on Grandda! Just a little further," Clara urged, turning the page.

"Cape Sago, Day 4?, I cannot be sure of the count, for I took ill shortly after my last entry—a result of pathogens carried by the abnormally prolific insects I'm sure, though our native guide insists it is a curse laid to protect the valley we were approaching. It is easy to see the source of this superstition, as our expedition was indeed forced to turn back when the disease spread to more than half our ranks in the first day, and the other half within a few days following. Only three of us made it through alive: myself, our native guide, and the teenage son of a man we hired to help us pack in our gear.

"I must relate something I observed in the hours before I fell ill, though my memory may have been distorted by the fevered imaginings I later experienced. I was out in the jungle trying to count how many varieties of hiliblooms I could find in a mile radius (I encountered some with the most intriguing spirals on their leaves!) and lost my bearings due to an unexpected patch of fog. I climbed a tree to see if I could find the camp, and off to the east I saw the most incredible sight: A valley, barely visible between two worn mountains, with trees that looked taller and broader than any we had encountered thus far. A river passed through the gap and must've joined with the one near our camp, but it appeared to originate at a spring high on the other side of the valley.

"Even from my distance I could see that the valley was the most beautiful place I have ever laid eyes on, with plants of all colors, and birds whose plumage was so bright I could see them from miles away. After determining the right direction and climbing back down, I made my way back to camp, only to come down with a virulent fever before I could relate what I had seen. When I next woke, we were miles away and my memory of the place was hazy..."

"This is it." Clara whispered, afraid if she spoke the words aloud her discovery would vanish, along with her hope. "Great-grandfather found it. The Land of Origin."

Clara ran downstairs, the journal clutched to her chest.

"Mama! Papa! I know how we can fix this! I found—"

The house was eerily empty. Usually around this time her mother was preparing dinner.

A note on the kitchen table caught her attention. "Went to the meetinghouse to consult with the other families. Will be home late. Love Ma and Pa."

"They left for the meeting without me!" Clara tossed the journal on the table, annoyed. How long would they insist on treating her like a child?

She stared at the journal for a moment before snatching it up once more. Her discovery couldn't wait until they got home. They needed to know now.

Clara grabbed her coat and tucked the journal safely into an inner pocket, then rushed out the door. A drizzling rain had started while she was in the attic, and she instantly regretted not grabbing her hat, but there was no time to lose. If they reached a decision before she got there, they'd be unlikely to listen to reason. Her people were generally egalitarian and would ask for input before forming a decision, but they could also be a stubborn lot. Once a choice was made it may as well have been set in stone.

Clara reached the meeting house and hesitated outside the big double doors. Her hair was dripping wet by now, and her boots muddy. She heard her father's voice through the door and pressed her ear to it. If she could avoid a scene, she would.

There's no reason to go barging in—

"It looks like we're about done here. We will plan to leave for Draunland by the end of the month—"

"No," Clara whispered.

She pulled the journal from her coat pocket and flung the chapel doors aside. Everyone turned in their pews to face her, their discomfort and alarm apparent on their faces.

"We don't need to flee to Draunland. We have a better option." Clara walked down the aisle with purpose, straight

25

toward where her father stood behind a podium on the stand.

"What are you doing?" Her mother whispered as Clara passed her seat in the front pew.

Clara glanced at her, then resolutely continued to the podium. She stood next to her father who had turned to her with an inscrutable expression, and held up the journal toward the congregation.

"This is an account by my great-grandfather Henry Karrow. He was an explorer and botanist, and based on what I have read, I believe he found the Land of Origin."

The room went silent. Clara stood holding the journal aloft, unsure what to say next. All eyes were on her. She glanced at her father.

"And where is this land he discovered?" Her father asked, his voice level but his gaze flickering back to the congregation as the shocked silence began to give way to whispered conversations and murmured expressions of doubt.

"Um, that is, it's—I haven't read the journal in its entirety. We would need to do more study to determine the route, but he was on a jungle expedition overseas and he describes a valley that matches everything we know!"

She opened the journal to the relevant entry, and read the description her great-grandfather had written. The congregation's murmuring grew louder.

Her father put a hand on the journal, lowering it to the podium as she finished the sentence. "That sounds... intriguing, but we cannot know if it is the Land of Origin, nor whether what he saw was real or the result of his imagination. He himself admitted as much in the section you just read to us."

"He describes plants centuries old in the area nearby!" Clara argued, "And ones that grow quickly. Trust me Father—"

"We can discuss it later. Now is not the time—" Her

26

father trailed off as a calm, clear voice interrupted their argument.

"And the Divine One put forth his hand and called forth the waters, which came flowing as though from an endless spring. And it spilled forth and from it sprang life of every kind." Clara's mother stood, holding her worn copy of The Book of Beginnings in the palm of her hand. As she read, Clara was drawn in by the sense of wonder and reverence in her mother's voice, a cadence and lull as familiar to her as breathing.

She flipped to another place in the middle of the book and read again, "And lo, the place from which we came was a land of plenty. Indeed a land from whence the leaf and vine could multiply and never die." She turned a page and continued, "And thus we know that this place of origin shall be a refuge, encircled by gates of stone and winged sentries. Where the sapling can grow stout and tall..."

Clara stared at her mother in awe as Kate met her eyes and nodded ever so slightly before turning around and addressing the congregation with tears in her eyes.

"My grandfather was not a believer. He couldn't have understood the significance of his discovery, but when my parents joined the church decades later, I always wondered if it had something to do with the stories he told of the places he traveled—that maybe my father had faith in the Land of Origin because he had grown up with firsthand accounts of the miraculous places that exist in far off lands. I never imagined there was a record of these travels... We cannot let such an opportunity pass. I agree with my daughter. It is time to act upon what we believe."

Kate turned back to the front and sat. Clara saw her father meet her mother's gaze and something passed between them. He nodded. "It seems the time has indeed come for us to seek the Land of Origin."

Silence reigned for the second time that night, and then the whispers and murmuring grew again. A man in the back stood, and Clara recognized him as Herst the wheelwright.

"We can't pack everyone in a boat and ship them across the sea on a whim," he said, flinging an arm toward the rest of the congregation. "You said yourself that this man, who was not one of us, had seen many undiscovered lands. How can we be sure this is the Place of Origin?"

"Didn't you hear the scriptures my mother just read?" Clara said, trying to rein in her annoyance. Her father placed a hand on her arm and shook his head in warning.

"We will consider the matter closely, you can be sure Goodman Herst. For now, let us assume it is worth investigating and discuss possible courses of action."

Clara saw many people nodding in agreement, excited whispers overpowering the doubtful murmurs.

"We could send a small party," a middle-aged housewife in the front row suggested.

"Who would we send?" her neighbor asked.

"I think it would be prudent to send a select few whose skills could be useful on a voyage." Clara's father said, "This is a tenuous lead at best. It doesn't make sense for everyone to go."

The noise level rose as the congregation considered this. Clara watched as some thawed to the idea while others grew colder.

A woman near the back stood. "If we can prove the Land of Origin exists, the government will have to reconsider this law, won't they?"

"It's a possibility, but not one I would pin our hopes on," Clara's father replied.

"Isn't the point of finding the Land of Origin so we can return to it? Why should we try to convince the government they're wrong if we're leaving anyway?" A man sitting in front of the woman asked, turning to face her.

"It would buy us more time," her husband spoke up, putting an arm around his wife, "It might be easy for you to just pick up and leave, but some of us own businesses. Leaving means selling our assets and contacting clients... doing that in a month is next to impossible. If there is an option that means we can stay here longer, I'm all for it."

"Even if it means you'll be arrested in the meantime?" The man shot back.

"The law just forbids teaching that Aldonia isn't the Land of Origin or Final Destination. As long as we keep our mouths shut for a few months, we'll be fine," another person chimed in.

"We covered this before the young lady interrupted. Staying is too risky. We can't just wait months for an expedition to return," Herst grumbled, "and I'm certainly not getting in a boat that doesn't even know where it's going!"

"No one is forcing you to go on the expedition!" a man in the back called.

Clara's father held up his hands and the noise level decreased.

"The option to flee to Draunland still stands," he said, speaking loudly over the lingering discussions. "It may be necessary for those who stay behind to flee regardless of their thoughts on investigating this new avenue. For now, let us adjourn and return home to consider our individual concerns. If you would like to be part of the expedition or have ideas for funding it, you may contact me directly."

"And if we still want to leave?" A woman Clara knew had five young children at home called out.

Clara's father turned to Mr. Herst. "Goodman, would you be willing to coordinate with the other families who wish to leave for Draunland and notify me of your plans?"

The bulky man nodded, looking less petulant now that he was in charge of something.

Clara felt a thrill of excitement. They were actually

doing it! Plans still had to be worked out, and she would have to scour the journal for information on where to go, but this was a start.

"Let us end on a note of peace and unity as we leave this meeting." Clara's father closed his eyes and bowed his head. The rest of the congregation followed suit, except Clara, who looked at her father as he recited words she'd heard a thousand times. "Oh Divine One, thou who is with us from beginning to end. Bless us with thy guidance, increase our knowledge, and lend us thy strength, until the day when we are called home to the place where it all began. Amen."

Never before had those words carried so much promise.

CHAPTER 4

Travel Plans

"**A**bsolutely not." Clara's father waved his hand, dismissing the notion, just as he had done the evening before. A breakfast plate sat in front of him with steam rolling off it, but he ignored it and turned his attention back to the almanac in his hands.

Clara watched him for a moment.

How can he be so calm? What use is it to read an almanac when there's little hope of keeping the farm?

"But father—"

He gave Clara a stern look, but she didn't take her seat at the kitchen table next to her mother as she knew she ought.

"The journal was my discovery, I have to go on the expedition!"

"I said no. You're far too young to—"

"I'm not a child."

"That may be so, but you are my child."

So you will do as I say. Clara finished his sentiment in her head.

"Your father is right," Kate said, placing a hand on Clara's arm, encouraging her to sit. She looked into her mother's eyes and saw only concern and love there, though Clara wondered what her mother would say if it were her decision to make alone.

Clara took her place next to her mother. "What do you think?"

Kate moved her hand down to grip Clara's. "I think your place is with us."

"What if we went together as a family?"

"Your mother and I have to stay with the congregation. We have a responsibility to look after their welfare, especially in times of need." Clara's father turned to face her. "Those staying behind have had their world shattered and will be living under constant fear of arrest. Many have already been struggling to make ends meet, with the increased persecution it will only get worse. That is where we should be placing our focus."

"But aren't you curious—"

"Those chosen for the expedition will take care of everything else. All we can do is hope they find The Land of Origin."

"But we could help! I have the journal." Clara dug into the bag hanging from her shoulder and held it out. "I've read it cover to cover."

"That's enough, Clara!" Her father slammed his hands down on the table between them.

Clara froze, wide-eyed. She couldn't remember a time when her father had raised his voice.

"Give the journal to me, please." Her father held out his hand. Clara's mother looked between Clara and her father.

"Warren," she whispered. "The book should be Clara's. It's her inheritance."

"And she can have it back when all this is over. Right now we need it to make preparations for the journey," Warren said, "The journal, Clara, now."

She wanted to stand up to her father, raise her voice

louder than his, stomp her feet, and demand to be heard. She winced. The image of a petulant child begging for sweets came to mind. No matter how much she wanted this, she would not get her way if she acted like that.

Clara looked at the journal in her hands and rubbed her thumbs over the worn leather one last time before handing it to her father.

He stood and took it to the other room, leaving the women alone. Clara's lip quivered. She crumpled into the chair next to her mother and stared at her clenched hands in her lap through hot tears.

"He wants you to be safe." Kate pulled her daughter close. Clara rested her head on her mother's shoulder and let the tears fall onto her pale, green dress.

"I know," Clara whispered. She hoped if she kept her voice quiet enough, her mother wouldn't be able to sense the anger bubbling below the surface. "But am I any safer here? Everything is changing one way or another. Why does it matter if I am on a ship to the Land of Promise or part of a caravan to Draunland?"

"I have wondered the same thing."

Clara lifted her head from Kate's shoulder and studied her mother's profile. Her nose had a gentle slope to it and her eyes were bright. Her frame was feminine and slight, nothing was rough or out of place. Everything about her was inviting, loving, as if life had never tried to wear her down, though Clara knew that was far from the truth.

Though she had the same coloring as her mother, Clara was taller and more wiry, like her father. Her temperament diverged from Kate's even further than her appearance did. Even now, being in the presence of her mother's serenity made Clara more angry than she already was. Wasn't her mother upset by all of this? Had she always been so accepting of her life's circumstances?

And why can't I be the same way?

"Don't you want to be on the expedition too?" Clara

asked. Her mother pursed her lips for a moment.

"Perhaps at one time I would have jumped at the chance to sail away to unknown places. Much like someone else I know." Kate smiled. "Believe it or not, my dear, though I haven't left this town more than twice in my life, I have had plenty of adventures. Your father, this farm, my kitchen… you. I have never regretted the path I've chosen and I don't expect I ever will."

Clara looked at her hands again. How could she make her mother understand—?

Kate lifted Clara's chin and their eyes met. "But that does not mean I expect you to feel the same way."

A tear slid down Clara's cheek. "If it were your decision, would you let me go?"

"It's not what I would want, but I don't see how I would stop you."

"Why wouldn't you—why don't you—want me to go?"

Kate sighed. "You have a young soul, full of curiosity and optimism. It is one of the things I love most about you. I would hate to see it destroyed by unnecessary hardship."

Like having to abandon my home with little hope the new country will be any better? Clara pushed the negative thought away. Turning this into another argument would not help her case. *Mother's reply was loving and honest, mine should be the same.*

"You and father have provided the perfect childhood for me. I grew up daydreaming in treehouses and strolling through fields as my imagination ran wild. I may not have known as much hardship as some young women my age, and for that I am grateful, but it doesn't mean I can't learn to face it when it comes." The words sounded braver than she felt, but Clara hoped they were true. "Everything I am is because of what you have given me. No matter how hard things get, I could never forget that."

"You are a good girl, Clara Mae. Now," Kate stood and

straightened the apron that hung over her dress, "get out to the yard and start your chores. We're already behind for the day."

Clara nodded and walked out the kitchen door. She paused for a moment, leaning against it and trying to get her emotions under control. Try as she might, she couldn't reconcile herself to her parents' decision. She bit her lip, suppressing the urge to hit the wall in frustration. Instead she ran across the yard and through the gate, snagging her dress on a rusted nail. She gathered the dress in both hands and gave it a hard tug. The dress ripped free with a loud tearing sound, but she didn't care. She kept running and the wind knocked off her bonnet, leaving her heavy braid thumping rhythmically against her back.

As she passed the old, once-red barn, she whistled sharply and an old sheepdog joined her. They ran until Clara's throat burned and her legs ached, all the way to the western edge of her father's land where rows and rows of apple trees waited patiently for picking.

She sat beneath one of the trees to catch her breath and leaned against the trunk, keeping out of the shade so she could feel the morning sun on her face. She reached up to grab a ripe, red apple and yanked it off the branch.

"How can I hope to return to my everyday life of chores and obedience and monotony when I know there's a grand adventure just within reach?" She scratched Champion behind the ear, his big brown eyes looking up at her as if he felt her sorrow as deeply as she did.

She threw a stick for him, watching his black, white, and brown fur bounce as he raced after it between rows of apple trees. His cares evaporated in an instant and she was envious of his ability to leave them behind.

"Mother would let me go... or at least, she wouldn't stop me. Father won't even consider it, yet he's letting Frederick take the reins on the expedition. We're practically the same age!" She bit into the apple and some juice dribbled down her chin. She wiped it with her sleeve and kept going.

"It's not just that I want to go on the expedition. I've been hoping and praying for a change for so long that I almost feel responsible for what's happening now, like my longing for something more somehow caused this mess." Clara stared into the distance, then shook her head. Champion dropped the stick at her feet and whined up at her. She looked down, sighed, and scratched him behind the ears again. "That's silly, isn't it? My daydreams have no bearing on Parliament. I didn't cause this. Just power hungry people afraid of what they don't understand."

She lost her appetite. Standing, she launched the apple as far as she could, shaking her head as the dog raced after it as he had the stick. It was time for chores, though they seemed pointless now. They didn't have much time before they had to leave for Draunland. She would miss this place, but she'd rather be leaving it for the Land of Origin, not another country full of people who hated them.

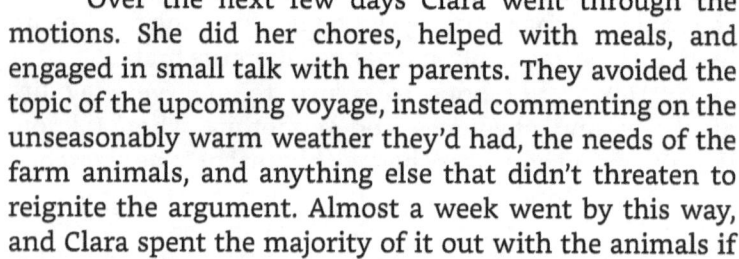

Over the next few days Clara went through the motions. She did her chores, helped with meals, and engaged in small talk with her parents. They avoided the topic of the upcoming voyage, instead commenting on the unseasonably warm weather they'd had, the needs of the farm animals, and anything else that didn't threaten to reignite the argument. Almost a week went by this way, and Clara spent the majority of it out with the animals if she could. Between the awkwardness with her parents and the fear that hovered beneath the surface, she was ready to burst.

One day, after finishing her duties outside, Clara walked back to the house and paused just outside the kitchen door, hearing voices within. She peeked through the gap in the curtains. Frederick sat with her father at the table, a piece of paper in front of him.

"I've told the others no more than one trunk each for clothing and personal items. I don't know how much cargo space the ship will have, but I worry about storing such things once we make port and have to trek through the jungle," Frederick said.

"A sensible thought," her father replied, "It might be better still to see if they are willing to share. It will be easier to book passage if some of you can work onboard, and sailors are rarely afforded the space for more than a rucksack."

Disappointment welled up within Clara again, and she sat on the step, leaning against the door. Part of her longed to hear the rest of their conversation, while another part wished she could just ignore it and get about with her chores. Her curiosity won out, and she stayed where she was as their voices carried through the open window.

"... actually Jode had a thought about that," Frederick was saying, "He has a friend from Estanya whose family is involved in the spice trade. They're leaving next week for Kordra and they may be open to taking us on to Cape Sago afterwards."

"That would be convenient. Have you inquired about the fee?"

"That's the best part," Frederick said, his voice rising in volume as he got excited. "Jode said they've been dabbling in research for the medicinal uses of plants native to the areas they trade from, and I think if we approach them right, we may be able to get them to fund the entire expedition."

"We will not lie to save ourselves the cost of passage," Warren said sternly.

"Of course not, Uncle." Frederick sounded contrite. "But this journal is full of scientific descriptions of plants native to that area, and if we are willing to provide them with that information—"

Clara jumped up at the mention of the journal. She looked through the window and saw Frederick motioning to the bag at his feet, where the brown leather peeked out above the canvas.

Father gave it to Frederick? Tears pricked her eyes, and she turned to run back to the orchard.

"Clara?" Her mother's voice startled her, and she turned to see Kate walking toward her from the chicken coop, a now-empty bucket of scraps swinging from her hand. "Why are you waiting outside?"

Clara opened her mouth to reply, then covered it with a hand to control the sob she felt coming.

Her mother's brow furrowed with concern as she drew closer. Her eyes flicked to the window and understanding registered on her face as she caught sight of the two men inside.

"The goats need more food," she said gently, handing the bucket to Clara, "why don't you go out to the orchard and gather the rest of the fallen apples? I expect it'll take you all afternoon."

"Does he really think Frederick will take better care of the journal than me?" she said in a pained whisper. "Frederick is barely older than I am, why does he get to go and I don't?"

"Frederick's father has given his blessing for the boy to go. And a few years is a lot at your age." Kate smiled at her fondly.

"Father wouldn't give his blessing no matter how old I was," Clara muttered.

"Perhaps not," her mother agreed. "Now, go spend some time under the trees, I'll make your excuses to your father."

Clara nodded and headed out to the orchard. She appreciated what her mother was trying to do for her, but even fresh air, the smell of ripened fruit, and seeing the sky through the leaves wasn't going to be enough to heal this pain.

CHAPTER 5

Repercussions

Afew days later Clara was helping her mother make apple jam when a frantic knock sounded at the kitchen door. Kate handed Clara the spoon and motioned for her to keep stirring the bubbling pot of fruit, then dried her hands on her apron and opened the door. A short man with dark hair and a scraggly beard stepped inside, his brow furrowed and his hair windswept.

"Is Warren here?" he asked, glancing around frantically.

"He's downstairs," Kate replied, "I'll go get him. Please Jonah, take a seat. Clara, get the goodman something to drink."

Clara served the anxious man a glass of the apple juice they'd pressed that morning, then returned to her position by the stove to prevent the jam from burning. Her mother returned a moment later, followed by her father, who looked calm, but strode quickly enough that Clara could tell he was anxious.

"Thank Divinity!" Jonah said, jumping up, "Warren you have to do something, Herst has been arrested!"

Clara's father closed his eyes, setting his mouth in a

grim line. "Tell me exactly what happened, Jonah."

The man quickly relayed the events that had taken place, how Herst had gotten in an argument at the market and the shopkeeper had accused him of treason. "The soldiers hauled him off to jail and threatened to bring in his family too if he didn't comply!" Jonah finished, wringing his hands in agitation. "And now Serin is fixing to march in and demand his release, and her with two littles at home who'll be left parentless if she gets herself arrested as well —you have to talk some sense into her."

Clara's father grabbed his hat and coat from their hook by the door. "I'd better go, Kate. If I'm not back by dinner, don't wait to eat. I'll try to send someone with word if I'm going to be longer."

Kate nodded and clutched her amulet, murmuring what Clara knew was a fervent prayer under her breath as Warren and Jonah ran out the door.

"I hope he can talk some sense into her," Kate said worriedly, "Serin is nearly as hot-headed as her husband."

"She has to know the soldiers won't listen to her," Clara said, ladling the hot mixture into a jar her mother held up, her hands wrapped in a towel to protect against burns.

"Maybe, but sheer stubbornness may drive her to try anyway." Kate set the jar far back on the counter and grabbed another one for Clara to fill. They lapsed into silence as the familiar work drew their attention.

When the last of the jam had been scraped out of the pot and into a jar, Kate wiped the rims while Clara grabbed the bowl of wax they'd set near the stove to melt and began spooning it carefully atop the jam. Her mind wandered back to that day in the market. Her cheeks flushed again as she thought about the condescending way that man had treated her, even if he had given them the wax. Maybe people in Draunland would be better. Somehow she doubted it.

Warren returned late that night, worry lines seeming permanently etched above his brow. He ushered in two small children with frightened eyes, whom Kate immediately whisked away to soothe with mugs of hot milk.

"Serin didn't listen to you?" Clara asked, placing her father's dinner plate in front of him on the table.

"She was gone before we even got there," Warren said, his shoulders drooping in defeat. He nodded his thanks to her for the food, but didn't touch it. "I spent the afternoon trying to track down where they'd taken her and submit pleas on her behalf, but I can't do much without risking captivity myself."

"What will this do to the preparations for relocating to Draunland? Does anyone know what progress Herst had made?" Clara asked.

Her father sighed, rubbing his forehead with one hand. "I don't know. I'll have to make some inquiries about it tomorrow."

"What are we going to do about the kids?" Clara asked, "We can't just take them out of the country with their parents imprisoned here."

"I don't know, Clara. We may have no choice." Her father sounded so tired.

Clara's mother walked over and rubbed his shoulders. Warren reached up to hold one of her hands, and Clara could see how upset he was by how tightly he grasped it—like a drowning man searching for something to pull him out of the depths.

"Warren," her mother said softly, "We can worry about this in the morning. Eat. Rest. Things will look better on a full stomach and a good night's sleep."

Clara's father kissed Kate's hand, holding it to his cheek and closing his eyes for a moment. Then he sat up straight and began to eat his dinner.

Her mother nodded with satisfaction, and looked

over at Clara, who was watching her parents with worry-filled eyes. Kate smiled and wrapped an arm around her, kissing her on the side of her head. "No more questions tonight. The Divine One has a plan, if we seek it in faith, He will reveal it to us."

Clara leaned her head against her mother's, then looked over at the two little ones who sat silently at the other end of the table, their faces far too serious for children.

"Come on, let's get you two to bed," Clara said, disengaging from her mother and holding out a hand to each of them.

"Will Mommy be home tomorrow?" the three year old asked, her eyes round and solemn. Clara looked at her mother, then knelt down in front of the child. "We don't know, but we can pray for her, would you like that?" The girl nodded, grasping Clara's hand. "And after that, I can tell you a story. Have you heard the one about the cow with purple ears?"

Both children giggled, shaking their heads. Clara smiled and guided them out of the room, glancing back at her mother, who mouthed a silent "thank you" before taking the empty milk mugs to the sink.

———— ❖ ————

Clara brought the children to help with her chores the next day, trying to keep them busy to avoid having to answer questions about their parents. She smiled as they joyfully chased after the goats, and coaxed them into reaching carefully under the chickens to collect the eggs. By the end of the week, she was exhausted from trying to keep them distracted.

"You're doing good work here, cuz," Frederick said. Clara nodded mutely, watching the children play. Frederick watched them too.

"We're leaving tomorrow, you know. I'm here to

talk to your father about the final preparations." Frederick turned toward her, his eyes shifting downward. "I know you're disappointed not to be on the expedition. Don't tell Uncle Warren, but if it were up to me, I'd take you in a heartbeat."

Clara looked up in surprise. "Really?"

"Sure," Frederick rested his forearms on the fence, his hands casually dangling over the other side as he looked out at the field. "You're smart and resourceful. And you're not afraid to take on hard tasks." He nodded toward the children as evidence of this. "I'd take you over Old Johnny any day."

He rolled his eyes upward, and Clara cringed. Johnny was a widower in his sixties, physically capable of anything the expedition might require, but thought he always knew best and was known to complain about every little thing.

"He's really going with you?" Clara asked, picturing the old man telling the ship's captain that they were hoisting the sail the wrong way.

Frederick nodded. "He insisted on it, and Uncle Warren thought the expedition would benefit from his 'experience'—apparently the old whiner used to be a trapper in his youth."

Clara covered a giggle with one hand. "What, did he tell the animals they were walking wrong, and it distracted them so they fell into his traps?"

Frederick snorted.

"Clara!" Her mother's stern voice came from behind her. "Speaking poorly of others is an unattractive habit, and an unseemly form of entertainment."

"Sorry, Mama," Clara said contritely, turning to face her.

Kate's expression softened. "I know this has been hard on you. Don't let that affect how you treat your elders."

Clara nodded, looking at Frederick, who mouthed

"sorry."

"Now, I came because I saw Mrs. Henderson walking up the lane. I assume she wants you to watch her kids again."

"I can keep an eye on these two for a minute," Frederick said, "When they're done I'll bring them back to the house to wash up."

Clara nodded and followed her mother back to the house. They paused at the kitchen door, hearing raised voices within.

"Mrs. Henderson I assure you Clara had no intention —"

"Maybe not, but that's the worst of it, isn't it? You lot can't help spreading your poison, you don't have to mean harm to do it!"

"I'm sorry this has caused you trouble," Warren said, using a tone Clara recognized as his "forcing myself to stay calm while I'm talking to an irrational person," voice.

"Sorry doesn't begin to cut it! I've got the schoolteacher breathing down my neck about the things Robbie mentioned in class. I've half a mind to tell her exactly who put those ideas into his head. You tell that daughter of yours to keep her mouth shut before she goes getting innocent folks arrested!"

Kate looked at Clara with wide eyes. Clara looked back with bewilderment.

"What is Mrs. Henderson talking about?" Kate whispered. Clara shook her head in confusion. She hadn't watched the Henderson kids for weeks, and she had never tried to convince them of her beliefs.

The front door slammed, and Clara peeked inside to verify that the woman was gone before opening the kitchen door.

"What was that about, Warren?" her mother asked, worry stitching her brows together.

Clara's father was pale, and he sat, drawing a hand

across his face.

"Apparently one of the Henderson kids said something about the Land of Origin in school. Verna is afraid he's going to get arrested and she blames Clara—something about a story she told last time she watched them."

"But that was over a month ago!" Clara burst out, "Before the law was even passed!"

"I know. This isn't your fault Clara, you did nothing wrong. But I don't think the officials will care about that. They're trying to make examples of anyone they can."

"Would they really arrest a child?" Kate asked, bringing a shaking hand to her mouth. "Surely Verna can be reasoned with."

Warren looked grim. "You heard her—if she thinks it'll protect Robbie then Verna will undoubtedly point the finger at Clara. We have to get her to safety."

"Could we hide her? The caravan for Draunland should be ready to leave in two weeks. She could stay at my brother's, or maybe in the root cellar... we could move some things to hide a portion of it," Kate said.

"I'm not going to hide in a dark hole for two weeks!" Clara said, horrified at the suggestion.

"It wouldn't work anyway," Warren said wearily, "The soldiers could search anyone we might send her to, and it would endanger them as well."

"What are we going to do then?" Kate asked, looking at Clara with fear-filled eyes.

This is my chance, Clara realized.

"I could go with Frederick," she said, trying not to let her eagerness show. "They're leaving tomorrow. If the soldiers come looking for me you can have them check the copy of the ship's manifest at the port—I'll be out of the country and they won't be able to do anything about it."

"Clara, we've talked about this—" her father started.

"She's right Warren." Kate held Clara's hand and

looked into her eyes before turning to Warren. "What else can we do? It's safer for her to go with them than to stay here."

"How is it safer to send her on a ship with sailors and other riffraff and then through a jungle your own grandfather nearly died traversing?"

"I—"

"Frederick will be there," Clara cut in, "he will look out for me Papa, you know he will."

"Frederick is barely more than a boy. He knows little more of the world than you do."

"What are we supposed to do then?" Clara's mother asked, her voice weary. Clara squeezed her hand. She knew how hard it was for her mother to argue, especially with her father.

"We must find someone they cannot tie to us, perhaps a distant relative of one of my contacts at the market. She can stay closer to the Draunlandian border, and we can pick her up on our way out."

Clara threw her hands up in disgust. "You'd rather send me to a total stranger than give me what I want? Why do you—"

"Clara." Her mother's voice was sharp. Clara snapped her mouth shut and stood holding back tears. Kate turned to her husband, setting her chin firmly and fixing him with a stern look Clara knew all too well. It was usually directed at her though, not her father.

"We don't even know if such a person exists, or whether we could find them in time. We cannot ask someone else to endanger themselves for our sake, you said it yourself. Especially a stranger."

"It would only be for a few weeks. Verna might take that long to stew herself into taking action," Warren muttered.

"Or she might go to them tonight. And when the soldiers come looking for Clara? What do we tell them?

Would you have us lie? Ask others to lie for us? Tangle ourselves in a web of fear and deceit when there is no need? Clara's solution makes sense. She can go and we can tell them she is gone. She would be safe from them and we could still retain our integrity."

Warren sighed, looking between his wife and his daughter. There were tears in his eyes. Clara suddenly felt guilty for putting him in this position, for pushing him so far. Deep down, she knew he was acting out of love.

"I need this, Papa," she murmured, taking his hand. "I've been so angry—so afraid—since the proclamation. This is a way for me to do something about it... a way to feel a little more in control." She looked intently into his eyes. "I'll be all right."

He nodded, swallowing and squeezing her hand so hard she thought her fingers might break.

He finally let go, meeting Kate's eyes and nodding reluctantly. She smiled sadly and nodded back. Then he cleared his throat and looked at Clara. "Go pack your things. You'll go home with Fredrick tonight, in case Verna goes to the soldiers today—it will buy us a little time. Tomorrow, you'll be on the ship to Kordra. I pray the Divine One keeps you safe."

CHAPTER 6

Departure

C lara breathed in the salty ocean air mingled with the smells of animal waste, half-rotten seaweed, and sweaty men working on the docks. She grinned.

"What is that awful stench?" Frederick wrinkled his nose.

"It's not awful, it's the smell of freedom and adventure! Which one is our ship?" Clara shifted her pack so it sat more comfortably on her shoulder.

"The Perseverance," Frederick replied, pointing to a tall, triple-masted schooner a few docks down.

Clara quickened her pace, excitement welling up inside her. She couldn't believe she was really here. The port was crowded and she had to shoulder her way past people of all different ethnicities to reach the ship. Every once in a while she caught a glimpse of the silvery ocean through the forest of ships on their left.

Frederick caught up to her at the gangway and set down his heavy trunk with a grunt. Though most of their companions were bringing only what could fit in a heavy-oiled rucksack, he had bought a stout, waterproof sea chest with the express purpose of protecting the diary and other valuable supplies they needed for the journey. It fit right in with the pile of other trunks waiting to be loaded into the cargo hold.

"Don't go running up the walkway, I don't want to have to fish you out of the water." Frederick said, grabbing her pack as she was about to do just that.

"It's four feet wide!" Clara protested, turning to make a face at him, "I'm not going to fall off."

"Let's not risk it, all right?" Frederick gave her a tense look and moved past her up the gangway, walking with a slow, steady stride. Clara rolled her eyes and followed him.

The view of the port was even more dramatic from this angle. A line of ships stretched down the coast ahead of them, from huge trading vessels to smaller sloops and fishing boats. On one side lay a bustling, chaotic jumble of people moving to and from the harbor, carrying luggage or unloading cargo; on the other, the open ocean.

Clara looked out over the water, watching it glisten in the sunlight. Her foot teetered suddenly and she looked down, realizing that she'd unconsciously moved right to the edge of the plank.

Maybe Frederick knows me a little too well.

She turned back to the ship and hurried to catch up with her cousin. At the top of the gangway they were met by a clerk who marked their names down on a roster and asked after their luggage. While Frederick spoke to the man, Clara let her eyes wander over the ship that was to be her home for the next month.

The deck was crowded with sailors readying for their departure, checking ropes, loading cargo, and moving up and down the rope nets that connected to the masts with a speed and grace Clara hadn't expected.

Her eyes were drawn to a figure standing on a raised section of the deck. His back was to her, and the sun illuminated his silhouette. His dark, wavy hair glistened in the sun and his partially tucked, white button-up shirt had the sleeves rolled to his elbows. The sea breeze plastered the shirt to his torso and the muscles in his back tensed as he gestured to the uniformed man standing next to him.

"This day keeps getting better and better," Clara whispered.

"What was that?" Frederick asked, coming up behind her.

"Oh, nothing." Clara snuck another glance at the man, wishing he'd turn around.

"Come on, let's get you settled." Frederick offered his arm and Clara took it, about to give up hope that she would see the man's face. Luckily it was a long journey. She was bound to run into him eventually.

Just then, he turned and their eyes met. Clara smiled.

He's even more handsome than I imagined! Those eyes and, wait... I've seen those eyes before. Clara's smile slipped.

"The man from the market!" She glared at him, turning up her nose. The man raised an eyebrow and went back to his conversation with the uniformed man.

"What man?" Frederick asked, leading Clara to join the fifteen or so other Seekers who stood clustered together off to the side.

"I just thought I recognized one of the sailors, that's all."

Clara half-listened as Frederick greeted the others and began explaining Clara's presence. She continued to sneak peeks at the raised deck, somehow hoping she'd been mistaken and the man was just a look alike for the one who'd been so condescending almost two weeks earlier. A few of the Seekers greeted her warmly, drawing her attention back to the group. Clara smiled and murmured some brief acknowledgements of their welcoming words.

Frederick pulled a list from his satchel and began methodically checking off people and the supplies they'd brought. Clara let her gaze drift back to the odious man, who was still talking to what must be the captain of the ship, and then forced herself to look out over the harbor instead.

The bustling crowds were comprised of people from all different nationalities and walks of life. A cluster of rich merchants in top hats and sleek coats stood outside a blocky warehouse that sailors in ragged cutoffs and loose shirts labored to fill. Just one ship over, a group of dark-skinned Katarans in vibrant purple, scarlet, and turquoise robes bedecked with heavy gold jewelry oversaw a similar operation. The sailors in this case were shirtless and wore brightly colored—but equally ragged—skirts that wrapped around their waists and between their legs. Around them, other shades of foreigners, some with wide, darkly hooded eyes, others with their hair pulled to the tops of their heads and flowing down in long tails, wandered across the pier, lugging trunks or carrying packs to or from the passenger ships.

It was more variety in higher quantities than Clara had ever seen. She grinned. *Bless Mrs. Henderson and her big mouth.* This trip was going to be the adventure of a lifetime, and without the angry accusations of that over-anxious busybody, she would never have been allowed to come.

A disturbance at the entrance to the port drew her attention, and Clara squinted at the shaded gateway. The crowds were parting for a group of men in deep blue coats with two horizontal white stripes that wrapped all the way around their chests. The early morning sun glinted off their bayonets, held rigidly upright by their sides as they marched across the quay.

Soldiers.

Clara's face went white and she tugged on Frederick's sleeve, pointing. He turned and saw the soldiers, his eyes widening in alarm.

"What are we going to do?" she asked, her voice coming out as a little more than a frightened squeak. She hadn't expected soldiers to actually come after them.

Mrs. Henderson had always been all bluster and no action, a fact Clara had conveniently ignored when convincing her father to let her come. Her hands wrapped around Frederick's bicep and she hid herself behind him.

"We don't know if they're here for you," Frederick said, tracking the movement of the group as it headed straight for their ship.

"Certainly seems like it," Charles, a burly middle-aged man with a neat beard said, stepping up next to Clara, "or at the very least, here for us."

Frederick spun on his heel, making Clara lose her grip on him, and headed for the raised deck where the captain stood. "Stay with the others!" he called as Clara tried to follow him, "Try not to be too visible."

She hung back reluctantly, allowing Beth Ann, a young widow whose presence surprised her, to push her to the middle of the group.

"Maybe we should all split up and try to blend in, or go belowdecks," she suggested, watching Frederick approach, not the captain like she'd expected, but the man from the market.

"Won't do any good," Old Johnny grunted, "If they're here for us they'll find us regardless, and if it looks like we're trying to hide, it'll make us seem guilty of something."

The others accepted this mutely. Clara bit her lip. *So, instead we just do nothing?*

The man Frederick had spoken to was looking at the soldiers with narrowed eyes, his arms folded across his chest. He exchanged words with another man carrying a ledger who Clara recognized from the market, then grabbed a rope and swung down from the deck, landing near the gangway and striding down it confidently. The man with the ledger approached the captain, who immediately began shouting orders at the sailors. They hastened their preparations and began dropping the cargo on the deck instead of carrying it below.

Clara twisted the corner of her apron anxiously as the soldiers approached the end of the dock, where they were met by the man from the market. She edged closer to the railing, hoping to overhear their conversation.

"Don't worry cousin," Frederick said, returning to her side, "Desmond Andreyas is the heir to Estanya's foremost merchant house. The soldiers won't want to cross him."

"And if he decides the hassle isn't worth it?" Clara asked worriedly.

Frederick hesitated. "He won't."

The soldiers' voices raised, and Clara caught snippets of the argument occurring on the dock, words like "heretic" and "troublemakers" carrying across the water. The merchant stood across from them, his feet planted firmly as he used his hands to elaborate upon whatever he was telling them. The breeze shifted, and his voice, low and melodic, finally carried across the distance.

"That provision only applies to native born Aldonians, Captain. But the law is still new, so I understand why you wouldn't be familiar with the details yet." How could a voice so beautiful also drip with so much condescension? Clara almost felt sorry for the soldiers.

The lead soldier glanced at the man to his right, who frowned and gave a small shrug. He looked back at the haughty merchant, an uncertain furrow between his brows. "Regardless, I must insist you give me access to your ship so I can gain custody of the heretics. Whether you are breaking the law by sheltering them is irrelevant—they have still broken the law and must be brought in for questioning."

"You are mistaken," Desmond replied smoothly, "My ship is registered to the port authority in Estanya and is therefore foreign soil. They are not currently breaking any Estanyan laws that I know of, and you have failed to present me with any proof that they have broken Aldonian law."

"They are Separatists!" The soldier sputtered, "They are breaking the law just by existing."

Clara clenched her hands, any sympathy she'd felt for the soldiers evaporating.

"I respectfully disagree," Desmond said, unwavering, "The law forbids expressing Separatist sentiment, not believing it. None of them have tried to convince me that Aldonia is not the Holy Land itself, so you'll forgive me if I err on the side of caution. Return with a proper warrant signed by the embassy with permission to extradite them from Estanya, and I'll see what I can do."

The soldier opened his mouth, then closed it again. He glanced back at his fellow soldiers and scowled, his hand clenching around the barrel of his musket. "Very well. May I at least receive your assurances that you will remain in port until this matter is resolved?"

"You may not," Desmond responded tersely. "Time, as they say, is money. I cannot delay the launching of my ship or we could miss important appointments in other ports. If you return with haste perhaps we can come to an agreement. Until then, I have a ship to prepare and a cargo to secure. Good day, Captain."

The soldiers had no choice but to turn around and march back the way they had come. Clara grinned widely. Perhaps her initial judgment of the man had been too hasty. True, he may just be a stickler for protocol and more concerned with making money than obeying a foreign government, but he'd still protected them, hadn't he?

Desmond had reached the top of the gangway and Clara hurried to follow Frederick as he approached the man. "Thank you," she blurted, as Frederick opened his mouth to speak. Her cousin gave her an irritated look. Desmond glanced at her, then his eyes flicked back to Frederick. "She is the one you spoke to me about last night?"

Frederick nodded. Clara's anger at the merchant returned. He hadn't even acknowledged her gratitude! She took a deep breath, reining in her temper and focusing on the fact that regardless of his attitude, his actions had shown compassion.

"Very good. She can start work immediately. Meanwhile, get the others to help my sailors. We need to get the cargo loaded and set sail before those soldiers decide to come back. I'd rather avoid another confrontation."

"Start work?" Clara asked, confusion clouding her face.

"We don't usually take on extra passengers last minute without securing a substantial fee, Miss Bowman." The man finally addressed her directly, though he was busy scribbling something on a ledger and passing it to the same scribe who'd approached him earlier. He didn't even look up.

"In lieu of such a fee, I've been assured you will work for your passage. You've been assigned to the galley for the duration of the trip. You can report belowdecks for further instructions."

Clara ground her teeth. She was supposed to spend the trip trapped in a stinky kitchen belowdecks? She wouldn't even be able to see the launch!

"We appreciate you making an exception for her." Frederick said, laying a hand on Clara's shoulder in warning. "And for keeping the soldiers from taking us into custody."

His grip on her shoulder tightened and Clara forced a smile onto her face. "Yes, thank you again," she said, the words tasting bitter.

Desmond Andreyas, heir-to-Estanya's-foremost-merchant-house, barely glanced in her direction.

"Gratitude is unnecessary. I didn't do it for you."

"Then why did you?" Clara asked, narrowing her

eyes.

Desmond was already turning away. "Excuse me, I must get back to running my ship."

"Of course," Frederick replied, steering a red-faced Clara away.

"Can you believe him?" Clara whispered, "How arrogant do you have to be to refuse thanks?"

"He's a little preoccupied trying to get us away from here," Frederick said, "I don't think he meant offense. Now hurry belowdecks while I get the others loading, we don't want to delay our departure."

Clara pursed her lips and looked around. She asked a passing sailor for directions to the galley, and was directed to a hatch in the middle of the deck. As she pulled it open, she was assaulted with the pungent smell of fish and brine, mingled with the musty, stagnant smell of mold.

"The smell of freedom and adventure," she muttered to herself, feeling the irony of her earlier statement twisting her insides. Holding her breath, she descended the rough wooden ladder rung by rung. A sailor above closed the hatch with a thump, the sound echoing inside her with a finality that filled her with despair. She'd traded the threat of possible incarceration for the reality of actual imprisonment.

"Oh, get a grip!" she berated herself. "It's not as though you have to spend the entire voyage down here... right?"

She squared her shoulders and marched down the dim hallway to face her fate.

CHAPTER 7

Voyage

A cool breeze blew across the deck and Clara shivered, tugging at her sleeves to cover her wrists. She was on her hands and knees with a brush and bucket, scrubbing some sort of horrid stain. From the crimson color she guessed it was blood and from the stench, blood from a fish. Her stomach churned and she grimaced.

She sat back on her heels and grumbled to herself, "If I wanted to scrub floors I would have stayed in Aldonia." The boards were so faded and filthy and worn, she was convinced no one would know if she even finished her task. She wiped cold sweat from her brow, tossed her scrubber aside, and stood.

She was alone on this side of the ship except for a few sailors on the upper deck who were stacking crates in silence. There was a strict chain of command among the sailors and she knew these men were low on it. They had no authority over anyone—certainly not her—so she confidently strode to the railing and looked over into the blueish green water.

As filthy as the deck was, she much preferred it to working below. Apparently being "assigned to the galley" was a fancy way of saying she got to do all the menial and disgusting chores related to the kitchen, from washing dishes to chiseling plastered on food from the crevices and corners of the galley. When the undercook had suggested she go atop to clean up a mess, she'd jumped at the opportunity to breathe a little fresh air.

Clara smiled wryly. *Fresh air. Right. Is there anywhere on this ship that doesn't stink of fish?*

The excitement of going on the voyage had faded after a week of drudgery. The ship's cook was a cranky, red-faced man who didn't take excuses and "didn't have time to coddle a silly daydreaming farmgirl", so he'd passed her off to the undercook, who kept her busy from sunup to sundown. She hadn't even had time to talk to Frederick about their plans once they arrived at their final destination in Cape Sago, Kordra. There were a few ports between here and there, so there was plenty of time, but with the journal in Frederick's possession and her every waking moment consumed by chores, the Land of Origin felt as distant as the moon.

She sighed, gripping the rail and staring out over the endless blue water, tuning in to the rocking of the ship and letting herself relax for a moment. She really needed a change of pace. Maybe when they stopped to resupply in Kemford she could convince the cook to let her go with him to the market. The country of Joravel was known for its orchards, there were bound to be fruits she'd never seen before, or at least never had fresh.

Clara turned to get back to her work before someone could come up to yell at her for being lazy. A man came up from belowdecks and Clara did a double take as he walked toward her to get to the raised deck where the captain was. His shirt was tucked tight and his pants had perfect traveler's creases down each leg. His honey-blonde hair was combed to the side, not a strand out of place.

How many gorgeous men can be on one ship?

Hopefully this man didn't have the same attitude toward her that the merchant did. They certainly didn't look anything alike.

Clara smiled at him. The man nodded to her, never slowing his stride. Clara's eyes darted to the bucket surrounded by the large puddle of water and fish entrails she'd left in the middle of the deck. She opened her mouth to warn him, but it was too late.

The man's black boots slid across the slippery planks of wood and his arms flew out in an attempt to balance himself. For a few moments he wobbled like a child learning to ice skate, then he fell forward, throwing his hands out in front of him to break his fall.

Clara heard a *crunch* and she cringed. The man cried out and sat up, cradling his right hand close to his body, the front of his crisp, white shirt covered in brown-red fish guts. Clara ran and knelt down beside him.

"Are you hurt?" she asked, reaching for his injured arm. He pulled away.

"I wouldn't be if the cabin boy had done his job." The man stood, wincing. "I think my wrist is broken."

Clara swallowed nervously. She should tell him it was her fault, but she couldn't bring herself to confess. "Let me help you wrap it. With rest it should heal in a matter of weeks—"

"I'm a scribe. I can't write with a broken wrist! Not well, anyway." The man scanned the deck with narrowed eyes. "Where is that cabin boy, I'll toss him overboard."

The color drained from Clara's cheeks. She couldn't tell him now. She knew he wouldn't actually toss her overboard, but he was angry enough he might get her confined to the galley for the rest of the trip. She might prefer drowning to that. "You're the scribe?" she latched onto the topic, hoping to deflect his anger. "I didn't recognize you without your ledger."

He pulled the ledger from his satchel with his good

hand. "I don't go anywhere without it."

A sailor came down to their deck and approached the scribe. "We're missing two hogsheads of sugar."

"That's what we get for rushing out of port," the scribe grumbled.

"Hogsheads?" Clara grimaced, picturing the head of a hog stuffed with sugar.

"Barrels," he informed her. The scribe held the spine of the ledger in the palm of his hand and let it fall open. He attempted to use his thumb to flip to the correct page and when that inevitably failed, he lifted his injured hand.

"Let me." Clara held her hand out and smiled.

The man looked at her for the first time. He pursed his lips, meeting her eyes with a measuring gaze, then closed the ledger and handed it to her.

"Page fifty-seven, column four, row fourteen."

Clara fumbled through the pages, keenly aware of his eyes on her as she flipped through page after page of neat, slanted cursive. She found the spot and held it out for him to read.

"Good. Now, page sixty-four, column four, row twenty-six."

Clara flipped through and held the book up again, this time with her thumb marking the spot in the ledger so he could see it immediately.

"There should be eighteen hogsheads," he said, then looked at Clara, "Thank you for your help." He took the book from her hands and tucked it away. Clara raised an eyebrow. "How do you sift through the numbers so quickly?"

"Levi," the sailor interrupted, "We have eighteen, there are supposed to be twenty."

"The original order on October twenty-sixth was for twenty. A week later, we delivered two barrels to the market in Rausendel," the scribe replied, "The eighteen we have left are for six each to Kemford, Teldry, and Naasim."

"Ah, I wasn't aware we'd already off-loaded some, thank you sir. I'll update the sheet in the hold," the sailor said, hurrying off.

"You were very helpful." The scribe turned toward Clara. "I don't believe we've been properly introduced. I'm Levi Perez, Head Accountant for the Andreyas Shipping Company." He bowed his head to her.

"Clara Bowman," she replied with a small curtsy. "I'm sorry about your wrist."

"Not your fault," he said, his voice pained as he tried to bend his wrist back and forth, "I think it really is broken. Bother, the ledgers are going to be illegible if I try to write in them like this."

"I could help, if you want," Clara volunteered, feeling guilty for not correcting him about her involvement in his injury, "I can write."

"No, no, you're a passenger, I wouldn't dream of imposing—" Levi started to say, and Clara rushed to interrupt.

"I'm required to earn my keep, this could be how I do it. It's really no bother." She smiled at him again. Helping him would ease her conscience and provide an out from kitchen duty. Looking at ledgers had to be less tedious than scrubbing pots, and would certainly stink less.

"I suppose I do need the help and we don't have anyone else aboard without duties of their own." Levi returned her smile and motioned for her to follow him. "Desmond will have to approve your position as my assistant if you're to see the ledgers. Come." As they walked away, he indicated the mess and raised his voice to catch the attention of a nearby sailor, "Have someone get this cleaned up before anyone else gets hurt."

Clara avoided looking at the wet patch and squashed her guilt as Levi led her to Desmond's quarters. The scribe rapped three times on the door and Clara rocked on her heels, her hands clasped in front of her. *Please let this work.*

"Who is it?" Desmond's deep, accented voice called through the door.

"It's Levi, I—"

Desmond pulled the door open. His shirt was untucked and open at the throat, revealing a wide expanse of his muscular chest. Clara blushed.

"Oh good, Levi, could you help me with this blasted button…" he trailed off, seeing Clara and eyeing the stain on Levi's shirt. Desmond cleared his throat. "What's this about then?"

Levi's facial expression stayed neutral—a little too neutral. Clara couldn't help but notice the difference between the unkempt merchant and the orderly scribe. Perhaps Levi wasn't as approving of his boss's appearance as he tried to look.

"I've hurt my wrist. This lovely lady has volunteered to assist me until it heals. Could you sign an approval form so she can see the ledgers?"

Lovely? Clara's cheeks turned a deeper red and she looked down at her shoes.

"How did you hurt your wrist?" Desmond asked, fumbling to do up his buttons. "And don't give me that look Levi, you're rather frightful yourself right now. I ripped my other shirt helping to fix the rail and this one has infernally tight buttonholes."

Levi's expression flickered as he glanced down at the mess on his shirt.

"Someone left a patch of filthy water on the deck and I slipped," he said defensively.

"Someone?" Desmond cocked an eyebrow and looked at Clara.

"Yes, that inept cabin boy, I suppose. That's how I hurt my wrist. It's probably broken. Now can I have the approval form or not?"

"*Someone* left a mess on deck, hmm?" Desmond smiled and it looked as if he was trying not to laugh.

"What's the matter with you?" Levi looked perplexed. "I think we've established that."

Clara narrowed her eyes at Desmond, her embarrassment overshadowed by desperation. *Please don't ruin this for me you arrogant prig.*

"We'll have to talk to the galley maid about that, since I assume it was the mess Oberon made gutting fish earlier today.

"I'll be having words with him about that then," Levi said through clenched teeth, growing impatient. "Now about that form?"

Desmond chuckled and turned away to rifle in his desk drawer for a paper and pen. He scribbled something and signed it, then handed it to Levi. "Don't worry about talking to the cook, I'll take care of it."

Clara's eyes widened. Sure, she wanted the job, but she didn't want the other galley maid to be tossed in the brig because of her mistake. Or maybe he was going to tell the cook that she had caused this whole disaster and she'd be stuck belowdecks the rest of the journey!

She opened her mouth to speak, but Desmond caught her eye and winked. Confusion killed the words she was going to say. Was he actually helping her?

"I appreciate it," Levi said, turning to go. Clara glanced at Desmond one last time, blushing again at the amount of exposed skin, and moved to follow.

"You might want to learn to control that blush of yours," Desmond called after her, "as we get closer to the equator most of the deckhands will be working shirtless."

She spun to glare at him, but he'd already shut the door.

"I apologize for him," Levi called over his shoulder as he began to walk down the corridor. Clara nodded but didn't say anything. She wondered if apologizing for Desmond was part of Levi's job description, the way the merchant went around doing whatever he pleased in whoever's presence, like he owned the place or something.

Well, he does own this particular place... but that's beside the point.

Levi pushed open the door to his quarters. There was a bed in one corner with a chest at the foot of it, a small desk in another, and two chairs. Next to the desk were bookcases filled with ledger books. Clara glanced around for anything that might tell her more about her new boss, but came up short. She wondered if the lack of personalization was due to a private nature, secrecy, or perhaps there wasn't much personality to work with in the first place.

Clara stood in the middle of the room, unsure what to do with herself. Levi took the seat at his desk and began pulling things from his bag. As he did so, he caught a glimpse of his shirt.

"If you'd excuse me, I'll go change and then we can get started." He opened the chest and pulled out a crisp, new shirt, and trousers. Clara turned around. She'd seen enough underdressed men for one day.

"You don't have to turn around," Levi said.

"Uh," Clara stammered and stayed where she was.

"I mean, I'm not... you don't have to worry about—"

Clara heard something metal drop to the floor, maybe a belt?

"What I mean is, I wasn't planning to change here. We may be sailors, but some of us still have a sense of propriety."

Clara heard the clank of metal as whatever had fallen was retrieved from the ground, followed by rushed footsteps and the slam of a door. She turned around to find herself alone in the scribe's office. The space felt so unlived in, so bare.

Clara thought back to her room at home and felt a pang of homesickness. She missed the garland of dried flowers that hung above her bed and the stuffed dog her grandmother had made that sat on the edge of a paint-chipped shelf. She longed for the hand stitched quilt that lay at the foot of her bed and the stack of books and letters heaped on the windowsill. Her heart ached knowing she may never see that room again. Even more than her things, she missed her parents. Were they all right? After the ship's near escape from the soldiers at the port, she hadn't even considered that maybe they'd go after the Seekers who were still there. Now she worried.

Looking around, she wondered if there was anything Levi missed. If this room was anything to go by, there wasn't much he cared about except his job.

Clara sighed, taking a deep breath and going to the porthole in the middle of the wall to look out at the ocean. It was just as beautiful as she'd always imagined, but she hadn't expected to be so homesick.

A little while later there was a light rap on the door and Levi entered, looking as pristine as he had before the unfortunate event on deck. A plain white cloth was wrapped tightly around his right wrist. He motioned with his other hand for Clara to take a seat and she did so, placing her hands in her lap and crossing her ankles as her mother had taught her. She felt it was the proper thing to do in situations such as this, but she couldn't know for sure. Besides babysitting and helping her father and mother, she had never had a real job, especially one so far outside of household and familial responsibilities (she wasn't going to count the last week in the galley, that wasn't a job, that was torture). She had never imagined herself doing something like this, but she was open to the possibility of anything that kept her away from the unfortunate smells she'd been subjected to so far on the voyage.

"Thank you for volunteering to do this, Clara." Levi busied himself with straightening the items on his desk and Clara nodded, worried that if she opened her mouth he might change his mind about letting her help him. He turned to the bookshelf and pulled out two ledger books with his left hand, placing one on the desk and holding the other out for Clara.

She rubbed her thumb over the cover and turned the book over in her hands. It reminded her of her great-grandfather's journal, but without the charm of age and use. Clara flipped through the thin, leatherbound book filled with neat, blank columns and rows. It was identical to the one Levi had pulled from the shelf, with the exception of the first few pages of his being filled out.

Clara peeked over at his book to get a better look but he quickly tilted it out of view. Their eyes met for a moment and Clara's ears burned with embarrassment. *Mother always told me to mind my manners and keep out of other people's business. Three minutes on the job and I've already messed it up!*

"Sorry." The tips of Levi's ears turned pink too. "Force of habit."

Clara's lips turned up in a small smile. She still felt like she'd done something wrong, but recognized that Levi probably felt similarly. He looked down at the page in front of him and sighed.

"The information contained within these books is more than just numbers. They represent the whole of the Andreyas Shipping Company, everything from personnel to shipping dates to individual barrels. We are very careful about who has access to them. In the wrong hands, these books could be the cause of the Andreyas empire's downfall, but in my hands they're the key to its success." Levi closed the book carefully and looked at Clara.

"Ha." A short laugh escaped Clara's lips before she could clap a hand over her mouth.

Levi raised an eyebrow. "Something funny?"

"No, no." Clara shook her head. "It's just... Who would be interested in these?"

Levi's eyes seemed to ignite at her question. "Competitors! We have competing companies on three continents, but we are the best. They either can't keep up with our shipping speed or our prices, often both, and are set on stealing our clients and discovering our suppliers."

"Really?" Clara asked, "Has anyone actually tried to take a look at your books?"

Levi colored slightly. "Not to my knowledge. And we're going to keep it that way. We have very strict protocols in place to avoid any such thing from happening."

"Protocols I need to learn?" Clara asked, wrinkling her nose.

Levi nodded. "Of course."

He went on to explain in great detail how exactly the books were stored, when it was acceptable to access any of the older copies, who was allowed to see the current ledgers of each kind, and what forms anyone else had to have if they were to be allowed the privilege.

Clara bit her lip, trying to file away all the information for later. She didn't want to disappoint him.

"Wouldn't it just be easier to lock them up and never let anyone else on your ship?" she said wryly.

"We don't often let anyone else on our ships," Levi answered, either missing or ignoring her joking tone. "Not without proper background checks. Desmond has made an exception for your people, and I'm not sure it was the wisest choice—nothing personal of course."

Clara held back a snort, clearing her throat to hide the choking noise that emerged instead.

"Do you need some water?" He reached under his desk and grabbed a canteen and held it out to her. Clara took a sip and set it on the desk between them. Levi's eyes darted toward it and she watched his fingers fidget before picking up the canteen and placing it back on the floor.

Clara glanced at it, mentally rolling her eyes. "We

can get started with whatever work you should be doing instead of explaining things to me. I think I'd learn faster that way."

Levi smiled, "Of course, let's get to it."

CHAPTER 8

Land-Ho

Over the next few days, Clara learned all there was to know about the inner workings of the Andreyas Shipping Company. She had assumed that their work would be rather light since the initial accounting for cargo had already taken place and they wouldn't be changing anything until they reached the next port.

She was wrong.

Levi worked tirelessly, checking and double-checking their purchase records from each supplier in Aldonia, reviewing their contracts for the merchants in the next port, and preparing new paperwork for future shipments. Clara helped him by fetching the appropriate volumes and making notes in the designated spots of the current ledger.

There were also safety protocols in place that, in Levi's words, "were imperative to the survival of the Andreyas Shipping Company." She was expected to learn them inside and out and follow them impeccably. Clara was fascinated by Levi's ability to train her while maintaining the high standard he held himself to, and at the same time remember the minutiae of each deal the company was involved in.

"That's what good record keeping does," he told her when she asked if he'd always had such a keen memory. "Now could you hand me volume three point seven? I need to know exactly how much mint we're acquiring in Kemford. We may have to reshuffle the cargo to account for the differences in weight from the sugar we're offloading."

After a week, Clara was finally starting to feel like she was getting her feet under her, and then Desmond announced that they'd be making port that afternoon. The flurry of preparations that followed made their previous work look lazy. Levi had Clara pull all the relevant ledgers and load them into a satchel to take with them when they made their deliveries. She copied forms in triplicate.

"One for us, one for the merchant, and one to store back in headquarters," Levi explained, raising an eyebrow at her incredulous expression. "Redundancy is the soul of good record keeping."

Clara sighed and continued meticulously filling in the necessary details on various forms. She had just finished the last form in a stack when she heard a sailor shouting up above. She looked up excitedly and Levi chuckled. "Go ahead, I can pack these. Nothing quite like your first view of land after weeks on the ocean."

Clara smiled at him and hurried out onto the deck. Birds circled the mast and flew on ahead, toward a smudge on the horizon that grew closer every minute. Before long the smudge had become a line of ships docked in a haphazard row, beyond which lay a bustling sea port that dwarfed the one they had left in Aldonia. Clara laughed and twirled around, stumbling into a sailor who grunted in annoyance, and finding her balance again moments before hitting the deck railing.

"Careful there cuz," Frederick said, catching her arm and helping her steady herself. "You don't want to topple overboard."

"Sorry, it's just—"

"Land?" Desmond volunteered, stepping up from behind Frederick, that same condescending smirk she'd grown to hate playing about his lips. He glanced at the port and then at her, his expression softening. "No matter how many times I travel, it is always a relief to see it."

Clara narrowed her eyes as he walked away, found the captain, and conversed with him in low tones while the captain shouted occasional orders to the sailors. Was he messing with her? Or had that been sincere?

"Come on, we'd better go talk to the others," Frederick said, pulling on her arm. "Desmond wants me to go ashore with him so we can discuss supplies for the jungle trek once we reach Cape Sago. The market here may have some of what we need for better prices than the other ports along our route."

"Are you going to leave the journal with someone here then?" Clara asked. Frederick stopped, turning to look at her.

"Are you volunteering to take it?" he asked, hesitance in his gaze.

Clara flushed red, feeling like a schoolgirl called out for trying to hide the fact that she hadn't been paying attention. "No! I'm going ashore too. Levi needs my help."

Frederick raised an eyebrow. "That's working out pretty well for you, isn't it? Does he know yet that you're the reason he broke his—"

"Shhh!" Clara said, her eyes flicking to where Levi had just emerged from belowdecks.

Frederick snorted, shaking his head. "The situations you land yourself in. Remember that time whe—"

"Shouldn't we be asking the others if they're going ashore?" Clara interrupted, before he could bring up some embarrassing story from her past.

Frederick nodded, pressing his lips together and

giving her an amused look. "And anyway, I'm keeping the journal with me. Seems like a safer bet than leaving it on the ship—I'm not sure if I trust the sailors. Some of them have given us shifty looks."

"Shifty looks?" Clara asked skeptically. She looked around at the sailors, and one lifted his chin in greeting. The man behind him glanced at her amulet though, and then dropped his gaze quickly. Clara sighed. There was always that. She'd hoped these men would be more open-minded than the people back home. It seemed prejudice was a trait one could find anywhere.

Frederick steered her over to where some of the other Seekers had congregated on the deck.

"We're going ashore with the businessmen. If anyone else wants to come I need to know. We can't risk leaving someone behind in Joravel because they left the ship without my knowledge."

Old Johnny snorted. "I'm stayin' put. These sailors are likely to go diggin' through our things if we all go off-ship."

"I'd like to go," Beth Ann said, her voice timid.

"Me too," her sister Marta chimed in. "We've been doing naught else but mendin' for the sailors all day long. It would be nice to see the sights."

"We could all go," a man the age of Clara's father said. She didn't know his name, though she'd seen him at services in the past. "Except Goodman John of course," the man added hastily when Old Johnny opened his mouth to argue. "He can stay and watch our belongings."

"Is that wise?" Charles grunted, "Joravelians are likely to take the Aldonian side of things, aren't they? What if there is an extradition order out for us?"

"Mr. Andreyas will be making discreet inquiries before we disembark," Frederick explained, "If he finds that Seekers are in danger here, we will hide our amulets, and the rest of you will stay on the ship. No one would be able to tell what we are."

Clara looked at her cousin in shock. "I will not," she said, defiance in her tone.

The other Seekers' glances darted between her and Frederick.

"Clara, think about this for a second. It could be a matter of life or death."

"I'll take my chances." Clara crossed her arms over her chest and Frederick started to turn red, as if he had been holding his breath too long. He yanked her aside by the arm.

"I told your father I would watch out for you. I swore over this very amulet that I would protect you." He gripped his own medallion in one hand, holding it in front of her face.

"It doesn't seem like that promise meant much if you're so willing to hide the very thing you swore over. I tucked my amulet away before, at the market. I couldn't very well stand to look at myself if I made the same mistake again."

Frederick turned his back to Clara and ran both hands through his hair. Then he stood up straight and turned toward her again. "You're an adult, so do what you will. I pray, for your sake, that there is no extradition order in Joravel."

Frederick began to walk away and she quickly looped her arm through his and walked next to him in silence. She had never fought with Frederick before and she already regretted what she had said to him. Insinuating that his faith meant little to him was a slap in the face, especially since he only had her best interest at heart.

Perhaps she had been too hasty in saying she wouldn't tuck her amulet away again… It wasn't what she wanted to do, but was she prepared to die for it? She wanted to cry over the fact that she even had to ask herself that question. She had no right to judge her cousin for his choice.

"Frederick, I—"

"You are too rash, Clara. We do not always need to agree, but I need the respect of our group if I'm to be any sort of help on this voyage. You have every right to question my decisions—"

"That's what I'm trying to—" Clara interrupted.

Frederick held up a hand to silence her. "And every right to make your own, but there are better ways to discuss these things. In the future I hope you take the time to think through each side of the situation before jumping to a conclusion, and be able to justify your choices."

Clara nodded and leaned her head on Frederick's shoulder. He was starting to remind her more and more of her father. Frederick had always been her friend, with as much authority over her as she imagined an older brother would have had. She recognized that he was stepping into a new role here on the ship, just as she was trying to do. And although she was bothered that they were not on equal ground, she was comforted that someone on this ship cared about her as much as he did. "I'm sorry," she whispered.

Frederick pulled her in for a hug. "It's okay. Look." He pointed to the docks, which were nearly upon them now.

Clara turned. The line of ships she'd seen from a distance had become a veritable forest of masts that blocked all view of anything beyond. The sailors' activity on deck intensified, men shouting and pulling ropes and casting a big heavy anchor overboard as the ship approached a long empty dock at the end of a line of similar sized ships.

Clara joined Levi near the bow, taking the thick ledger he held and giving him a stern look.

"Didn't the ship's doctor say you shouldn't lift anything heavy with that arm?"

"He barely even counts as a doctor," Levi sniffed,

"He's just a sailor with a little medical training. The man always errs on the side of caution, that way if he ever gets hurt he has an excuse to lounge about like a no-good—"

"Are you insulting my employees again?" Desmond said, walking over. He was dressed to the nines and carried a pouch that jingled with coins. Gone was the disheveled sailor, this was a businessman ready to negotiate.

"Wouldn't dream of it," Levi replied. Clara snorted, then turned red when Desmond looked her way.

"How long until we're ready to disembark, sir?" Frederick asked, coming up behind Clara with a few of the others trailing behind him.

"Not long," Desmond replied, "They've nearly got the gangway in place. I'll go on ahead and talk to the port master. They've got to inspect our cargo and calculate tariffs before anything can be unloaded. You all can wait here, just stay out of their way. Should go quickly, they've done this a thousand times."

It all went as smoothly as he'd said. After a quick chat with a tall, uniformed man wearing a tricorn hat, Desmond returned to the ship accompanied by a burly man and a severe looking woman holding a ledger much like Levi's. The three went belowdecks and then emerged a few minutes later and did a quick circuit of the deck. The woman wrote something neatly on her clipboard and handed the form to Desmond, then made lengthier notes on the page beneath before exiting the ship and handing the form to the port master.

Desmond walked back over to Clara's group. "I didn't ask directly, since doing so would draw undue attention to us, but it appears the locals are aware of the recent law change in Aldonia. It has caused some degree of unrest here. We should tread lightly, but I do not think you are in direct danger."

Frederick nodded. "We'll be careful."

Clara walked down the gangway, Desmond and his

crew in front of her, Levi beside her, and the rest of the Seekers behind her. When it was her turn to step onto the dock, she took a deep breath to steady herself. She'd been warned that it was hard to transition back to land after being out at sea so long, but somehow she hadn't believed it until she actually stepped off the ship.

Her legs wobbled under her and her stomach turned as everything around her continued rocking with the waves while she stood still. A reassuring arm wrapped around her shoulders and gently moved her forward. She closed her eyes for a moment and rubbed her thumb over the compass around her neck while she was led away from the ship. She was afraid if she opened her eyes, the commotion of the port would make her more dizzy than she already was.

"I see you kept your compass visible."

Clara opened her eyes just enough to see Levi nodding to the amulet in her hand, keeping his arm steady around her. It felt strange to have him so close to her, even if he was awkwardly stiff, as though keeping as much distance between them as he could while still keeping Clara supported. She wasn't sure if she was grateful for that distance, or offended by it.

"Yes, I did." She opened her eyes a bit more, dropping her gaze to her feet when the sunlight reflecting off the ocean nearly blinded her.

"May I ask, why?"

Clara stopped walking and turned to face Levi. His arm dropped to his side. Was he asking about her compass because he thought she made the wrong choice? If that was the case, she supposed he may have the right to ask her to hide it if he believed it would affect her ability to do her job. After all, if she was arrested it would be a pain for him to have to train someone else to help him. Or maybe he was simply curious and she was being paranoid because of Frederick's chastisement of her impulsive choices.

Regardless, Clara could only answer his question one way.

She stood tall, willing her legs not to shake. "Because I am not ashamed of who or what I am. I have done nothing wrong."

Levi pursed his lips and seemed to study her for a moment before nodding and continuing on ahead of her. Clara watched him jog to catch up with Desmond.

The conversation had been far too one-sided. She had no idea what Levi thought of her choice, though she could guess, and it left her feeling even more off-balance.

"That was very brave of you," Frederick said, placing a hand on her shoulder, "Stupid, but brave."

Clara swatted at him and he smiled, but his grin was fleeting. Behind it Clara could sense tension. She swallowed and walked on ahead, steadier now as she acclimated to land. Frederick was worried. If Clara was being honest with herself, so was she.

CHAPTER 9

Port

C lara watched Frederick cup an orange citrus fruit in his hands and hold it to his nose, taking a deep breath in. "I wonder what kinds of fruit grow in the Land of Origin..."

"I think I remember reading about something resembling a lemon in great-grandfather's journal, except it didn't grow on a tree and was a reddish color." Clara knew there were other fruits too, but that was the closest she could think of to citrus.

She let her eyes roam the market, the energy of the place similar to the one at home, but that was where the resemblance ended. Instead of unevenly spaced, sturdy wooden booths, there were rows of colorful canvas tents staked into the dirt-covered ground. The people were more colorful as well. Their clothing blurred together, each movement creating a lively, moving rainbow. Clara smiled. This was exactly the kind of place she'd envisioned visiting when she'd left home.

"I wish we could afford a few of these. I keep having dreams where I have scurvy and all my teeth fall out." He put the fruit back in its basket, casting a longing glance before turning to Clara.

"I wish we could afford them too. Hard, stale biscuits are getting old. I would do anything for a cup of Ma's fresh apple juice and some scrambled eggs." She sighed and forced herself to look away from the fruit, only to catch Desmond's eye. He smiled at her and then nodded to the merchant, who began stacking boxes of the fruit off to the side.

Clara pursed her lips, remembering her first encounter with Desmond. Did he think she was impressed by the way he threw money around? Did he fancy himself some sort of savior because he bought them some oranges? Or maybe she was assuming too much, and he'd intended to buy the fruit all along. She flushed. *Not everything is about you, Clara.* She'd heard her mother say it a thousand times, but apparently the lesson hadn't sunk in yet. Something about Desmond just put her on edge, made her want to lash out.

Clara turned and realized Levi was motioning for her to begin marking the number of crates in the ledger while he spoke to the merchant.

Since Levi's memory for detail was far superior to her own, Clara had made up a system that worked for her when keeping track of inventory. She pulled a loose sheet of paper out and tallied each crate that was set aside, knowing she could transfer the final tally over to the ledger after double-checking the amount when everything was brought aboard the ship. Levi thought the practice was messy, but she assured him it was much neater than having to correct it in the ledger after failing to keep everything straight in her mind.

As she tallied, Levi chatted cordially with the merchant about future inventory, business as usual—*more like business as always*—while Desmond and Frederick talked animatedly with a man in a gold and red cloak.

The men all laughed and Clara briefly wondered

what they were talking about, what topic besides her own embarrassment could make Desmond laugh.

She went back to tallying, hoping in the name of The Divine One that she hadn't missed any crates. Out of the corner of her eye she saw Frederick stick a hand into his bag for a moment and then stop, his brow furrowing. She looked up from her ledger, inadvertently catching Desmond's eye. Frederick pried the bag open with both hands and looked inside. Then he took the bag off his shoulder and dropped to the ground, digging frantically.

Clara's eyes widened, and she closed the distance between herself and Frederick, forgetting about her task entirely. "Where's the journal?" She knelt beside him, taking the bag in front of her and searching through it herself.

It wasn't there.

"I—I don't—"

"There!" Desmond shouted. The man in the red and gold cloak was barreling through the crowd, leaving a sea of confused and angry market goers in his wake. Clara thrust the ledger at Levi and dashed after the man, but Desmond was already on it. He leapt over some crates full of figs and ran along the outskirts of the crowd, dodging people and jumping over a cart loaded with Joravelian greenfigs.

Clara tried to follow, scrambling over things with much less grace. The man in the cloak looked behind him, realized he was being followed, and darted between two tents. Clara turned down the nearest opening she could see and turned again to run down the narrow alleyway between booths, where she assumed he was going. It was much less crowded, with only a few workers here and there presumably taking a break from the swarm of people in the market. Clara held her skirt up out of the way and sprinted, eyes searching ahead. No red or gold stood out to her. Had he ditched the cloak or had she lost him? Maybe the man had turned again somewhere. It had been a mistake letting him out of her sight—

Desmond and the man tumbled out of the gap to her left, knocking her to the ground as they fought over the journal. Clara watched, half-dazed, as Desmond landed a punch squarely in the man's gut with one hand while pulling the journal from his grasp with the other. The man in the cloak doubled over, gasping for breath and falling to his knees. Desmond turned immediately toward Clara and rushed to her side. "Are you hurt?" he asked, helping her to her feet and handing her the journal. Clara shook her head, brushing off her dress with one hand while she clutched the journal in the other. Desmond turned to deal with the thief, but in the few seconds he'd been occupied with Clara, the man had run off.

Desmond peered down both sides of the alley and sighed, straightening his jacket, and running a hand through his hair. He winced as he accidentally brushed a bruise on his forehead, then tasted a bit of blood on his lip with his tongue.

"Here," Clara fished out a handkerchief and gave it to him. Desmond took it, his eyes holding hers for a moment as their hands met.

She looked down. "Thank you. This journal—it means everything to us."

Desmond nodded and offered her his arm. "We should get back to the others."

———— ✦ ————

By the time they reached the rest of the group, the bruises on Desmond's face were more defined and beginning to turn black and purple. Clara felt sick, realizing how much danger he had put himself in for them, how much danger she'd put herself in by running after them. She wrapped her arms around herself. What would have happened if Desmond hadn't been there and she had tried to fight the thief herself? She shuddered at the thought.

"Clara!" Frederick ran to them and held Clara at arm's length, looking her over. "What in the name of The Divine One were you thinking, running off like that?"

"It was stupid, I know. I shouldn't have done it. But look." Clara held up the journal.

"How did you...?" Frederick took the journal from her before catching a glimpse of Desmond's face. He drew in a sharp breath. "Mr. Andreyas, thank you. You've done our people a great service."

"Glad to be of assistance. I know what the journal means to you." Desmond nodded to Clara and she nodded back. Whether he was being sincere or playing a role she didn't know, but right now she was too grateful to care.

"We should get you back to the ship." Levi was beside Desmond now, his eyes never leaving Clara. He didn't seem concerned about his friend at all. She wondered how often Desmond got himself into scrapes like this. "We wouldn't want our business partners to see you like this."

"I think we should all go back," Frederick said to the group of Seekers that congregated behind them. "We have a lot to discuss." He held his hand out to Clara for the journal. She hesitated, meeting his eyes and setting her jaw stubbornly. He raised his eyebrows, looking pointedly at the ledger Levi held. Clara reluctantly handed him the book and took the ledger back from Levi.

They returned to the ship, pausing only to converse briefly with the sailors handling their purchases. Clara looked back over her shoulder as she stepped onto the deck, regretting that she'd been unable to see more of the port. It seemed unlikely Frederick would allow her to set foot on land again after this.

"I've given it some thought," Desmond said, turning to Frederick as they boarded the ship, "the journal might be safer kept in my quarters, where I can keep it behind a locked door."

Clara tensed, looking sharply at Frederick and hoping he wouldn't allow the journal to be taken from them.

"With all due respect," Frederick said, "I don't think that's a good idea. This journal may be a means of increasing revenue for you, but to us it is our only hope of freedom. If we turn it over to you, how do we know you'll keep your word and bring us the rest of the way there, rather than leaving us behind and using its information as you see fit?"

Desmond's expression darkened. "I have risked a great deal to let your people on my ship. I could have given you up to the soldiers in Aldonia. I did not. Yet you insult me by questioning my honor?"

There are more important things at stake here than your ego. Clara mentally rolled her eyes.

Frederick looked uncomfortable, but stood his ground. Levi stepped forward hurriedly to lay a hand on Desmond's arm. "I'm sure he didn't mean any disrespect."

"I appreciate your generosity sir, truly," Frederick said, "but the other Seekers, they have a stake in this too, and they would not be pleased if I gave up such a precious item to a non-believer."

Clara looked from one man to the other, the tension in the air pressed in on her.

Desmond shook off Levi's hand and folded his arms across his chest. His black eye made him look even more imposing. "I have a lot invested in this too, even if I don't share your faith. Keeping that journal safe is more important than the petty feelings of some—"

"What about the records cabinet?" Clara blurted.

All three men turned to face her. The other Seekers had finally noticed something was amiss and drew closer, listening in. Clara swallowed, face growing hot. Levi was giving her an inscrutable look, and she hoped he wasn't going to be annoyed with her for infringing on his precious ledgers' safe space.

"The records cabinet," she repeated, softer this time. "It's where they store the company's accounts and other paperwork to ensure their safety." Frederick looked unconvinced, but Desmond was nodding thoughtfully.

"It would be as safe as we can keep anything on this ship," he said, "In fact, the thief probably thought those ledgers were what he was getting when he raided your satchel."

"Wouldn't keeping the journal with them be less safe then, not more?" Frederick set his mouth in a stubborn line. "I fail to see how that would be any better than giving it to you."

"But I'd be able to look after it," Clara said hurriedly, "I could check on it anytime we need to access the other files, but no one else would be able to get through the safety protocols they have in place. It's the best of both worlds, safe but also under the care of one of our own."

The other Seekers within earshot murmured expressions of agreement.

Frederick sighed. "All right. If you agree Mr. Andreyas, it is acceptable to me."

Desmond looked over at Levi. Clara could see him trying to gauge how vehemently his friend was likely to object. Levi's jaw tightened momentarily, and then he sighed, rolling his eyes. Desmond smirked and turned to Frederick. "Miss Bowman can keep the journal with the ledgers. I would, however, like to begin meeting with you to formulate a plan for when we reach Cape Sago. I'd like to study the journal and see for myself the likely benefits of these plants you mentioned."

Frederick nodded and shook Desmond's hand. "Thank you, sir."

He turned to Clara and held out the journal. She took it from him and held it reverently in her hands.

"Don't think I didn't notice that you basically get to keep this now," Frederick murmured. The corner of his mouth tweaked up in a smile.

"I was just using my head and thinking things through," Clara replied quietly, "like you wanted me to."

Frederick patted her shoulder. "Get to it, then."

Clara hurried off to Levi's quarters, whipping the door open without knocking. She gasped when she saw Levi sitting at his desk, staring at a ledger.

"How did you get down here so quickly?" Clara asked, regaining her composure.

"I was no longer needed on deck, it seems you made all the decisions for me." He still hadn't looked at her.

Clara bit her lip. *I guess I didn't think this through after all.*

"But what's done is done." Levi held out the key for her, eyes not moving from the ledger in front of him.

Clara took his hand between hers for a moment. "Thank you." Their eyes finally met and Clara could almost feel Levi's icy demeanor melting.

She took the key from him and knelt down in front of the ledger cabinet that sat on the floor.

"Why is that journal so important to your people?"

Clara fumbled with the key in her hand. Levi had barely spoken directly to her about anything since getting into port. She knew he hadn't agreed with her decision to wear her compass, and he probably thought she was reckless for trying to protect the journal by chasing the thief.

She moved a few ledgers around and found a nice, tight space for the journal to stay.

"Well," Clara locked the cabinet and then stood to take her seat across from him. "Finding the journal was a blessing. We lost everything because of what we believe, but this proves we were not forsaken. It's a beacon of hope for us, a new start."

Levi seemed to consider this for a moment, but shook his head. "I suppose I don't know enough about what you believe to properly understand. Why do the other Aldonians hate you so much?"

Clara shrugged. "I don't know why. We believe in a Divine Creator like everyone else in Aldonia. We believe that we'll be accountable for the way we live our lives, so we should do our best to help others and work hard at our jobs. The only thing that makes us different is our belief that the Land of Origin isn't some spiritual allegory, it's an actual place."

"And you have to search it out?"

Clara hesitated. "The doctrine is a little less clear there... It's there, waiting for us if we should need it, but even among my father's small congregation there is some dispute over whether we are required to move there should it be found, or whether that will only be required when the Divine One reveals it is time for the Return. Regardless, my people need a safe place to live now, and most of them wish to settle there... if we can find it."

"And this journal, it tells you the way there? Why have none of you searched it out before?" Levi's eyes were inscrutable.

"We only just discovered the journal. And it doesn't say the place in it is the Land of Origin, not exactly. But my great-grandfather's descriptions fit everything I've imagined about it, and I have to believe I found the journal when I did for a reason."

Clara sensed he didn't agree with her. She felt the same way she had on the docks when he walked away from her without saying what he wanted to say. "What?"

"You can't possibly have any proof that the place written about in the journal is the one your God promised."

Although that was true, Clara still didn't doubt that the land her great-grandfather found was the Land of Origin. "I know enough. I suppose that's where faith comes in."

Levi leaned back in his chair, the closest Clara had ever seen him to slouching. His brow furrowed. "I could never do that."

"Do what?"

"Be like your great-grandfather. Or like you, for that matter."

"In what way?" Clara looked into his deep blue eyes, trying to decipher what was going on behind them.

"Going wherever some siren call beckons you and risking everything you have to find it."

"My great-grandfather was like that, perhaps. I don't know about myself. I've only recently had enough freedom to find out."

Levi held her gaze for a moment and Clara wondered why he had asked her about the journal in the first place.

"It's about time for supper. You can head down early this evening." Levi picked up his pen, flipped to a new page in his ledger, and scribbled down a few numbers.

Clara pursed her lips. She wanted to ask him what he was thinking and why he was dismissing her, but instead she stood and turned to leave.

"I have never risked anything," Levi whispered.

"Maybe there just hasn't been anything you care enough about," Clara said. She looked back and held his eyes for a moment, his gaze unreadable. Then she left, slipping through the door and down the hall to the galley.

CHAPTER 10

Plague

Everything was off-kilter for the next few days. Clara vacillated between wanting to get Levi to open up more and wishing she could just sweep it all under the rug and go back to how things had been before. So she kept her head down and tallied cargo, updated ledgers, and helped him prepare documents for the next port.

She wasn't sure if the awkwardness was one-sided or if he felt the same way. But he never mentioned it, so neither did she. Eventually they settled back into a comfortable rhythm, and Clara relaxed. She enjoyed Levi's company, even if he didn't understand her beliefs. And it seemed like he enjoyed hers, even if she wasn't always as meticulous as he might hope.

Sea travel had lost its shine by now. Clara had reacclimated to the ship's rocking more quickly than she'd expected, and wondered if she'd have another difficult transition to land when they reached the next port. If she was allowed to go ashore, anyway.

That day seemed so distant. Levi said they wouldn't make port for another week, and Clara found the days since the last port blurring together in her memory. Had she checked the food stores two days ago or three? When had they passed those distant cliffs that Levi said marked the halfway point between ports? With nothing but open ocean on both sides for days at a time, the voyage felt interminable. She began to see why Levi was such a stickler for protocol—writing down the precise dates and times of each inventory check made it easier to track how much time had passed, though checking the ledgers for such details brought her less joy than it seemed to bring him.

At least she had the journal. At the end of each day, when Levi left for supper, she stayed behind for a few minutes to pour over the entries about the Land of Origin. She'd already read the whole thing cover to cover, now she looked for details and clues that might help them follow the same path her great-grandfather had taken.

"Cape Sago, Day 8, We have finally found a local willing to act as a guide. Uashaam says he knows the jungle well enough to help us find our way as we study the flora and fauna of the region. He is insistent that we leave in all haste, there are some local legends surrounding this area of the jungle, and he fears we may be prevented from going if our scholarly motives are uncovered. For this reason, rather than entering near the village, we are to travel a half day's journey northeast toward the next village before we turn toward the jungle..."

Clara wrote "starting point" and listed the timeframe beside it, then scanned the next few pages for a description.

"Cape Sago, Day 9, Tonight we camp within the boundaries of the jungle. The variety of plant life here is astounding, as is its natural disposition toward both order and chaos. Almost I am persuaded to believe it was at one time cultivated by the natives, though they have since abandoned it. For example, the point at which we entered the jungle was marked by a stand of trees encircling three large rocks. So perfectly symmetrical was the layout that

I immediately inquired whether it was a shrine to some native deity…"

Clara smiled. Her great-grandfather's journal entries were so focused on recording the details of the plants he encountered that she had learned little about him as a man, but she was beginning to see him as a deeply curious soul who wanted to understand everything he could about the world around him. She jotted down his description of the landmark and where it was referenced, then continued her search for relevant information, creating an exhaustive index of where to find details about their route, supplies, and use of the jungle's own resources.

Frederick met with Desmond regularly, requesting the journal from her every few days, presumably looking for the same kinds of information. Clara had asked to be included, but so far they'd scheduled meetings precisely when Levi said he couldn't spare her. Since it was her fault he couldn't do the work on his own, she didn't put up a fuss. Even if he still didn't know that.

She stewed over the fact that it was undoubtedly Desmond's doing that she wasn't in the meetings and not Frederick's—at least she hoped that Frederick knew her value and would want her there. She couldn't figure Desmond out. There were times when he seemed half-way decent and others where decency was nowhere to be found. The past few days of monotony and redundancy had provided her with an abundance of things to be annoyed at the man about.

Finally, the call came from the scout that land had been sighted. Clara let out a sigh of relief and kept working on the ledger Levi had asked her to finish. She knew now that it would be hours until they actually docked, and if she pushed through now, she wouldn't have to come back to a half-finished task. Levi glanced up at the commotion on deck, then at her, smiling faintly as he read out the next few numbers for her to copy. When they reached the end of the page, he closed his ledger and stood up.

"Get these stored away and grab the ledgers we need for port. Then we can go up top and get an estimate for when we'll need to leave the ship."

Clara jumped to her feet and marked the page she was on, then stacked the two copies carefully and returned them to the cabinet, marking on a special chart that they'd been replaced. Then she checked out the one they needed and closed and locked the cabinet securely. Levi watched her lock it and made a notation on another chart as he took the keys and put them safely in his breast pocket.

They went up on deck and Clara took a deep breath. The sea air was still salty, but now she could detect a faint earthy odor—a sort of warmth that told her they were drawing near to land. Levi sought out Desmond and Clara went to the rail, looking out at the port. It seemed less chaotic than the last one had. She supposed that was because it was further from the busy trade lanes.

A lone rowboat approached the ship, and Clara recognized the sailor within it as one who had smiled at her over dinner the night before. Raoul? She thought that was his name. Spending every day locked up with Levi had given her little time for learning much about the sailors. She waved as he drew nearer, and was surprised to see a dour expression on his face. He stayed back a ways from the ship, calling out for a tethering line and connecting it to his boat when they cast him one.

"What's going on?" Clara asked, walking over to where Levi stood.

"The port's too deserted. Desmond sent a scout to see what's wrong. Don't want to dock and risk our cargo if there's war or plague in the region."

Desmond was leaning over the rail a few feet away, conversing with the man in the rowboat. He straightened suddenly and motioned for the sailors to cut the tether, a grim expression on his face. He started calling orders to raise the anchor and turn the ship around. Clara looked from him to Raoul, who was rowing back to shore.

"Well, I guess we'll be putting those ledgers away," Levi said, sighing in a way that Clara had come to recognize as him reining in his frustration.

"But, the sailor—we can't leave him behind!" Clara turned toward Levi, her eyes wide with shock.

"If it's plague, that's company protocol. He had contact with someone here, and that means he may have caught it. He'll be well cared for by the company's liaison in the region, don't worry."

"But what if he hasn't caught it? You're all but guaranteeing he will now!"

"It's not our place, Clara," Levi said gently, "Desmond makes these kinds of calls. It's better if we just do our job and carry on as before."

Clara snapped her mouth closed, inwardly seething. Maybe protocol was a good enough excuse for Levi, but not for her. Nothing justified leaving a man to die.

The other Seekers who had come up on deck were starting to ask questions, calling out to the sailors who efficiently worked the lines and cranked the windlass to raise the anchor back onto the ship.

"What are we doing?"

"Why are we turning around?"

Desmond looked up from where he was speaking to the captain. He walked to the edge of the foredeck and shouted for silence.

"Unfortunately we will not be able to make port here. We will press on and try for another nearby city, but it is likely we will not be able to make landfall until we reach Naasim.

"Why?" Old Johnny's voice rang across the deck. He had his arms folded and a sour look on his face.

"There is vidirian fever in the region. For the ship's safety it is best we avoid anywhere that has had recent contact with Teldry."

The Seekers hushed. Clara could see they were as stunned as she was by this turn of events.

"Because we cannot know for certain when we will be able to restock, water will be rationed starting immediately. We will evaluate our reserves and draw up a schedule for distribution, giving preference to those whose work is more physically demanding."

Clara raised her eyebrows. That seemed premature. She could tell the other Seekers felt the same way. They began to murmur to each other again, confusion and irritation evident in their tones.

Desmond held up a hand and they quieted. "I know this isn't something many of you have had to deal with, but the sailors have been through this kind of thing before and if we all stick to the schedule, we'll be able to make it to the next port. Anyone with complaints is welcome to come to me for further explanation, but be warned: if I catch you sneaking extra water, the punishment will be swift and severe." He fixed them all with a stern look and then turned away.

Clara was torn between anger, fear, and disbelief. She started toward Desmond, ready to give him a piece of her mind and toss a tether to Raoul herself. After only a few steps, she heard Frederick's voice, calm and reassuring, behind her.

"I'm sure Mr. Andreyas has his reasons for rationing the water supply—"

"He's treating us like criminals," one of the other Seekers argued, "Saying we'll be severely punished if we don't adhere to his dictates."

"He's already left a man to fend for himself in a land riddled with plague!" This voice was a woman's, too abrasive to be Beth Ann, her sister maybe? Clara turned back as murmurs of agreement echoed among the Seekers. There would be power in numbers, if the others came with her to confront Desmond—

Frederick put his hand up, calling for silence. He reminded her of her father again, the way he quietly commanded the group's attention, and to Clara's recognition, their respect.

"I will entertain no more negativity or disrespect toward Mr. Andreyas. We do not have to agree with everything he says, but while we are on his ship we will abide by his rules."

There were a few murmurs again, but this time Clara was hesitant to join them. As strange as it was, Frederick was their leader, just as her father had been back home. Frederick had asked her to think before she acted, and she could do that now. Backing him up would do more good than trying to argue with someone as stubborn as Desmond.

"My cousin is right. There is nothing we can do about the way things are on this ship, but we can continue to take care of each other and make sure we all make it through to the next port." Clara looked up at her cousin, who smiled down at her.

"You heard the girl. Back to your duties."

Frederick wrapped an arm around Clara's shoulders and gave her a quick squeeze. "Thank you."

Clara nodded and hurried off to Levi's quarters. She was sure the change of plans would have thrown him into a frenzy and she wanted to be there to help.

Sure enough, Levi was pacing his quarters, flipping through a ledger with his good hand and mumbling to himself. "...something like this happens, it's hours and hours of work for me."

Clara closed the door behind her and Levi jumped.

"I didn't hear you come in."

Clara leaned against the door. "Seems like I'm not the only one upset by this turn of events."

"Of course I'm upset by it. All that time we spent this

week getting papers ready was for nothing. We can't very well use the contracts and receipts we've dated or—"

"I know, but now you've got some help." She smiled, hoping to bring him back to his normal, even-tempered self. He was a calming influence on her, something she was beginning to see great value in.

"I suppose that's true." Levi pulled the key out of his pocket. He tossed it to Clara. "Eyes up."

She caught it and unlocked the cabinet. "Does this kind of thing happen often?"

"Plague? Occasionally. More often in lesser developed regions. Vidirian fever is one of the worst."

"Is someone left behind every time?" Clara whispered. Instead of grabbing the ledgers that needed to be updated, she ran her fingers over the soft spine of the journal instead. Levi had opened up to her once before. Maybe he would be okay talking about what was on her mind now.

"Clara," Levi's voice was stern. "We talked about this."

"No, you talked about it. You said you were fine with leaving Raoul behind, you were fine that he was sentenced to death."

"Of course I'm not fine with it. Raoul is a good man, a good sailor. I've known him nearly as long as I've known Desmond!"

"Then how could you watch that happen to him and not be outraged?"

"It's not my job to—"

"Right. Not your job, not your place... or is it because you won't stand up for anything? Too afraid to take the risk?"

Levi was taken aback, the hurt apparent in his eyes. His voice was low and yet it rang in Clara's ears. "It's clear to me that you haven't seen enough of the world to see this situation for what it is. And you obviously don't know me well at all. You're young and naive and don't have a single clue what happens every day off your farm!"

Hot tears sprang to Clara's eyes. "If that's so, I won't be much help to you this afternoon and I really should be going."

She ran out the door and let it slam closed behind her, running down the hall and wiping the tears that fell freely as she went.

How could I have been so stupid? She had thought Levi was becoming her friend, someone she could potentially confide in. Instead it was blatantly obvious that her thoughts and feelings weren't welcome. She heard a door in the hallway open and turned to see Levi step out.

"Clara, wait."

She turned her back to him, wiping the last of the tears away, hoping he hadn't seen them, and went straight for the ladder. She climbed as quickly as she could with the journal in one hand.

"Ah, Clara." Desmond and Frederick opened the hatch just as she reached the top. "Perfect, you already have the journal. We were hoping to use it to verify the distance from our next port to Cape Sago. Can Levi spare you a minute?"

"Actually—" Levi started from below her.

"Of course he can," Clara said, clambering out. "He believes I should get to know more of the world anyway." She closed the hatch, feeling a bit guilty as she glimpsed Levi's hurt expression at the bottom of the ladder.

Frederick gave her a concerned look, obviously taking in her red nose and the catch in her voice.

"Let's go, the sooner we start the sooner I can get back to my duties." Clara pushed past them and walked toward the meeting room before he could say anything.

Frederick and Desmond followed her. They joined a group of men including Old Johnny and a sailor she thought was the first mate, and soon the group was deep in discussion about the best place to start their expedition into the jungle.

Clara had a hard time focusing on the meeting. She couldn't get the expression on Levi's face out of her head, and when Desmond asked for her input on the plan they'd already sketched out, she said something noncommittal without really listening to him.

Get it together Clara! she berated herself after Frederick shot her a look. She tried to listen more intently for the rest of the meeting, but didn't find another opportunity to jump in before Desmond was called away by one of the sailors and the meeting was abruptly adjourned.

"Are you feeling all right?" Frederick asked as he handed her the journal to lock back away. The others were filing out, hardly sparing a glance for her.

"I'll be okay, I just—being away from home is harder than I thought it would be." Clara felt tears well up again unbidden.

She'd said the words as an excuse, but as soon as she spoke them she felt their truth. She did miss home. She missed her mother's gentle voice, her father's reassuring presence. The farm that Levi had so callously mocked had been her whole world, and if things went right on their journey, she might never call it home again. *If things go wrong I probably won't be able to call it home again either.*

She felt a pang of worry for her parents. They'd be leaving for Draunland shortly, if they hadn't already left. Had all the necessary preparations been made? Had they been able to sell what they needed to pay for their journey?

A wave of deep guilt washed over her. She had been so focused on the expedition and whether or not she'd be on it, that she'd paid little attention to the plans for Draunland. She desperately wished she had done things differently. If she had, maybe now she'd have a better idea of how her parents were faring.

Frederick patted her on the shoulder. "I know it's

hard. Being among strangers and working constantly doesn't help things either."

Clara took a steadying breath and clasped the journal tighter. She still had Frederick, and she still had the journal. It was a connection to her great-grandfather, and therefore her mother. Her mother, who had trusted her to go on this journey, to find a place where they could be safe, together.

Clara stood a little straighter. "I'll be fine. You're right, I'm just tired and today's events were…trying. Next time I'll be more attentive, I promise."

Frederick nodded and left, going to see to his other duties. Clara sighed and made her way back to the office, rapping the door twice with her knuckles before going inside. Levi looked up as she entered, then went back to organizing the papers he'd been working with.

Clara stood in the doorway uncertainly for a moment, then straightened her shoulders and walked across to the cabinet to return the journal to its place, marking it down on the chart and returning the key to the hook they kept it on for easy access while working.

She took her seat and Levi silently handed her a stack of papers labeled "Port Teldry corrections for undeliverable goods: plague" in handwriting a touch less neat than she knew he preferred. He'd gotten pretty good at writing while wearing the brace on his wrist, but she knew it pained him if he did it too much. He must've been working at a snail's pace while she was gone.

"I'm sorry for leaving," she said stiffly, "I—"

"Copy those, please," Levi cut in, not looking up from the ledger he was examining. Clara sighed and picked up a pen.

CHAPTER 11

Water

The next couple days were some of the worst of Clara's life—they even rivaled the days she'd spent thinking she wouldn't be able to come on this voyage. At least then she'd been able to drink water.

As it was, Levi barely talked to her other than what was absolutely necessary to do their work, her lips were chapped from constant thirst, and she was developing a headache she suspected was due to dehydration. The crew continued to go about their duties, but their interactions were less jovial than before. General grumbling increased among the passengers and sailors alike, and more than one scuffle broke out in the line to get water, which was only available twice a day.

They passed another settlement along the coast, this one visibly flying a plague flag, and Clara overheard Desmond conversing with the captain about whether they should continue hugging the coastline in search of another port or strike out to open water so they could reach Naasim more quickly. The concern in his voice scared her.

After breakfast the next morning, Clara went on deck to get some fresh air before her morning tasks. In addition to the anticipated sunshine and salty air, she was greeted by the horrifying sight of Charles lashed to the mast. His cheek was bruised and puffy, the left eye swollen shut.

She ran to the man and yanked at the ropes around his bloodied wrists.

"No use," he panted, "sailors don't tie loose knots."

"What happened? Who did this to you?" Clara said, brushing away the unkempt hair that fell into the man's eyes.

"My own fault. I tried to steal water." He met Clara's gaze and she saw remorse and desperation there. "I was just so thirsty."

"I'm going to get help."

Clara ran to find Frederick, aware that she would be late for work but not caring to do anything about it. *Levi would tell me to let it go anyway.*

When she found Frederick with another group of Seekers, she made a few quick apologies and pulled him away. She didn't want to alarm them with what she knew, especially if Frederick could fix it before they even had to know.

"Do you know what's going on up there?" Clara motioned to the upper deck. "Charles has been tied up and beaten and—"

"I know, I'm so sorry I couldn't catch you before you ran up there, I was just telling the others to steer clear of the deck until his sentence has been served."

Clara stared at Frederick, letting his words sink in. "You knew? And you're just going to let Desmond get away with this?"

"It's his ship Clara. There's nothing—"

"Charles is your responsibility! Desmond has no right to treat him like a common criminal just for being thirsty! You have to talk to him, you have to—"

"I already spoke with Mr. Andreyas this morning. He

came to me as soon as they discovered Charles trying to break open one of the casks. I've done everything I can do."

"Well I haven't! I'll give him some of my water, I—"

"Clara, don't be foolish. He's still receiving his water rations, and if you don't drink what you're allotted you'll be of no use to anyone."

Clara glared at him sullenly. Frederick sighed. "We're meeting again before midday to study the journal, will you come?" He held her gaze with his own, the look in his eyes challenging her to live up to his expectations.

"Fine," Clara replied, her voice clipped.

"Good," Frederick said, his expression softening. "We need you there Clara. You know the journal better than anyone. But after last time... well, having the journal kept in your care was called into question."

Clara felt another spike of anger. *Of course, Desmond still wants to keep it with him!*

"You need to come and you need to put aside all this resentment. Focus on the purpose of this voyage."

Clara watched him walk away, then closed her eyes and tried to center herself. *Focus on your purpose.* She turned abruptly and went down to the office. She spent the morning taking notes on the journal. Levi glanced at her a few times, but she ignored him. His wrist was almost healed. If he didn't insist on using the most perfect handwriting he'd be able to keep up with his work fine on his own now. If he was slowed down by her lack of cooperation it was his own fault.

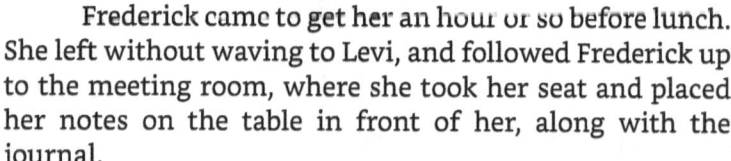

Frederick came to get her an hour or so before lunch. She left without waving to Levi, and followed Frederick up to the meeting room, where she took her seat and placed her notes on the table in front of her, along with the journal.

"Now gentlemen," she started, as soon as Desmond

had called for order but before he could say anything more. "I realize I haven't been available for most of these meetings, but after considering everything I heard last time, I've evaluated your proposals and come up with a number of alternatives based on the information found in my great-grandfather's journal."

Desmond raised an eyebrow at her boldness, but Clara ignored him. Frederick couldn't seem to decide whether to be horrified or amused. She ignored him too. Instead she turned to Old Johnny.

"You indicated last time that without a proper map of the area, charting a course is useless and we should focus instead on determining what supplies to take with us into the jungle. I've drawn up a list of every supply mentioned in the journal, as well as a list of additional modern items that seem likely to help in the kinds of situations my great-grandfather talks about. I've noted which of these items we already have aboard using the inventory ledgers, and which we will need to secure at the next port."

Old Johnny took the lists from her, scanning them and grunting in a way that seemed to indicate he was impressed. She felt a twinge of apprehension, hoping he didn't find anything that would prove she didn't know what she was doing. She had used every ounce of knowledge she had gained from the journal, as well as drawing on adventure novels she'd read and the stories of recent exploration in the paper back home. It was all just speculation, but hopefully she'd gotten some things right.

"You have a lot of netting listed here," Johnny said, stabbing the page with a finger.

"To keep the bugs away," Clara said, "they carry some really dangerous diseases there."

"We can take rosemary and sage to burn and it'll do near as good a job... or whatever smelly herb is cheap and available in large quantities," Johnny said. "Works better than draping the whole camp in nets and will be significantly lighter. It also won't slow us down if we need to pack up in a hurry."

"Excellent," Clara said as Desmond opened his mouth to say something. She made the change to her own copy of the list, then handed Desmond a paper. He accepted it, closing his mouth.

"These, as near I can tell, are all the landmarks mentioned in the journal, in order and with page numbers to reference his drawings of them. We can't know exactly where to start without seeing the landscape, but he says they traveled east after picking up their guide at the village, and entered near a particular tree formation. We can ask around if the place still exists and start our expedition from there."

"This is incredible, Clara," Frederick said, leaning to look over Desmond's shoulder. "How long did it take you?"

Clara blushed, then raised her chin. "I made most of the lists this morning, but I couldn't have done it if I hadn't already studied the journal front to back many times."

"One might wonder why we even bothered meeting without you," Desmond said wryly.

"Yes, one might," Clara replied, her tone clipped. She was bordering on insubordination, but she didn't care. They needed her and he should know it. This whole voyage had been her idea from the beginning.

She pulled a few other lists from her stack: animals they might encounter, plants they could eat and ones they should avoid, and other useful bits of knowledge she'd gleaned from her great-grandfather's detailed writings. It was unfortunate that Levi was still mad at her, he would've been impressed by her organization and use of redundancy to keep track of it all. At least she hoped he would have.

The others examined her lists and gave input on what may or may not be useful. Some items she added to her list of supplies, others she argued against and ultimately left off. Desmond put his foot down only twice, citing the expense of certain items and giving cheaper alternatives in their place. Other than that he mostly sat back and listened, watching her as she listened to the others, argued with them, and pointed to evidence in the journal on occasion to prove a point.

When the conversation began to die down, he gathered the papers, rapped them into a neat stack and handed them back to her before addressing the room.

"Thank you all for your input. We seem to have this thing in hand finally. You may go."

Clara took the stack of papers and rose.

"Not you," Desmond said, "A word please, Clara?"

Clara turned to face him and he motioned for her to sit. She did so, crossing her arms and holding her chin high. Whatever he had to say couldn't be good, it never was where Desmond was concerned. But Frederick was right, she needed to think about why they were on this voyage and what was at stake.

She thought of her mother, who was probably facing life in a new country surrounded by people who were different from her... No matter how much resentment Clara had toward Desmond, she was determined to handle the rest of their conversation with grace and temperance, for her mother's sake, even if it took all of her self-control to do so.

"I have to say, I'm impressed with you, Clara."

Clara blinked. *Is he serious?* "Thank you, Mr. Andreyas."

"Desmond, please." He tapped his fingertips on the stack of papers in front of him. "This is exactly what we needed to get us started. We've been going in circles the past few weeks, if I'm being quite frank. I'd hoped you would bring this kind of energy to the last meeting you attended, but I see now that perhaps you were simply as disappointed as I was with the lack of enthusiasm and knowledge from this lot."

Clara pursed her lips, which were dry and cracked from thirst. She wondered briefly if there would ever be a situation where the man said something she found palatable. She doubted it.

"Levi says you've taken nicely to the books. He speaks quite highly of you, actually. I want you to work with him on making sure all the supplies we've agreed upon are accounted for before we embark into the jungle."

"I believe Levi's wrist is healing quite well. I doubt he will need my assistance much longer." She looked down, tugging on the corner of her apron.

"Maybe so, but I want your eyes on this. If he can handle his own duties, then you take this on and have him consult. We will all benefit from having multiple eyes on the numbers."

"Yes, sir." Clara glanced up at Desmond. His full attention was on her and she felt the intensity of it. It was like he had his own gravitational pull, drawing her in with his dark brown eyes that somehow shone even in the dim room. Clara looked down at her papers and cleared her throat, wishing she had something to drink.

"We'll need to know which account the funds are to come out of. Then there is the amount of each product... Exact prices would be preferred as well, but if we need to use estimates Levi always says it's best to err on overestimating the cost of each item."

"Let's add that to the next meeting's agenda."

As he scribbled some notes, Clara's anger started to boil again. She would have to keep working closely with Levi even when his wrist was fully healed, which would be miserable if the awkward silence between them continued, but other than that, the conversation had been going well... Which made her even more mad. How could he sit there like nothing was amiss when a good man was tied to a mast, by his orders, at that very moment? How could he ignore the fact that everyone under his care was wasting away from thirst?

I need to get out of here. Clara stood. "If that's all you need, I should be getting back to my duties." She turned on her heel and made long strides toward the door.

"Wait a moment," Desmond said.

Clara closed her eyes, took a deep breath, and faced him. "Yes?"

"I wanted to ask once more if you feel comfortable having the journal stored with the ledgers. After the last meeting—"

A laugh escaped Clara's lips. "You mean after the last meeting when you called my authority to keep the journal —which belongs to my family, by the way—into question because you wanted it for yourself?"

So much for grace and temperance.

Desmond raised his eyebrows and sat back in his chair. "Are you always this passionate?"

"Where injustice is involved."

"Your hurt feelings count as an injustice?" Desmond smirked. He thought this was amusing, like a game of jacks. Did he even realize how much his decisions affected other people?

Clara stood and put her hands flat on Desmond's desk, leaning in. "This has very little to do with my feelings and everything to do with how you treat the people in your care."

"And how is that?"

"Should I start with a few days ago when you sent a man to his death in a rowboat to die far from everyone he knows and loves?"

Desmond's smirk faded and he sat up in his chair. "Now hang on—"

"Or how about just this morning, when you had a man beaten within an inch of his life because he was afraid of dying of thirst?"

Desmond was quiet for a moment and then stood. "Is

that all?"

"No. You have an air of condescension about you that makes you completely unapproachable. You throw out these dictates like we're your prisoners and expect us to follow them without a second thought, but there's no reason to heed your orders without the respect that comes from knowing you're a decent human being!"

Desmond came around the desk and stood inches from Clara.

"I've heard quite enough." He stared down at Clara, his height making her feel small, but she stood her ground. "The decisions I make on this ship are life or death. Yes, I sent a man to quite possibly die on foreign soil. Yes, I made a gruesome example of a thief. And I'd make the same decisions a million times over. I have an aura of haughtiness? If that keeps people in line, so be it. Have you seen what vidirian fever does, Miss Bowman? If I'd let Raoul back on this ship every one of us could have died right along with him, covered in our own blood and filth."

Clara recoiled at the thought. "He might not have even had it! He barely even—"

"But if he did start to show symptoms, what then? Would you have had me throw him overboard? Keep him locked away from everyone else with no one to care for him? Condemn someone else to care for him and risk a second life?"

Clara opened her mouth to argue, but he kept going right overtop of her.

"Even if I did, we don't have the resources to care for someone with severe illness. Leaving him there was his best chance for survival, as well as our own."

"And Charles?" Clara said stubbornly, beginning to see she had made a hasty judgment but unwilling to let the injustice she had witnessed above slide.

Desmond sighed. "I regret that had to happen. But if I let one thirsty man drink freely from a cask, I am taking it straight out of the mouth of another. What if he had stolen that water today and it meant there wasn't enough for Frederick or Old Johnny?"

"I would find another way to—"

"There is no other way, Clara! If the punishment is light, desperate people decide they'd rather take the punishment than live with the thirst. And then we run out of water and everyone dies. This is how things must be if we want to survive. There is no cure for vidirian fever, there is no more water. This is it. Can you see now why I may seem unapproachable? I cannot let myself care more for the individual than for the whole. I have a job to do, a responsibility to these people."

Clara was silent and looked down at her feet. Her face burned and tears threatened to spill from her eyes, which was the last thing she wanted. She had embarrassed herself enough for one day.

She felt like a fool, accusing him the way she had. Levi and Frederick had both tried to tell her to trust Desmond's judgment and she had disregarded it completely.

Desmond tilted his head, trying to catch her eye.

"I'm sorry," she whispered.

Desmond's voice was soft and quiet, "If it seems I have taken these responsibilities lightly, I apologize and assure you I do not. Who do you think has to tell Raoul's wife and family what happened, if he doesn't survive? If you think you feel bad about this, try looking in the eyes of a child and telling them their father will never return."

Clara winced, closing her eyes and feeling more miserable than she thought she ever had in her life.

Desmond put a hand on her arm. His touch was more gentle than she would have expected. "Do you know why I had you stay after the meeting?"

Clara looked up at him, his face only inches from her own. She shook her head.

"I believe you can do this job better than anyone else on this ship. Even if someone else read that journal over and over, their heart wouldn't be in it as much as I know yours is. I believe that to be an asset, do you?"

"Yes," Clara whispered.

"Then we are in agreement."

Desmond left, giving Clara time to gather her things and wipe her tears before she had to face the others.

CHAPTER 12

Preparations

After a good night's rest, Clara woke earlier than usual, still undeniably mortified by her actions the day before. Underneath it all, though, she felt hopeful. She had a real purpose, a real place on the crew, and she had found a way to show her worth. If only she had shown it and then kept her mouth shut.

She knew she was lucky Desmond had been so forgiving. He could have told her to forget the whole thing after she'd torn him apart for simply doing his job. She cringed at the way she'd thought she had some sort of higher moral standard than Desmond, when really she didn't have a single clue what went into his decisions. She just didn't have enough real-world experience.

Just like Levi said.

Clara groaned and fell back onto her bunk, burying her face under her pillow. Thinking about her conversation with Desmond made her realize how terribly she had treated Levi as well. He had opened up to her, tried to extend an arm of friendship (which she knew had to be difficult for him), and she had completely disregarded it and judged him as a calculating and callous man when he was really just looking out for her. If she wanted to do her job well and be happy on the rest of this voyage, she needed to make things right with Levi.

She combed through her hair and pulled it up into a bun, then smoothed out one of her better dresses and put it on. It hung loosely on her frame and her uncovered arms were more angular than they had been when she'd left home. The voyage had not been kind to her body, leaving her more frail, dehydrated, and malnourished than she'd been on the farm. Her mouth watered thinking of the fruits and vegetables her great-grandfather had described in the journal. She couldn't wait to pull them right off the vine and sink her teeth into them.

Shaking any thought of food from her mind, she pulled a shawl over her shoulders and stood tall, heading straight for Levi's quarters. It was about an hour earlier than she usually started her day, but she guessed Levi would be awake and ready. Everything about Levi made her believe he was an early riser.

Clara knocked lightly, not wanting to disturb anyone else at this hour. She heard shuffling behind the door and then it opened, revealing a rather disheveled Levi, still in his clothes from the day before.

"Clara!" Levi tried smoothing down hair that showed he had clearly slept on one side of his face.

"I didn't mean to wake you," Clara said, barely able to suppress her amusement. She had never seen so much as a wrinkle on the man's clothes and yet here he was, looking like a schoolboy who was late for class.

"I thought you were Desmond. I mean, if I had known it was you—" Levi finally looked at her and stopped trying to tuck in his shirt, regaining a little composure. "Is there something you need?"

"Yes, actually." Clara felt a bit silly for coming here unannounced. She should have known Levi would feel uncomfortable with something so sudden, but she needed to say this to him before she lost her nerve. "Could we talk for a minute?"

"Of course, umm, do you want to come in?" He held the door open, looking embarrassed. The bed in the corner was still unmade. "If you'll just allow me a minute to tidy things up—"

"I was actually hoping you would come up on deck with me."

Levi glanced down at himself. He quickly finished tucking his shirt and slipped on a belt before pulling on his shoes. He held the door for her and they climbed the ladder to the lower deck, and another to the upper deck.

They were alone other than a few sailors getting ready to end their shift. Everything felt sluggish this morning, even the wind barely blew. It was calm and quiet. Clara breathed out, her inner world settling to match the outer one. This was how she had often felt with Levi. It was good to have it back.

"I'm glad you came to find me this morning." Levi put his hand on the rail beside hers, barely an inch away.

"You are?" Clara's heart skipped a beat. She hoped he was feeling the same way she was, that he wanted them to mend the rift their argument had caused as well.

"I'm afraid I spoke too harshly before—"

"Please don't say that." Clara put her hand on top of Levi's. "You were right. I was foolish. You were trying to help me and I dismissed your guidance without a second thought."

Clara moved both of her hands to the railing in front of her. Levi slid closer to her and Clara leaned into him, just enough that she could feel the warmth of his arm on her shoulder.

"I wouldn't have listened to me either, the way I spoke to you." Levi said quietly, "I don't know what got into me. I promise you, it was out of character."

"I wouldn't have asked you here this morning if I

thought it wasn't." She nudged him and he looked down at her, seeming to study her face for a moment before settling on her eyes.

"What are you thinking?" Clara whispered, asking the question she had wanted to ask him so many times before.

"That we should have done this sooner."

Clara looked away, wondering if he meant apologizing or something else entirely.

There was commotion on the lower deck as the sailors switched shifts, signaling that breakfast would be served any minute.

"I'd best be getting back," Levi said. "After breakfast we'll get started on those supply lists, yes?"

"Yes."

Levi smiled and walked backwards a few steps. "Good."

Clara turned back to the ocean and smiled too. She was glad to have her friend back.

The next few days were easier. She didn't know if it was the renewed warmth between her and Levi, or that she'd grown used to feeling thirsty and tired all the time.

Then they reached the bottom of the last cask of water, and tension on the ship spiked. The navigator assured them all that they'd be making port that very afternoon, but those who hadn't received their water ration struggled even to speak civilly to the others. One of the sailors, all of whom had shown incredible discipline until now, ended up confined to the brig for striking the cook when his portion size was smaller than his companion's.

Clara saw now that Desmond's harsh rationing had, if anything, been too generous. *Please,* she prayed, *Get us to the next port before anyone dies.*

Just when Clara was beginning to fear the navigator's calculations had been off or he'd been lying to keep their spirits up, land was sighted. The cheer that rose from the deck was subdued, but only because their throats were all parched and dry, not from lack of feeling.

This stop, thankfully, went much smoother than the others. The cargo was efficiently unloaded and tallied, new provisions taken on, and they pulled back out to sea that same day. Clara stayed on the ship and worked on tallying the new supplies while Levi handled everything on shore. His wrist was finally healed, and he'd insisted they'd work faster if they divided the work.

She ran into Desmond as she was leaving the hold, a ledger under her arm and her pencil tucked behind her ear.

"Oh," she said, stopping abruptly as he stepped off the ladder and turned toward her, "hi."

"Hello Clara," he nodded curtly, then stood for a moment, looking past her at the entrance to the cargo hold. "Almost finished taking inventory?"

"Yes sir," Clara said, "I just tallied the final cask of water. I assume that's the last of the new cargo anyway. The sailors stopped bringing more down and the one I talked to didn't seem to think there'd be any more..." She snapped her mouth shut, realizing she was babbling like an idiot.

"Good." Desmond's eyes crinkled a bit at the corners. Was he *laughing* at her? Clara's temper flared, but she quickly tamped it down. She had misjudged him too many times already, maybe this time she could give him the benefit of the doubt.

"So, um, how are the preparations going for the expedition? Levi said you have a good handle on things, but that preparations are never really over...but then again, he's Levi, so..." Desmond spread his hands out to the side and rolled his eyes.

Clara smiled. She'd known Levi and Desmond were friends, but somehow she'd always thought Levi only put up with Desmond because he was his boss. That was another thing she had probably misjudged.

"He's actually not being finicky about that," Clara said dryly, "There is still a lot to do, even without triple checking and recording everything in multiple places. But we're working on it."

"I appreciate your dedication," Desmond said, "Not everyone would have been capable of working so hard under such trying circumstances." Desmond indicated the water barrels, then put a hand on her shoulder. Clara was suddenly aware of how close they were standing in the dim, narrow corridor. She looked up at him and for a moment neither of them moved. Then Clara broke her gaze and looked past him at the ladder.

She cleared her throat. "I'd better get these numbers to Levi," she murmured, stepping around him and rushing up the ladder. She paused to catch her breath at the top, then shook her head and moved through the passage to Levi's office.

They were now only days away from their final port, and every spare moment they had was spent planning for their arrival.

"I want to have packs for each individual stocked with a small supply of food, water, basic first aid supplies —"

"Won't that make for an awful lot to carry? How far do you expect we'll be trekking from shore?"

Clara pulled out a roughly sketched map Desmond had helped her make from the information in the journal entries. "My great-grandfather saw the valley after several days of travel inland. It's possible that some people could stay in the village with the bulk of the supplies, but those venturing into the jungle will need to carry everything they need to make it to the valley and back... Unless we try to forage. My grandfather does mention a number of fruits and vegetables among his plant descriptions."

"Hmmm, probably better to be careful and bring what we need, despite the weight. Identifying plants can be a tricky business, we don't want to end up poisoning ourselves because we fail to notice a slight difference in leaf shape or misinterpret a description."

Clara nodded. She'd had similar thoughts.

Levi jotted something down. "How many people do you expect on the expedition inland?"

"About ten—seven of us and a few sailors. That will leave a somewhat equal number in each group. Some of the Seekers have already expressed preference for one group or the other to Frederick."

"I don't imagine it will ultimately be up to them which group they're in."

"What do you mean?" Clara asked, furrowing her brow.

"I'm assuming Desmond will divvy up the assignments based on what skills and capabilities each individual has."

Clara thought about that for a moment. She wasn't sure any of the Seekers had skills that would be useful traipsing through a jungle, other than Old Johnny—if he was to be believed. If she hadn't been in possession of the journal, she knew she wouldn't have anything of value to offer either.

"That's a good point. I think we should have a few training meetings before the expedition begins, for those who are interested. That way everyone can be prepared and learn the skills they need to stay safe."

"Noted." Levi jotted this down on a separate sheet of paper, one they were compiling with information specifically for Desmond. "Now, about the supplies—"

"I used the inventory ledgers to make the lists. I thought it would make sense to make use of materials we already had—" Clara snapped her mouth shut, realizing she should have asked Levi before using the information in the company's confidential ledgers without asking him. "I'm sorry I didn't ask first."

Levi smiled and shook his head. "If you're on company business, the information is open to you. You're as good as any of our accountants now. Speaking of..."

Levi opened a drawer in his desk and pulled out a leather book. It was similar to the ledgers, but a lighter shade of brown. It was thicker and shorter in height than they were as well.

"This is for you."

Clara turned the book over in her hands. Clara opened the cover to find "The Voyage of Clara Bowman" written right in the middle in Levi's unmistakable, perfect handwriting. Clara ran her fingertips over the print.

"I picked it up for you at the last port," Levi said. "I thought you might like having a place to keep a record of your adventures, like your great-grandfather did."

Clara closed the cover and held the book tight to her chest. "I love it. Thank you, Levi."

"Clara," Levi put down his pen and took a deep breath. "I—"

There were three sharp knocks at the door and Frederick barged in. He was grinning and couldn't seem to stand still. "We've made it to port."

Clara dropped everything and ran out the door, "I'll be right back to put things away," she called over her shoulder, knowing it probably wouldn't help. Levi would still be annoyed she'd broken protocol, but she had to see it for herself.

She reached the deck and darted between the busy sailors as they hurried to do all the little tasks that went with docking a ship.

A rough wooden dock extended out toward them from a sprawling collection of straw huts. The village was old-fashioned, but the dockside was still crowded with people and warehouses. Clara couldn't see anything beyond the buildings, so she climbed the shrouds to get a better view.

Not quite like climbing a tree, she thought as they swayed and rocked with the lapping of the waves.

She hooked an elbow through the rope and hung out as far as she dared. The warm breeze caught her hair and teased it out from her loose bun, whipping it behind her as she gazed in awe at the sight before her.

Beyond the village a tangle of green spread out in all directions as far as she could see. Far to the southeast, she could just make out mountains rising into the distance, darker green than the jungle around them and shrouded in mist.

The Land of Origin is out there somewhere, she thought, excitement rising within her, *we're finally here!*

CHAPTER 13

Village

Clara stepped off the ship and made her way slowly down the gangway and away from the docks. She'd spotted a patch of white sand below some cliffs and couldn't resist the urge to take off her shoes and bury her toes in it. There was work to do, of course, but it would still be there after she took a moment to savor the fact they'd arrived in one piece.

She opened her satchel and rested her hand on the two journals that resided there. The ship's captain had orders to take the ship back to Estanya in a few days, with the cargo the sailors were currently loading, then return for them. The trip would take him almost a month, and hopefully they would be waiting for him here, having discovered the Land of Origin. Until that time, Clara was in possession of the journal.

She fingered the spine of the second journal, the one Levi had given her. A warm glow filled her chest when she thought about him, but it was always accompanied by a flutter in her stomach. They had reached a point where they were finally understanding each other, getting along in their work, and developing into (she hoped) close friends.

She bent down and scooped up a handful of sand, letting it fall through her fingers, and wondered if friendship was enough for her or if there was something more she wanted.

The lie of omission she'd used to become his assistant still hung over her head. She no longer feared that he'd hate her for being the one who left the mess he'd slipped on, but it was still an awkward weight on their relationship. The lie had been left alone for too long to bring it up without seeming like she'd been intentionally keeping something from him. He finally seemed to trust her, respect her. If she told him now he'd see her as an immature child again.

Clara sighed, and turned to put her shoes back on.

"It's comforting somehow, isn't it?"

Clara jumped, whirling around and nearly falling over. Desmond caught her, one hand on each of her arms, and set her back upright.

"Sorry, I didn't mean to startle you." He gave her a sideways grin and cocked an eyebrow. She used to think that was condescending, but maybe he was just easily amused. Clara blushed. *Confound this man! I can never seem to figure out what he's thinking!*

"Did you come to join me?" she asked, trying to recover her dignity. She looked up at him and realized how close they were standing. His warm hands were still resting on her arms, loosely gripping her just below the shoulders. Desmond seemed to realize it at the same time she did. He let go, tucking his hands behind his back, and cleared his throat.

"You should probably get your shoes back on, there are some pretty nasty little crabs that live in this region. You're going to want all your toes for our trek through the jungle."

He looked at her sidelong, and Clara narrowed her

eyes at him, trying to determine if he was being serious. Desmond just smiled and turned to walk back to the ship. Clara hastily bent to grab her shoes. She didn't know if he was joking or not, but she wasn't about to ignore his advice and find out the hard way.

When they rejoined the others, Clara hurried to help Levi with the long list of supplies they'd been working on.

"What were you doing over there?" Levi asked, hardly glancing up from his list.

"Just walking in the sand."

"You shouldn't do that around here. You never know what kinds of things are lurking in the sand. Half of the animals and plants we come across will probably be poisonous."

"Yes, I've been warned already," Clara said. She looked over at where Desmond was giving last minute instructions to the captain. Why had he come over to get her? He could have just as easily sent a sailor.

Levi finally pulled his eyes away from his checklist. He followed her gaze.

"He didn't tell you your feet would fall off, did he?"

Clara looked at him sharply. "No, just my toes."

"Crabs or spiders?"

"Crabs."

Levi snorted and returned his focus to his work. "Des always has liked that joke."

"But you just said—"

"There's likely to be broken shells, spiny sea creatures with poisonous prickles, or sharp rocks." He checked the last box on his list and tucked the ledger under his arm. "But as far as I know, no vicious crabs."

Clara rolled her eyes up toward the sky and sighed. "Well, that's a relief. Should we get started?"

They quickly organized the Seekers and the members of the crew who would be joining them in the jungle. Levi assigned one group to secure lodging for the night and another to guard the cart of supplies they'd unloaded from the ship. The last group—to which he assigned Clara and himself—was responsible for obtaining the remaining supplies they would need at the market that bordered the harbor.

"Wait a moment, Levi." Desmond's interruption stopped him from tucking his ledger away. "I want Clara to come with me to ask around about a jungle guide. We're going to need a local to help us."

Levi glanced at Clara, then back to Desmond. "She would be more helpful with supplies Des. She knows these lists inside and out."

"As do you, I'm sure. Clara knows the journal better than anyone else, and she can describe the area we are looking for and the kinds of things we expect to encounter. Sorry Levi, I'm going to insist."

Clara looked at Levi, trying to gauge his reaction. He huffed and scratched out her name on his list, then glanced up and caught her watching him. He rolled his eyes toward Desmond and gave a minute shrug. She smiled, glad he wasn't too angry. Talking to locals sounded much more exciting than buying supplies—or more likely, marking down supplies while Levi bought them. Even if she did have to put up with Desmond while doing it.

The others dispersed, going about their tasks, and Desmond nodded toward the path. "Shall we?"

Clara took her cue from his mock formality and curtsied to him, then began down the dirt path, which led away from the dockside market and into the cluster of huts. Despite her outward nonchalance, she felt the weight of what she was setting out to do. These were the first real steps toward everything her people had been striving for, and though she was proud to be the one to take them, she'd be lying if she said she wasn't scared.

Desmond stopped a passing villager, a native man with deeply tanned skin and reddish-brown hair. Clara hung back and looked past the huts into the sprawling jungle that rose behind them. The place looked dark and mysterious, and more than a little dangerous. She felt her breath catch as a small flock of birds took flight with a raucous screeching off in the distance. For the first time, she confronted an unpleasant possibility.

What if we fail?

Desmond had finished his conversation and motioned her forward. The path into the village was winding and oftentimes unclear. Though the huts had looked close together from the ship, they were more spread out than she'd originally thought, and the spaces between were still mostly ungroomed. Weeds covered in thorns with small white flowers crowded around their feet and nipped at Clara's dress. She pulled it up to about mid-calf, but then the plants pulled at her socks.

Clara put her hands on her waist, letting the dress fall back around her ankles. Breathing became more difficult as they climbed up a steep slope. It was apparent to Clara that during the month at sea she had lost much of the physical stamina she'd gained on the farm and it made her worry about what was to come. Would she be able to make it through the jungle in one piece? What about the other Seekers?

Desmond was starting to pull ahead of her, though she could tell he was trying to slow down for her sake. She didn't understand how he seemed unfazed by the physical exertion, since he had been on the ship all that time too. She supposed he had been walking the deck and helping the sailors while she spent her days sitting in an office, but it still surprised her.

So far, the huts they'd passed had seemed unoccupied. The man Desmond had asked for directions was the only villager they'd seen. Clara wondered if that was because the people were busy elsewhere or if they were hiding inside, away from the strangers.

Desmond turned where the path forked and began to skirt the edge of the village. Clara looked down the other way and saw a smaller market, one probably intended for locals instead of foreigners, like the one near the docks. People bustled here and there between more densely clustered huts, while children played in the open space between them.

We should head that way so we can talk to the shopkeepers. They might know something.

Desmond clearly had other plans. He called to her and she hurried to catch up, deciding she'd wait to see his destination before suggesting anything. The foliage around them became more dense with various types of palm trees springing up in all shapes and sizes, interspersed with large, fragrant flowers.

Clara reached out and stroked a soft, red petal. "Beautiful," she whispered.

"They don't have flowers where you're from?" Desmond raised an eyebrow.

Even Desmond's sarcasm couldn't dampen Clara's wonder. "Not like this." She rubbed the petal between her thumb and index finger. "My father planted a rosebush for my mother when I was young. It's taller than me now, but the blooms never get this big."

Clara's smile faltered. Homesickness mingled with worry seemed to come in unpredictable waves, brought on by the most bizarre things. She was in the most beautiful, exotic place she'd ever been but it felt wrong to enjoy it when she didn't even know where her family was, or if they were okay, or if she would ever see her home again.

"Are you all right, Clara?" Desmond's accent made her name sound almost regal, like a different name altogether. His version of her name somehow felt more fitting for the woman she wanted to be—one who stood her ground and made things happen.

"Yes, I'm fine." She nodded and cleared her throat,

glad there was someone to pull her away from her own thoughts.

"Good. I was thinking we could start with the village chief. He will know the trade routes and neighboring villages, and be able to connect us with other leaders in the region. He will surely know of someone to lead us through the jungle."

"That is a good idea. In addition to a guide, I'd like to find out more about my great-grandfather. The journal doesn't give much information about him as a person. He mostly recounts the scientific side of things." Clara's brow pulled together in thought. "I hope the chief is married."

Desmond laughed. "Married? Why?"

"In my experience, wives are the ones that know the goings on of the village."

"And the men are oblivious?" Desmond almost sounded offended as he held a leaf the size of Clara's torso aside so she could pass.

"Well," Clara wanted to roll her eyes at Desmond's pride, but squashed the urge. "When was the last time you gossiped about anything with one of your sailors?"

"What does that have to do with—" Desmond pursed his lips as understanding dawned on him. "Oh."

Clara giggled and Desmond offered her his hand as she stepped over a tree root that was sticking out of the dirt.

"I also think we will find great value in the memories of those who were alive around the time my great-grandfather would have been here. The journal mentions the tribes in this area passing down stories and legends orally. With any luck, there may be someone old enough that remembers him coming through this area or had a relative that came across his path."

Desmond considered this. "Did your mother ever speak of him?"

"He died before she was born and her father wasn't

a talkative man. She thought her father's silence on the subject stemmed from the personal differences between the two men."

"What do you mean?"

"My great-grandfather wasn't a Seeker, my grandfather was."

"I don't see why that would cause a problem."

Clara stared at Desmond's back, perplexed. He had seen firsthand how the people in Aldonia and Joravel dealt with them. Even lawmakers and soldiers, those charged with the responsibility to protect people, treated them with contempt.

"You're the one who told me I should hide my amulet in the marketplace." Clara pointed out. "People don't understand us, so they target us to try to make themselves feel safe. When my grandfather converted, his father didn't understand why he would choose to become a Seeker when all it did was cause problems for him. But I suppose you've never felt like an outsider in your own home."

Desmond stopped walking and turned toward her. "Maybe not in my own home, but I have traveled my whole life, Clara. I was born in Estanya, but as soon as I was old enough to swab decks my father had me on his merchant ships learning the family business. I have been an outsider everywhere I've ever gone."

Clara met his eyes, surprised that he would open up like that to her. "So you know the feeling."

Desmond nodded, his expression unreadable. "That frustration when no one will quite meet your gaze... the pit in your stomach when people shift from friendliness to wariness once they identify you as 'different'... I hate that feeling. It's why I've tried to train away my accent. I speak five different languages, and I've taken painstaking care to ensure I sound as close to native-born for each of them."

Clara smiled, unsure how to respond to something so deeply personal. He really did know the feeling. She latched onto the last part of his confession, hoping to shift the conversation away from her unfair assumption. "For the record, I like your accent." It was true. For all his faults, when he spoke she couldn't help feeling drawn in by his voice.

Desmond's eyes narrowed, like he was unsure if she was teasing him or not.

"I do!" she protested, "I noticed it was stronger on the ship than when we met in the marketplace. I imagine that's because you aren't focusing on it as much as you are on shore."

Desmond pursed his lips again. "I suppose."

"Now," Clara said, stepping past him on the path and continuing toward the large hut she could see at the end of the path. "Let's go make use of some of those languages you know—I imagine someone here will speak one of them!"

CHAPTER 14

Chief

The chief's hut was much grander than the others, about twice the size with a white exterior instead of sandy brown. Big, bright green plants with wide seaweed-like leaves lined the home, springing up at the feet of vast palms adorned with coconuts. The smell wafting out of the hut was thick and sweet.

Clara's hands started to sweat. She thought of when her father would meet with important church leaders in the parlor of their home. She would often be asked to set the table or bring tea in at such events, but she had never really been part of them. Now here she was, heading into a situation she was ill-prepared for and feeling ashamed of her inexperience.

If only mother was here. She would know what to do.

Clara smiled. She may not have had much experience in these situations, but her mother did. She couldn't count how many times she'd watched her mother counsel with her father or host luncheons with such grace that it made Clara proud to be her daughter.

All I have to do is try to be like her.

"Are you ready?" Desmond asked. Clara nodded, his

presence a welcome reminder that she wasn't doing this alone. Funny how quickly things could change. Only a week ago she would have rather done *anything* alone than with him.

They walked down the white stone pathway that led to the door and were met by a guard holding a handmade spear. Desmond bowed to the man and Clara curtsied, following his lead. The guard addressed them in a language Clara had never heard before and Desmond answered without hesitation in the same tongue. She smiled. Desmond thanked the guard who held the door for them, and they stepped inside the hut.

The door shut with a gentle swish, leaving them alone in a dark room. The only light came from a row of candles on the back wall, illuminating a depiction of what Clara guessed was their deity. A ball formed in her stomach. She knew they would have to be careful how they spoke in case the tribe was hostile toward differing beliefs —something her great-grandfather hadn't needed to worry about, as a scientist with little religious inclination.

A tall, sturdy-looking man with silvery-white hair emerged from behind a curtain and Desmond stepped forward to greet him. A loose wrap made of thin gauzy material covered the chief's broad, dark chest, and tied at one hip, where the ends dangled over a skirt tightly woven from thin reeds. Clara stood to the side, feeling like more of an accessory to Desmond's outfit than a participant in the conversation. Her breathing became more shallow and panic started to rise to her throat.

Why am I even here? He doesn't need me at all!

Just as she had made up her mind to bolt out the door and join Levi in the market, Desmond put his hand on Clara's back, easing her forward. The chief began to talk animatedly and Clara forced a smile, nodding as if she knew what he was saying.

Desmond leaned down, his lips so close to Clara's ear

that his breath moved the strands of her hair next to her cheek. His voice was low and soft. "Chief Tarrue says he welcomes us to his village."

"You have a lovely home," Clara said, a smile still plastered to her face even though her heart was pounding out of her chest. "The pottery is gorgeous."

Desmond translated for her and the chief nodded his thanks and continued talking, waving an arm toward a shelf that held several pots with various plants inside. Clara recognized some of the cuttings as smaller versions of the plant that grew outside.

Clara stepped up next to the chief and gestured to one of the cuttings, asking if she could take a closer look. The white-haired man nodded enthusiastically and Clara took the small pot from its resting place and held it in her palm. The red and orange designs on the pottery were delicate and more detailed up close.

"What kind of plant is this? I noticed them outside." Clara spoke directly to the chief and waited for Desmond to translate.

Desmond leaned in toward Clara and whispered, "He says the plant is called paashia grass. It is placed strategically outside of their homes and around the village to ward off harmful pests."

Clara nodded and placed the pot back on the shelf. She thought about Old Johnny and his suggestion of purchasing herbs to ward off poisonous insects. "Ask him if they have someone we can talk to about harvesting or purchasing some, an herbalist maybe."

"But we aren't sure what Levi has already purchased —"

"If this is what the locals are using, it's what we want to use too."

"Levi won't be happy about it."

"I can help him reconcile the books." Clara lifted her chin in the air, a sparkle in her eye. "I think this is less about him and more about your pocketbook." Clara smiled mischievously and Desmond narrowed his eyes before turning to address the chief. There was a lengthy back and forth that lasted several minutes. Clara followed the conversation with her eyes and occasionally made out the word paashia, so she assumed she had made her point and a negotiation for the plant was underway.

Clara had only seen Desmond at work for brief moments in the markets and on the ship, but never in a negotiation like this. He stood taller, straighter, and all informality melted away. He looked and sounded like a real businessman, even though the words were lost to Clara.

Finally, the chief clapped his hands and laughed a deep, whole-hearted laugh, slapping a hand on Desmond's shoulder and shaking him a bit.

"We've been invited to a feast," Desmond said, offering Clara his arm. They followed the chief through the curtains into the depths of the hut. The sweet smell from earlier got stronger the further in they went and Clara's mouth started to water.

"You were a master negotiator in there," Clara whispered, nudging Desmond.

"The plant grows abundantly in this region, so he was motivated to sell."

Modesty was not a look she'd expected to ever see on him. "I still think it takes skill to navigate conversations like that when you haven't known the person more than an hour. What's your secret?"

"Trust," Desmond said. "Don't give the other side a reason to doubt you."

"That seems too simple."

"Simple, but effective. If you know you're going to follow through with your promises, then they'll believe that you'll follow through with your promises. And you extend the same courtesy to them. Obviously that's good for business..." He trailed off, seemingly lost in thought.

"But I suppose it is more than that. Where it really counts is when something goes wrong."

How had this become a deeper discussion of his trading philosophy? Despite herself, Clara was intrigued. "How so?"

"Some businessmen try to be tricky, to pretend they don't care about the outcome. But then if something unexpected happens the whole deal can fall through. I've found it better to be honest, but clear about your limits, then they'll know your heart when it matters most."

Clara pondered his words as they were led out the back exit and through a large garden to a long, wooden tabletop that sat on the ground, surrounded by thin, rectangular mats. The table was stacked high with foods Clara didn't recognize, but that only heightened her excitement. The plates and utensils hadn't arrived yet and Clara couldn't figure out how they would fit on the table.

The chief sat at the head of the table and motioned for Clara and Desmond to sit along the side to his right, with a woman Clara assumed was his wife on his left, across from them. The chief introduced the woman as Saana. Even in her mid sixties, the woman had a youthful glow and her silver-streaked golden hair reminded Clara of sunshine and moonlight. The feeling was reinforced by the warmth of the woman's smile.

Once the other people had found their seats, the chief stood to address the group. Clara waited patiently until he was done speaking and all at once everyone started snatching up the food. Desmond didn't hesitate and tore a leg right off a bird that resembled a large pheasant while Clara watched dumbfounded. She had gone into the evening trying to be like her mother... She could only imagine what her mother would have thought of this scene!

Clara pulled a few small, round fruits from a vine and popped them into her mouth one at a time. She chewed slowly, trying to catch bits of conversation with little success. Desmond chatted with Saana, his easygoing manner returning after the more serious conversation in the hut.

Without warning, boisterous conversations cut short and gave way to murmurs and worried glances.

Clara leaned into Desmond and whispered, "What happened?"

"I asked Saana about your great-grandfather's expedition through this area."

Clara wanted to throw her handful of fruit at him for not consulting her before bringing up the expedition. She should have warned him to tread lightly. Her grandfather hadn't said a lot about the natives, but he had indicated his guide had been afraid the locals wouldn't approve of them venturing into the jungle to study it. Clearly whatever Saana had said alarmed the other village people, and Clara needed to know why. "Did she remember him?"

"She did, though she was just a small child when they came through. He was one of only three men to have made the journey into the jungle and come out alive."

Clara's heart leapt. "How many expeditions have gone through the jungle over the years?"

Desmond relayed Clara's questions. "She says that many men the world over have died seeking The Valley of Paradise."

"The Valley of Paradise?" *Another name for the Land of Origin, perhaps?* Clara tamped down her excitement. "Can you ask her to elaborate on that?"

Desmond nodded. Saana's lips flattened into a straight line and she spoke in a pinched voice, one too quiet for most of the party to hear. "She says that The Valley of Paradise lies in the heart of the jungle, situated in such a way that no man has ever stepped foot there. The locals avoid venturing too deep into the jungle, to stay away from the valley and the curse that protects it."

Her great-grandfather had mentioned this superstition, but he hadn't put much stock in it. Clara pulled the journal from her bag and began to flip through it until she reached the last entry. Henry had seen the valley with his own eyes. If he had seen it, maybe others had too.

"She said there were other survivors." Clara closed the journal. "Are they still alive? Does she know where they are?"

Desmond hesitated a moment. The chief was leaning back in his chair, his previously jovial face now stoic. His wife whispered to him, concern clear on her face. Clara's anxiety spiked. She'd been too pushy. It was clear the village people today were as leery of these expeditions as their ancestors had been, and Clara had inquired too far.

Desmond stood and leaned over the table, grabbing a bottle of wine and refilling the chief's glass with a debonair smile. The familiar lilt of his voice drew Clara in and she felt the tension in the air defusing as Desmond's laugh rang through the air, inviting others to join him.

Clara kept quiet the rest of the evening, letting Desmond take the reins and smiling and nodding and nibbling as needed. The sun was beginning to set and people began to file out the back gate. Clara was exhausted from the outing, but she didn't want to leave without getting the information they needed.

The chief stood and Desmond followed suit. They helped the women to their feet and Clara placed her hand on Desmond's arm to get his attention.

"The survivors," Clara said through a forced smile.

"I don't know how to bring that up without—"

"Tell them the truth." Clara looked into Desmond's eyes. "I'm trying to bring hope to my people and they can help."

Desmond placed his hand on top of Clara's, and a little jolt went through her. He turned back to the chief and spoke slowly and deliberately. Clara silently prayed the couple would recognize her intent with her questioning, and that they could tell her where to find the remaining survivors.

Saana took Clara's hands in hers and the chief spoke directly to her as Desmond translated.

"Your great-grandfather was the only outsider who survived the jungle, along with two members of our tribe. One was a young man at the time, around fifteen years old and the other was a guide who often aided travelers in the region. The guide has long since passed to the Beyond and had no descendants. The young boy is still alive...but he might not be of much help."

Clara's heart skipped a beat. "What? Why?"

Desmond didn't have to translate that, Saana continued anyway.

"It's said that he left his mind in the jungle and though he never went back into it, he could no longer be among the tribe either. He became a nomad on the outskirts of the very place that alienated him from his own people. Every now and then he is spotted on the border between our territory and the Aanidesh territory. There's a hut there... If I were you, I would start your search there."

Clara thanked them both, and followed Desmond back out onto the path. He carried a large pack full of dried paashia grass. Despite the seriousness of their conversation, the chief had not forgotten their deal. A jumble of feelings tied knots in Clara's stomach, which was already too full from the delicious food. She was troubled by the fate of the boy, both because it meant he could be useless to them, and because it made their own expedition feel more dangerous.

They had left the hut much later than Clara expected. The sun was already setting, and the palm trees cast long shadows across the path as they worked their way back to the designated meeting spot.

Clara glanced at Desmond, who appeared to be deep

in thought as well. "I suppose we'll have to wait to go downshore till tomorrow," she said tentatively, hoping a conversation would lighten the mood.

He glanced at her and then around at the increasing darkness. "That would be prudent. We'll get started first thing in the morning. Hopefully Levi was able to get all the supplies and we can organize our expedition properly from the hermit's hut—if we can even find him."

"Do you think it's true?" Clara murmured, "What they said about him leaving his mind in the jungle?"

Desmond shrugged. "I think people in small villages like a good story. Could be that he just likes to be on his own, or the same illness your great-grandfather contracted left him a little funny. We won't know till we can talk to him."

"Does it worry you?" Clara asked, "The danger, I mean? I know you're on this expedition to discover new medicines and spices to trade... I can't imagine those are worth risking your life—or sanity—for."

Desmond stopped. He turned to face her, his expression unreadable. "Is it worth risking your life for?"

"The future of my people? The chance to live without fear and believe what we choose?" Clara said, her voice growing stronger with each word. "Yes, it's worth it."

Desmond smiled. "Then you don't need to worry about me. I made a deal with your people, and I'm a man of my word—whatever the dangers may be."

Clara smiled in return, then looked past him as Frederick appeared on the path ahead, a concerned expression on his face.

"There you are! We've been waiting for you two, I was starting to worry you'd been hurt or taken—"

"We're fine," Clara said, yawning widely.

"But thoroughly exhausted," Desmond added. "The chief graciously invited us to dinner, and our inquiries kept us late."

Frederick ushered Clara down the path and Desmond followed, until they came to a small inn. It was similar to the chief's hut in style, but had obviously been outfitted with modern conveniences by a foreigner or enterprising local, for those who visited the port.

Frederick showed Clara to the room she would share with the other two unmarried women on the expedition. She slipped in quietly and went straight to the washroom, where a huge tub waited.

CHAPTER 15

Supplies

Clara sat on the edge of her bed and combed through her wet hair, a contented smile on her face. Never again would she take for granted the simple luxuries of a bath and a bed. A dim candle flickered on the nightstand between her bed and Marta's. On the other side of her was Beth Ann, who had barely spoken a word all evening.

Clara had imagined at the beginning of their journey that they would have become close friends by now, but instead they were as unknown to each other as when they first started out. Between Clara's clerical duties and their... Well, Clara didn't know what the women had done with their time on the ship, but nonetheless they had rarely crossed paths.

"Isn't it nice to have our feet on solid ground?" Marta asked, laying back on her bed and stretching her arms above her head. Clara smiled her agreement and Beth Ann opened a book without acknowledging them. Marta continued, "I guess you ladies won't get to enjoy it much longer since you're heading out to the jungle shortly."

"Aren't you as well?" Clara asked.

"Not for all the money in the world," Marta laughed.

Clara scrunched her brow. "Then why did you come?" She knew that some of the Seekers had volunteered to be among those who waited in the village, but Marta's attitude seemed to go beyond that.

The woman sat up. She was ten years Clara's senior, a handspan shorter, and twice her width. She had short brown hair and squinty eyes, like she was perpetually trying to read something in the distance. "I didn't have anything going for me at home. Even before the new law, I was bound to lead a miserable life regardless of religious prejudice."

"Why do you think that?" Clara shifted on her bed and turned a bit further from Marta, so she wasn't looking directly at her.

"You don't have to worry about this yet, since you're still young and thin and whatnot," Marta waved a hand. "But once you reach a certain age, it's like someone waves a magic wand and you suddenly go from twenty-four and eligible to twenty-five and a leper."

Clara grimaced and turned her back to the woman, fairly certain that Marta's lack of companionship stemmed more from her abrasiveness than her age.

Marta didn't seem deterred at all. "You should be careful though, wasting these valuable years trudging through some forsaken jungle. You do want to get married, don't you?"

Clara opened her mouth to respond, but couldn't get a word in.

"My plan is to spend the next month in the village. I'll say I'm twenty-three again, fish around for a husband, and if they're not biting, I'll hop back on the ship and try the next port." She laughed loudly and Clara clenched her teeth. "From what I've seen, Estanya produces some pretty good looking men. Take Mr. Andreyas for example. I swear I spent half my time on the ship plotting how to—"

Clara blew out the candle between them. "Good night." She pulled the thin blanket over her shoulder and flipped onto her side, her back facing Marta. She didn't dare move in case the shuffling of her blankets invited another lesson from Marta.

Turns out not having her companionship on the ship was a blessing.

Clara stared beyond Beth Ann out the open window, the evening sky clear enough to see the stars. She wished her mind was like that tonight. Instead it was clouded by Marta's words, none of which she wanted to justify but at the same time they made her doubt.

Growing up, Clara had felt safe within the home her parents had established. They loved her and each other and took care of their farm with pride and dignity. Clara had assumed that would be her life as well, someday, even if she had hoped for more excitement, she'd known eventually life led to a family of her own, on or near the farm. It was simply how things were. Now it seemed more complicated.

She was an accountant, a voyager, and learning to become a leader. She had put very little thought into anything beyond finding the Land of Origin. Was she being too shortsighted? After all, what would be the point of reaching the promised land if she had no one to share it with?

On the other hand, she was young and had so much to see and learn and do. Would marrying slow that down or take away that possibility altogether?

Marta began to snore and Clara rolled onto her back. Beth Ann blew out her candle and all was dark.

No, she thought, *it would only enhance the thrill of the adventure to have someone to share it with. As long as it's the right man.*

---❧---

The next morning Clara helped Levi inventory their

supplies and triple check to be sure they had everything they needed. It was harder than Clara had anticipated to limit their supplies to only what they could carry on their backs, but somehow they managed.

Desmond had made inquiries about the route to the cottage on the edge of the jungle. Amaar, a local who had learned their language after years of serving foreigners at the inn, had overheard and volunteered to take them. The journey would take almost half a day and Desmond didn't want to come back this way afterward, so they couldn't forget anything.

Clara looked over the pile of tightly packed bags and frowned. Her back was aching just thinking about carrying one of them, especially since she still felt weak from the voyage. Marta surprised Clara by picking up a pack and joining her sister and the other Seekers waiting to leave.

"I thought you weren't going to go into the jungle?" Clara asked, her pen hovering above the place where she was supposed to write who carried what. She barely glanced at the woman, still put off by the conversation they'd had the night before.

"I don't plan to," Marta said, "but I'm not going to pass up an opportunity to get to know the locals... Maybe Amaar can escort me back here after I twist my ankle and can't continue." She waved at the tall man with dark hair and tan skin who was speaking with Desmond, then smiled bashfully and turned her eyes downward.

Clara looked at her in disgust.

Marta met her gaze and shrugged, rolling her eyes. "Judge all you want, everyone else does." She moved off to chat with the guide, easing her way in next to him and asking about the route they would take.

"Unbelievable," Clara muttered.

"Don't be too hard on her," Beth Ann said from beside her. The woman's voice was timid. Clara looked over, surprised to hear her speak, and felt like she'd been caught snitching treats from the cellar. Beth Ann glanced at her, then frowned and scuffed her foot. "She's had a rough go of it."

"Really?" Clara asked, "Aren't you the one whose husband died—" she stopped, realizing how callous she must sound. "I'm sorry, I didn't mean—"

Beth Ann met her eyes. "At least I know what it feels like, to be loved, wanted. Marta..." she trailed off, shaking her head.

Clara pursed her lips, wanting to point out that Marta was probably the one at fault for that, but that would be rude, so she restrained the impulse.

Beth Ann read her expression and caught on anyway. "She's never been easy to get along with, but she was a whole lot better before she got engaged."

"Marta was engaged once?" Clara asked, curious in spite of herself.

"Twice actually." Beth Ann's mouth twisted into a wry smile. "The first man—boy really—left for an apprenticeship in Kaufdel and never came back. We heard later he'd married his master's daughter. The second... he was much older than Marta. It was to be a marriage of practicality, not passion, but she seemed happy to have him..."

"He left too?" Clara guessed.

"Died," Beth Ann whispered, "Lung infection. Same winter my Derrick passed. After that no one wanted anything to do with us. It was easier for me though. Being a widow gives one a certain status... Being an old maid just makes people wonder what's wrong with you."

"I'm sorry," Clara said, feeling guilty for her judgment of Marta, "I didn't know."

"We came to Rausendel for a fresh start, you know. Moved in with Derrick's cousin and her husband last year... Didn't seem to help. Then that law passed and you proposed this journey... I was hoping it would give her something different to focus on." She sighed.

"Beth Ann—" Clara rested a hand on her arm. "I'm sorry. I didn't mean—"

"I know." Beth Ann patted Clara's hand and turned away.

Clara watched her leave, then turned back to look at Marta, who was still trying to flirt with their guide. Knowing what she had gone through made Clara want to feel sorry for her, but the way Marta held her head at an angle and rested her hand on the man's arm still irked Clara. She resisted the urge to clench her teeth and roll her eyes, instead turning her attention back to her clipboard. Levi wouldn't be happy if she lost track of supplies because she was distracted.

Throughout the course of the morning Clara had spoken to almost every person that was going on the expedition, Seekers and members of the shipping company alike, making sure every foreseeable need was met. Bags began to be separated into a pile for personal belongings and another for supplies. Each person would need to carry their own belongings and an additional pack of supplies needed for the expedition. Anything they couldn't carry with them would be left with the half of the company staying in the village, for use establishing a settlement if—when—they found the valley.

As each pile grew, so did the knot in Clara's stomach. She couldn't discern if it was nerves, excitement, or dread. She had spent her whole life waiting for a chance like this one and now she was on the precipice of adventure, wondering if she would be able to take the leap.

"Everything has been accounted for," Levi said to Desmond, tucking his ledger into his satchel.

"Then let's get moving." Desmond put on a wide-brimmed hat and tipped the rim at Clara, smiling. She caught her breath, cheeks flushing, then gave a quick smile before turning back to the supplies

The men tossed their bags on their backs and Clara searched among the Seekers' pile of belongings for hers. When she found it, she dragged it aside from the rest, with more effort than she was hoping it would take, and bent to pick it up.

"Don't lift it that way." Desmond squatted down and looped an arm through one of the straps. He held it out for Clara to slip her arms through, as if it weighed nothing. "Lift with your legs."

Clara stopped herself from quipping at him, and nodded instead. Once the bag was securely on her back, she was surprised. "It doesn't feel as heavy when it's on."

Desmond cracked a smile, letting go of the bag completely. Clara staggered a moment before catching her balance. She hadn't realized Desmond had been supporting much of the weight.

"Clara!" Levi gripped Clara's arms to steady her and darted a pointed look at Desmond, who laughed.

"Oh come off it Levi, she's tougher than that. A little teasing isn't going to break her. " Desmond flashed a smile at her, one that left her insides even more tangled, and motioned for his men to follow him. "Let's find ourselves a hermit."

CHAPTER 16

❖

Hermit

The guide led them out of the village eastward along a well-worn path. They kept the shoreline in sight, but traveled close enough to the jungle to stay on dirt and rock rather than sand. Clara peered into the jungle on their right, trying to catch glimpses through the tightly packed trees and undergrowth. Every once in a while she thought she saw something bright flutter in the trees, birds perhaps? Or possibly monkeys... Her great-grandfather had mentioned the troublesome animals causing problems for their expedition once or twice.

After an hour Clara found herself looking the other way—staring longingly at the cool water of the ocean. It was hot here. Somehow it hadn't seemed as extreme on the ship, or maybe it was all the extra weight she was carrying now. *Should've inquired about pack animals in the village,* she thought, *Maybe there is something here that can maneuver in that tangle of greenery.*

They stopped for a quick rest, readjusting pack straps and drinking from their canteens. Old Johnny also insisted they all check their shoes for pebbles and shift their socks if necessary. "Too many blisters now sets us up for a slower pace later. Better to take our time and start out right," he said firmly.

Clara was thankful for her sturdy boots, well worn but with plenty of life left in them. She was glad for the excuse to take them off for a minute though—her feet were, if possible, even hotter than the rest of her. She stretched them and rubbed her soles, but what she really wanted was to cool them down. She took her canteen and drizzled some water over them, sighing as the trickle of water hit her skin.

"What are you thinking?" Old Johnny snatched the canteen from her hand and the lid from the log she was sitting on and closed it tight, thrusting the closed canteen back at her. "Water is your most precious resource. Don't let me catch you squandering it!"

Clara rolled her eyes and packed it away.

"He's right, you know." Frederick stood behind her and lifted her bag so she could slide her arms through the straps. "We have to be mindful. We don't have a well or barrels to draw from out here."

Clara nodded. Just one more reason to find the hermit. Maybe he would know how they could replenish their resources in the jungle. The journal had mentioned a number of streams, but she didn't know if they'd be safe to drink from.

They resumed their journey, and soon enough Clara could make out a cluster of huts along the shore in the distance. Her heart skipped.

Their guide pointed out the village. "We are approaching the Aanidesh territory now. We will avoid their land to keep in line with an existing treaty that requires us to make them aware of any foreigners we bring into their region. It will take more time this way, but will avoid much unpleasantness."

He led them off the path toward the jungle. They passed between a few trees and rounded a cluster of large rocks, and suddenly Clara saw their destination—a dilapidated hut right up against the densely packed trees where the jungle really started.

Clara broke into a run, forgetting her fatigue and blisters. She heard someone calling to her, probably Levi or Frederick warning her to be careful, but she ignored him. When she reached the structure, she dropped her pack off to the side and knocked on the door, which hung crookedly but was fastened shut with some kind of rope on the inside.

When no one answered her pounding, Clara set about looking for another way in. The hut was sturdier than it looked from afar. The planks that made it up were gnarled, weathered boards overlapped in a haphazard manner, but upon closer inspection they were secured tightly together with no gaps to look through and the only window was too high for her to see into.

"No one home?"

Clara jumped, then turned to find Desmond grinning at her. She shook her head, giving herself time to regain her dignity before replying.

"The door seems to be locked from the inside—I'm not sure how that could happen, unless there's another way in and out."

"Or the old hermit died inside and has just been rotting away in there," Desmond said absently, inspecting the door.

Clara felt sick. Desmond looked over and cleared his throat. "Sorry, that was, um—he probably has another way in and out, like you said. Let's get this door open and we'll see if we can figure out where he went or when he was last here."

Clara nodded, glancing at the hut and suppressing a shudder. Desmond called one of the sailors over, a man Clara thought was named Vim. He examined the door carefully, then removed a large machete from his pack and inserted it between the door and frame, under the rope. After a bit of careful jiggling, the door swung open. Desmond looked at Clara.

"Do you want to wait out here while I have a look around?"

Clara shook her head, steeling herself against what they might find, and stepped through the doorway beside him.

It took her eyes a minute to adjust to the darkness within. With only one window, which was north-facing, there was little natural light except from some openings in the thatch on the jungle side of the hut. The air was a little stuffy, but nothing indicated the presence of a corpse, so Clara relaxed and looked around, her natural curiosity overcoming her fear.

There was a faint moldy smell that Clara attributed to the dampness of the jungle air, but as soon as Desmond pulled open a cupboard, the smell got stronger. Little brown bugs scurried in and out of holes they'd chewed in the back of the cabinet, taking pieces of flat, stale bread with them.

Clara wrinkled her nose and turned away from the bugs to examine the bed of giant, tropical leaves on the floor. She crouched down and felt one of them. Instead of the waxy feel she was anticipating, the leaf was dry and brittle.

"I don't think anyone's been here in weeks, if not months." Desmond rubbed the back of his neck.

Clara pursed her lips. "That's not what I was hoping."

"We gave it a shot."

Clara opened her mouth to speak again but Desmond placed a hand on her elbow and led her to the door. Clara found Frederick talking among the other Seekers and grabbed his hand to get his attention. He excused himself and Clara pulled him off to the side.

"He hasn't been here in months." Clara chewed on her thumbnail. "I'm afraid Desmond and his crew aren't going to be patient enough to wait for the hermit to show up."

"If he's really our best bet at making it through the jungle, I'm sure they'll want to wait. Let me talk with Desmond and see what he's thinking. We'll figure something out." Frederick gave her a reassuring smile and bridged the distance between the Seekers and the crew.

When Desmond saw Frederick coming, he raised his voice to the crowd. "It's time we gather our things and move into the jungle. While this stop was a worthwhile endeavor, it was ultimately fruitless. We can't waste any more time—"

"If the only rush is securing merchandise for your buyers, then we should wait." Old Johnny crossed his arms and narrowed his eyes. "We don't need to put ourselves in danger so you can make a little extra coin."

Desmond's eyebrows jumped up. "Isn't it your people who are determined to find the promised land?"

Frederick placed a hand on Johnny's shoulder. "I think what John is trying to say is that the hermit is our best hope for doing that. If we invest our time now trying to find him, it will pay off later. Our families are safe in Draunland by now. There's no need to rush this step."

"Draunland?" Amaar's brow furrowed. "Did you not hear about the civil war?"

"What civil war?" Clara asked, her heart dropping into her stomach. She looked at Frederick. He took her hand and squeezed it reassuringly before looking at the guide for an answer.

"We had news from one of the ships that came before your own a few days..." Amaar spread his hands. "War is in Draunland, the borders are closed. I'm sorry, but your families were probably not able to cross... and if they were, they are not safe there."

Clara turned and buried her face in her cousin's shoulder. All this time she'd imagined her parents' biggest struggle being leaving their home behind and integrating into a new culture. Never, not once, had it crossed her mind that they would be stuck in Aldonia with the new law or trapped in a war-torn country. Wherever they were now, Amaar was right. They were not safe.

"You see," Frederick said, shifting to put an arm around Clara and looking over at Desmond, "we cannot afford to fail. We need to look for the hermit so we will have the best chance of success."

Desmond looked at them and pursed his lips. His eyes flicked to Clara, something behind them she couldn't quite recognize. She took a deep breath, trying to calm her anxious thoughts, and stepped away from Frederick. She turned to the other Seekers, who all wore grim expressions.

"What do you think?"

"We don't have time to waste looking for someone who might not even still be around," Charles said, "I vote for us to continue into the jungle."

"We have the journal," Beth Ann said, surprising Clara. "The old man might not even remember the way—sixty years is a long time. I think we should go."

"Someone who knows the jungle is gonna save us time and trouble in the long run," Old Johnny grumbled. "Mark my words we're askin' for trouble if we try this without local knowledge."

Clara sighed, chewing on her lip. She looked out at the jungle and grasped her amulet. *Please Divine One, help me know what to do!*

The trees rustled, some animal within the thick green leaves chittering and moving away. The air hummed with the buzz of insects. The shadows beneath the trees seemed ominous rather than welcoming. Far off in the distance, a bird called.

Clara looked at Desmond, and he met her gaze evenly, giving a slight nod. His meaning was loud and clear —this was her decision. The others may have a stake in the matter and he might be in charge, but whatever she decided, he would back her.

She took a slow, steadying breath and peace settled over her. She looked at the empty hut, then back at the jungle. Between the trees she could see light filtering through the greenery. *It's just a jungle, your great-grandfather came out alive and so will you.*

"I think we should go," she said.

Desmond nodded once and started calling out orders, moving away to pick up his pack and have a word with Amaar.

"Apparently you're calling the shots, eh?" Old Johnny said sourly, hoisting his pack and fixing her with an inscrutable look. "Well, when people start dying, on your head be it."

"I—" Clara wasn't sure how to defend herself.

"Of the ones who spoke up it was three to two, John," Frederick said, "and we all went into this knowing it would be dangerous. It's not fair to put that on her."

Johnny grunted and moved off. Clara sighed, looking over at Frederick. "Thanks."

Her cousin pursed his lips. "You're right, there's no time to waste… but for the record I really wish we had been able to find this guy."

"Noted."

"You really are calling the shots now." Frederick nudged her with his elbow.

Clara pushed his arm away playfully and rolled her eyes. Desmond may have deferred to her in this, but she doubted he would continue to do so. "Come on, let's get going."

Levi met her where she'd left her pack. "Desmond wants to see you. He needs the map to ask that local about where to enter the jungle."

Clara nodded and picked up her pack, starting to head in the direction Levi pointed.

"Clara."

She turned to face Levi, but kept her eyes down, mind racing. Clara fiddled with her sleeve, wondering if she had made the right decision and hoping Old Johnny was wrong about where the fault would fall if someone got hurt.

Levi turned his head to catch her eye and when she met his gaze, he gave her a reassuring smile.

"It'll work out." He took both of her hands in his and squeezed them. Clara searched his face for any sign of worry or hesitation. There was none. She smiled, her eyes crinkling at the genuine happiness she felt from having his confidence. Levi tilted his head in the direction of the others. "You should get going."

Clara set off, but quickly spotted Marta standing behind the hut, looking out at the jungle. Amaar stood a few steps away, talking with Desmond. Marta glanced over at Clara as she approached.

"He'll be leaving soon," Clara said, nodding toward the guide.

"I guess it's time for me to have an accident." Marta's humor sounded a bit forced, and Clara looked at her more closely.

"You don't have to, you know. You could come with us."

Marta grimaced. "I already told you my reasons for coming, and they had nothing to do with the jungle."

Clara snorted. "See, that's where you're wrong. If all you wanted was a new pool of men to choose from you'd have gone to Draunland with the others."

"Couldn't have lied about my age then." Marta didn't meet her eyes.

"Still would've been a lot easier than a month-long voyage with no idea what kind of village we'd end up in." Clara sighed. She didn't even like the woman, why was she trying to convince her to come with them? *Because it's the right thing to do.*

"I think you wanted to come because you know deep down this is the chance of a lifetime," Clara said, "even if we don't discover the Land of Origin, you'll be a hero for trying. Stay here and you'll always wonder who you could've been, if you'd gone."

"Don't paint your own feelings onto me," Marta snapped, but her voice lacked conviction.

Clara shrugged. "Maybe, but I think you feel the same way."

Desmond motioned her over, and she left Marta still gazing at the jungle.

"Do you have the map?" Desmond asked. Clara nodded, pulling it out and pointing to a spot she'd marked.

"We don't know for certain, but my grandfather said they entered the jungle somewhere that looks like this. We assumed from his other travel information that it would be near this area. Any ideas?"

Amaar looked at the small drawing, with three rocks and a cluster of small palm trees surrounding them.

"There are a few places. The trees are now taller. But I think the place that matches most close is back a short walk. Near where we took our break."

Clara's eyes met Desmond's and he grinned. She grinned back. Despite the setbacks of the day, it was finally happening. They were going into the jungle.

CHAPTER 17

Jungle

The hike back toward the place they'd rested earlier was grueling in the afternoon heat. Clara eyed the shade beneath the trees and wondered if it might be worth it to go in just a little ways and stay on the border, but Amaar counseled against it. "Too easy to lose sight of the edge. You could get turned around and go deeper in, then miss completely the landmark you are looking for."

He accompanied them until the cluster of rocks was visible up ahead, then bid them good day and walked toward the ocean, distancing himself from the jungle as he headed back to his village. Clara looked at Marta, but the woman just waved calmly at their guide and turned to follow the rest of the group toward the cluster of rocks.

"What are you staring at?" she grumbled when she reached Clara.

"I thought you were going to go with him?" Clara said mildly. "Isn't that what all the flirting was about?"

"Found out he's already married. Now mind your own business." Marta shoved past her and made her way over to her sister. Beth Ann turned to give Clara a smile and shrug, then fell into step beside Marta.

Clara shook her head.

"You're a good leader, you know," Levi said quietly from behind her.

Clara blushed. "What makes you say that?"

"I overheard you convincing her to come along earlier. I can tell you don't even like her, but you didn't want her to live with regrets and you spoke your mind. You're selfless and honest—those are two qualities a good leader needs."

Clara's blush deepened, and she opened her mouth to respond, but Frederick called to them to hurry up, and Levi pushed her gently ahead. They caught up to the others, and Clara stared at the back of Levi's head as he passed her and went to talk to Desmond.

Selfless? Honest? Clara bit her lip. She felt like such a fraud. After all these weeks of learning a new trade and proving herself useful to the expedition, she had almost forgotten it was all built on a lie.

"Clara! Come here for a moment!" Desmond called.

She made her way over to where he and Levi stood, trying to push away her guilt.

"What do you think? Is this the place your grandfather described?" Desmond waved toward the cluster of stones and the scattered trees surrounding them.

Clara bit her lip. Were they close enough together? Did they fit the near perfect circle she'd read about in the journal? *I really don't know what I'm doing. How am I supposed to decide if this is what he saw?*

"Maybe?" she said, drawing out the word, sounding more uncertain than she wanted.

"Think carefully," Levi began, "this could be the difference between wandering around uselessly or actually finding—"

"I know!" Clara snapped, then took a deep breath. "Sorry. I am aware of the consequences if I get this wrong, I just have no idea how fast the trees grow or whether they've shifted over time... It's less circular than I'd imagined, but I can see how, a long time ago when they were small, these trees may have looked like a more round shape."

Desmond frowned. "Do you want to keep looking? We could follow the edge of the jungle and see if there is a better fit."

Clara looked at the sky. The sun was already dipping toward the horizon. According to the journal's map, if they continued any further along the edge of the forest, they would get into a rocky area and finding the landmark would be improbable. Though it would be problematic to enter the jungle at the wrong point, it would also be a waste to pace the edge of the forest looking for something they'd already found.

She closed a hand around her amulet. "This is the right spot."

Desmond eyed the lengthening shadows and then looked at the dense trees. "We'll camp here for the night, then start fresh tomorrow morning."

"But—" Clara protested, Desmond cut her off by laying a hand on her arm and dipping his head to look her square in the eye.

"It's no use getting lost in there in the dark. We'll have an easier time if we wait for morning, trust me."

She nodded mutely, and he turned to shout orders to the group. Before long they had their bedrolls laid out in a circle with their packs safely stowed in the center. They ate a simple dinner from the rations in their supplies and then turned in for the night. It felt strange to Clara, sleeping out in the open, with nothing but empty space between her and the men of the group. Between that and her anxiety about entering the jungle the next day, she was sure she wouldn't sleep a wink...

Bright sunlight on her face woke Clara early the next morning. Before long they had packed everything again and were ready to head into the jungle. Desmond's crew led the way, with the Seekers following close behind. Levi stayed back and fell into step with Clara. Side-by-side they took in the new sounds and sensations of the jungle.

It was darker under the dense canopy, and even though very little sun reached them on the forest floor, it somehow became hotter the further in they went. It was so humid Clara almost felt like she was drinking the air. The noises they'd heard from outside of the jungle the day before intensified and Clara found herself jumping every time she heard a monkey howl or a bird squawk. Her eyes darted after every rustling leaf and twitching shadow.

"How are you holding up?" Levi asked, his voice soft.

Clara smiled sheepishly. "I imagined the jungle differently, less alive or something. It feels like everything in here has a mind of its own, right down to the twigs." Clara squinted at a low hanging tree branch, squealing when the bark started to move. "See!"

Levi laughed. "It's a walking stick."

Clara tucked her hair behind her ears and took a deep breath.

"I'm surprised our fearless leader and accountant extraordinaire is afraid of a bug," Levi teased.

Clara stared at the ground. "I'm no leader... and I shouldn't have been an accountant either."

"What do you mean?" Levi's expression turned quizzical. "I was just teasing you about the bug thing—"

"I'm the reason you broke your wrist." The words rushed out of Clara before she could stop them and she let them flow, knowing if she didn't say them now, she might never muster the courage. "I'm so sorry! I wanted to tell you sooner and this is going to sound terrible, but I saw the opportunity to snag a better job and I took it."

Levi looked into the distance and clasped his hands

behind his back. Clara kept going. "And as we got to know each other I knew you would forgive me for the accident, but I didn't want you to think of me as the kind of girl that could be so irresponsible and selfish."

Clara looked up at Levi's profile, his jaw set, his lips pursed. She mentally kicked herself for saying anything, even though she knew she'd needed to. Maybe she was wrong about him forgiving her and now she'd jeopardized a professional relationship and friendship she really didn't want to lose.

Levi's eyes shifted to meet hers and his stoic expression melted into a grin.

"What?" Clara nudged him, smiling back despite the knots in her stomach.

"I've known you were responsible for quite some time."

Clara stopped walking. Levi laughed and reached for her hand, pulling her forward. The knots began to untie and for the first time in weeks, there was no weight on her chest.

"How did you know?" Clara looked down at their hands, still intertwined.

"As soon as Desmond said he'd take care of the matter himself. He doesn't tend to get involved in such petty affairs. I guessed he was trying to throw you a bone."

"Oh." Clara breathed a short sigh of relief. "I'm glad he did. If I remember correctly, you wanted to throw whoever was responsible in the brig."

Levi's smile faded. "Were you worried I'd really do that?"

Clara laughed and shook her head. "Maybe at first, but not after getting to know you! That all seems like a different lifetime now. I feel like a different person. Could you imagine me leaving a job half done now?" Clara shuddered. "You must be rubbing off on me."

Levi's smile returned, and he dropped her hand to

move a branch out of the way so they could continue forward.

They caught up to the others, who had stopped for a breather in a small clearing. Desmond was pulling a machete from his pack, the edge glinting in the sunlight that filtered through the trees.

"Is everything all right?" Levi asked. Clara frowned, seeing Frederick and Johnny digging in their packs for knives as well.

"We heard some rustling is all," Desmond replied, "Nothing to worry about, but we'd rather be prepared in case it is a wild animal or something that might attack."

Clara's unease deepened. She wanted to stop being so jumpy, but if Desmond was worried enough to pull out weapons...

It's just a precaution! He's being careful, that's a good thing, she told herself.

They continued trekking through the jungle, which got more dense the further they went. When they finally stopped for the night, Clara was more exhausted than she had expected. Something about traversing the uneven ground made what she'd assumed would be similar to a walk in the hills back home infinitely harder. They camped much as they had the night before, adding the paashia grass to the fire. Its smell wafted through the camp, sweet and sharp. The buzzing of bugs seemed to decrease, so it must be working. Despite her exhaustion Clara slept fitfully, jolting awake every time she heard a leaf rustle or one of the men snore.

The next morning they set out again, this time with more groans and at a considerably slower pace. Before long Clara found herself wiping sweat from her brow. It was difficult to believe that back in Aldonia it was nearly winter. They stopped to rest around noon, and Clara sank to the ground gratefully.

"How's everyone doing on water?" Johnny asked gruffly, taking a swig from his canteen.

Clara pulled her own out to see and bit her lip. There were only a few mouthfuls left. Had she really drunk so much already?

Judging by the looks on everyone else's faces, they were in a similar state.

"Right then," Old Johnny slapped his knee and stood. "First order of business is finding some. That journal of yours say anything about a water source?"

Clara kicked herself mentally and pulled the journal from her bag. Her great-grandfather's expedition had crossed a stream early on, but she couldn't remember if it was the first day after entering or a little later. She perused her notes, then turned to the relevant section. With each page she turned, the furrow between her brows deepened.

"Well?" Johnny asked impatiently.

"I, um, I mean, yes, it does mention a stream, but, well..."

"Spit it out already!"

Clara sighed, closing the journal. "We should have crossed it already."

Johnny grunted, pursing his lips, 'I told you so' written all over his face. Clara tucked the journal back into her pack, keeping her eyes down.

"What does that mean?" Frederick asked, standing and folding his arms across his chest. "Are we going the wrong way? Not even two days in and we're already lost?"

"Lost is a bit of an exaggeration," Levi said, "we could easily turn around and go back the way we came."

"So we're going to just give up?" Charles snorted. "You sailors sure have a stalwart nature, don't you?"

"It's not giving up to go back and get our bearings!" Levi looked annoyed. "We probably just entered the jungle at the wrong place."

Desmond put a hand on Clara's shoulder as the conversation descended into petty bickering. "Are you certain we should have crossed it already?" he asked in a low voice, "Maybe we just traveled a bit slower than they did."

"It says they crossed the stream well before midday the second day in the jungle... I think it's safe to say Levi is probably right." Clara felt tears prick her eyes, and she swallowed hard, trying to hold them back.

"Or maybe the stream changed course or dried up over the years," Desmond said, squeezing her shoulder in reassurance.

Clara nodded mutely, regaining a bit of control. She took a deep breath. "What now then?"

Desmond put his fingers to his lips and whistled shrilly. The argument ceased. "Listen up everyone. We don't know why the stream isn't where it should be, maybe something happened to it, maybe we're off by a few miles," he spread his hands and shrugged his shoulders, "but the fact remains that we need water. So we're going to keep moving forward. If we don't reach water by nightfall, we'll make camp and turn around in the morning. Now move out!"

Clara shouldered her pack and followed Desmond and the sailors out of the clearing. The Seekers grumbled and groaned, but they did the same. Charles walked beside Frederick just behind her, and she couldn't help listening in to their conversation.

"Listen Frederick, mister high-and-mighty up there is gonna be a problem."

"What do you mean?" Frederick's voice was light, questioning, but Clara could hear the undercurrent of tension in it. Charles' deep rumble was more difficult to make out, but she couldn't mistake the tone of discontent.

"I know he was in charge on the ship, but out here it's a different story. This is our mission, he can't just order us around and make unilateral decisions."

"He paid for all our equipment, I think that makes him more or less in charge out here too," Frederick replied, "but I'll try to have a word with him. I can suggest we take a vote before making any decisions about turning back."

Charles made an annoyed sound in the back of his throat, and dropped back to talk to Johnny. Clara glanced at Frederick and met his gaze, seeing the worry there.

"This is all going to fall apart, isn't it?" she asked, pausing for a moment until he fell into step beside her. Having charge of the journal was a huge responsibility, though she hadn't felt the weight of it until now. What if she was the wrong person to lead them? What if they weren't able to find the water source or the correct entrance and they were left in the jungle to die of dehydration and—

"Chin up." Frederick gently tapped under her chin with his knuckle. "We're just getting used to the jungle. Everyone will be a lot less cranky once we find some water and have clear proof we're on the right track."

Clara nodded, giving him a little smile of gratitude. She dropped back to walk with Beth Ann, who seemed to be having trouble with her skirts snagging on all the branches they passed.

"We should've worn trousers," Marta grumped, pulling her skirt from a particularly thorny bush.

Beth Ann shot her a look and rolled her eyes, but she struggled with untangling the lace at the bottom of her otherwise practical brown skirt from the same bush. "We just need to be more careful where we step," she said, puffing from the exertion. Clara helped her pick off the thorns that had tangled in the cloth, wondering how she had avoided this patch when she'd initially walked by.

"Dash-it-all!" Marta said, hitching up her skirt and tying two big wads of it together on the side. The knot was high enough to show off a considerable length of her bloomers, but Clara couldn't fault its effectiveness—Marta tromped off ahead of them and didn't seem to have any more problems.

Clara and Beth Ann looked at each other, then sighed and did the same with their skirts, though a bit more conservatively. They hurried after the others, but the trees had gotten dense enough that they only caught the occasional glimpse of Marta's gray dress and heard snatches of the men's voices.

"Does the ground feel squishier to you?" Beth Ann asked after a few minutes of trying to catch up. The jungle floor was a mix of sand and plant debris, but Clara thought maybe she was right.

"There's more moisture in the air too, I think," she said. Just then they heard shouting ahead.

"Maybe they found water!" Beth Ann pushed forward and around a clump of trees, with Clara close behind her.

They finally pulled within view of the others, who were standing in a small clearing. Clara stopped short. Why were they shouting? Beth Ann stumbled on a tree root, took a few steps trying to catch her balance, then twisted and fell on her rump. Except she didn't fall, she splashed, leaves and mud splattering Clara's skirt.

"Water!" Clara exclaimed, taking a step forward. Desmond, Levi, and Frederick started shouting, their voices overlapping and garbling the message. Why didn't they turn to face her?

Clara tried to take another step, intending to help Beth Ann up, and found that she couldn't move her foot. She looked down. Her boot was already sunk in mud over her ankles. She looked back up at the others. Desmond had twisted to look back at her over his shoulder, his lips forming the words and allowing her to differentiate his voice from all the rest: "Stay back! It's quicksand!"

CHAPTER 18

Bog

Clara stretched as far as she could, hoping she could reach solid ground, to no avail. She tried using her arms to yank her legs out of the sand, but they didn't budge. If anything, it made them sink further in. Her chest tightened, making it hard to breathe.

How are we going to get out of this?

The men were further out into the sand, spaced far enough apart that they couldn't reach one another. It was up to their thighs now and the frantic voices of sailors and Seekers alike rang in her ears. They were sinking too fast for comfort and if they didn't come up with a plan soon... Clara bit her lip.

Desmond's voice rang above the fray. "Can anyone reach a tree or a vine to pull themselves out? Keep your arms out of the sand if you can."

The company stretched and pulled themselves as far as the sand would allow, but no one was within reach of anything useful.

"Get rid of any extra weight." Desmond removed his pack and tossed it backward to Clara, who caught it and hurled it onto safe ground behind her. "Backpacks, shoes, jackets, anything that would cause you to sink faster." The others followed suit, but they didn't all have Desmond's strength or aim. Clara watched helplessly as many of the supplies she'd so carefully curated were trapped in the sand beyond her reach.

Clara took off her own pack and clutched it to her chest. It made her sick to think of tossing the journal where it could potentially be lost forever. She put her pack back on and resolved to only throw it to safety if there was no other option.

She locked eyes with Beth Ann, who was up to her hips in sand since she'd landed on her backside. Though she was composed as ever, there was fear in her eyes.

"What now, Desmond?" Clara called out to him.

He twisted to meet her eyes. "That's all we can do... Except pray."

Clara blinked in surprise. She'd assumed, based on his attitude toward her amulet when they'd first met, that he wasn't religious. Shame colored her cheeks as the other Seekers bowed their heads and mumbled earnest, recited prayers over and over. She closed her own eyes and started a prayer, but it was lost in the jumble of thoughts in her mind. This couldn't really be the end, could it? Swallowed by the jungle two days into their journey, with her family in desperate need of help, a world away?

Anger flared up inside her. What use was it to pray when there was no hope of survival? She supposed she could pray for her own soul to be saved, but she didn't feel like she deserved it. It was her fault they were in this position. If she'd been more careful at the beginning and made sure they'd entered the jungle at the right place, they wouldn't be here right now. Her grandfather's journal said nothing of quicksand. His expedition had never been here. As far as Clara was concerned, no other human being on earth had been to this forsaken pit and none ever would again.

A rustling came from the branches above their heads. The muttered prayers gave way to silence as the company gazed up at the trees.

"Whatever it is, I hope it eats us quickly," Marta muttered.

Beth Ann's face crumpled and she burst into tears.

"Was that really necessary?" Levi said crossly, glaring at Marta over his shoulder.

"I just—"

"Quiet!" Desmond ordered, his eyes fixed on the canopy above them.

Clara looked up, her heart rising into her throat.

"Caught in a pickle like a scurrytoad in nectar."

Clara shrieked as a gravelly, sing-song voice sounded from directly over her head. She craned her neck to see who had spoken, as the others started yelling for help. A wiry, shriveled man with deeply tanned skin and ragged clothing hung upside down from a vine an arms length or so above her.

"Shoosh shoosh, noisy bugs get eaten, don't ya know?" The man grinned, eyes wide and unsettling. The others looked at each other, confusion in their eyes, their calls for help faltering.

"So you're the one that was following us," Desmond said calmly. Clara didn't take her eyes off the man. His stark white hair stuck out in all directions from his head, even hanging upside down as he was. A short white beard that looked like it had been hacked off with little to no care for uniformity covered his cheeks and chin, the mustache a bit longer than the rest.

"Maybe. Or maybe you were following me!" The old man cackled and pulled himself rightways up on the vine with surprising dexterity. He hung out sideways, holding on with one arm and peering at Clara intensely.

"You're the hermit we've been looking for," she guessed, hoping he wasn't as crazy as he seemed. "We need your help!"

"You need someone's help, that's for sure. Maybe that someone is yourself!"

"Not just with this," Clara said, waving vaguely around her. "We need your help finding the Land of Origin. My great-grandfather—"

"Not gonna find much but grass and bones at the bottom of this bog. I suppose you'd like a hand?" The old man interrupted, flipping upside down again and stretching his hand out.

Clara reached for it, too startled to do anything else. The old man slapped her palm and snatched his own away before she could grab it. "Hand!" he shouted, giggling gleefully. Clara huffed in frustration and lowered her arm. The sand was at her midthighs now, the extra jolt having made her sink another few inches. Most of the others were almost to their waists, though curiously Beth Ann didn't seem to have sunk any further.

"Now see here!" Levi chimed in, his voice stern, "That's no way to treat a lady! You know we need help getting out of this quicksand, if you're going to be abusive we're better off without you."

The hermit rotated to look at him, blinking balefully, then shrugged and scurried up the vine.

"Wait!" Clara called desperately, "Please help us!" She opened her pack, which was nearly touching the sand, and pulled out the journal. The hermit stopped, eyes flicking between the journal and her face. Clara felt an inkling of hope. "Do you recognize this? It belonged to Henry J. Karrow, my great-grandfather. You knew him, right?"

The hermit lowered himself to the very end of his vine and swiped at the journal. Clara jerked her outstretched arm away from him, but it made her sink further into the sand. "If you pull us out, I can let you look at it."

The man narrowed his eyes, looking around at the

others. They'd seemed hesitant to say anything after Levi had nearly scared him away, but now they chimed in, pleading. "Help us!"

"Book first." The man reached his hand down again. Clara pulled the journal closer to her chest. The others immediately protested.

"Give it to him!"

Clara's mind raced with the possibilities. If she gave away the journal and the man took off, it would be no use to them anyway. They'd die here. Their families would be fugitives, or worse, and they would never know what happened to the expedition.

But if I give it to him and he helps us...

She sighed, feeling an ache of loss. "You can take it." Clara held the journal just out of the man's reach. "If you help us out of here." She extended it toward him.

He immediately snatched the journal from her hand, darted to another vine and swung to the ground. He sat back on his heels, flipping through the pages, a skeptical scowl on his face.

"You have the book. Now, help us!"

Cries of panic rose from the bog as the group slowly sank further and further. The hermit looked up. "Told you, need help from yourself!" He stared hard at Beth Ann, then went back to studying the journal.

The others groaned. Clara looked at Beth Ann. She still hadn't sunk any further. *If we stretch out more, we'll float!*

"Sit down, stretch out!" she called to the others, tossing her pack to dry ground and following her own advice. She laid back gently, taking a deep breath and praying she was right. For a moment, the awful feeling of her shoulders sinking into the muddy sand sent her into a panic, but she forced her body to relax and ever so slowly her legs floated up to the surface. She stretched her arms behind her and felt around, telling herself it was just like swimming in the bay, trying not to think of all the bugs and dead animals that were probably in the muck beneath her. There! She grasped a branch of some kind and pulled herself backwards little by little.

When she finally maneuvered her backside onto a tree root and hauled herself upright using the trunk, she found the hermit standing beside her, grinning from ear to ear.

"Helped yourself! Didn't I say?" He chuckled, stretching a long tree branch out to Beth Ann, who had lain back completely and was trying to maneuver herself to shore.

Clara gritted her teeth to avoid offending him again. *After all, he did stay to help.* She grabbed a long stick and used it to feel the ground in front of her as she walked around to where she could reach Levi and help him out. Desmond had already leaned back and worked his legs free, and was calling instructions to those around him.

In a few minutes, between Clara and the hermit, they had managed to free everyone from the quicksand. Clara helped Frederick find a safe place to stand and then went back, intending to retrieve some of their belongings. A few gurgly bubbles emerged from the center of the otherwise solid-seeming ground, and then it was smooth again—their packs were gone.

"Is everyone okay?" Desmond called, brushing wet sand from his hair with both hands. The sailors gathered around him, and a discussion about their predicament, and where the hermit fit into it, began. Clara made her way back to where she'd thrown his pack and picked it up. *All my planning, all the work we put into getting the right supplies... and this is all that's left.*

She looked around, trying to assess just how bad things were. The Seekers were all sitting on the ground, heads hung low, and there was very little conversation. If they were anything like Clara, they were feeling a mix of relief, exhaustion, terror, and gratitude.

She found Frederick resting his back against a log with round, red mushrooms sprouting out near his elbow. She sat next to him and leaned her head against his shoulder. "Some of the sailors are saying we have the hermit to thank for getting out of that mess. That's a good sign, right? Maybe they'll listen to us about needing him."

Frederick shifted and looked down at her, his lips pursed. Clara looked up at him quizzically. *Did I say something wrong?*

"I think we're awfully lucky he decided to show himself," Clara continued. "If it weren't for him—"

"Clara, Frederick," Desmond motioned them over.

Frederick sighed. "I don't think the hermit is the one we need to thank." He kissed Clara's forehead before getting to his feet, dusting off his trousers, and squaring his shoulders. Clara couldn't help but notice how much they'd broadened over the last few years. Frederick wasn't the same child she'd spent so many summers chasing through the fields. Her cousin was a grown man, and for the first time she felt that if she wasn't careful, she was in danger of him leaving her behind in childhood.

She reluctantly pulled herself to her feet and joined the men who, besides Desmond, looked haggard and downtrodden.

"Ah, there she is." Desmond smiled at her before turning to the group. "Now that we're all on solid ground again, we need to reassess our situation. We lost everything except four of our packs to the quicksand. Many of us no longer have adequate clothing. We are left with almost no food or water."

There was no shouting, no screaming or crying, no uproar. All eyes were on Desmond, and though there had been talk of discontentment surrounding Desmond's leadership before, there was none now.

"We may not have many physical resources left, but

I am hoping we have enough knowledge between us to secure what we need here in the jungle. First, we need water. Clara, we need to search the journal for every mention of water to see if we can find a source."

"The hermit has it. I didn't get it back…" Clara trailed off, realizing she hadn't seen the hermit since he'd pulled Beth Ann from the muck. The others looked around, and Desmond tilted his chin up, scanning the vines above them. Clara's heart sank, deeper than their packs had in the bog. She whirled around to check the jungle behind her, but it only served to confirm what she already knew. "He's gone."

CHAPTER 19

Abandoned

Unlike previous moments of panic, the Seekers and sailors seemed to take the news of the hermit's desertion with a sort of resigned hopelessness. There were no shouted suggestions or arguments, no muttered accusations or complaints. They were dejected to the point of agreement—no one could undo the decisions that had led them to this, and no one wanted to be responsible for the next one, which could very well lead them to their deaths.

Tears sprung to Clara's eyes, and she dashed them away angrily. *Crying won't help anything, focus on what to do next!*

Taking a steadying breath, Clara shouldered her pack. "We need to find clean water."

She maneuvered her way through the group, grabbing a stick to test the ground in front of her once she passed Desmond.

"There must be a source nearby," one of the sailors said wearily, "A spring or stream that feeds this bog. If nothing else, we can scoop this mud in a cloth and squeeze out a little water. It won't be much, but..." he shrugged.

"Thank you." Clara straightened her shoulders and turned to face the others. "I know this isn't ideal. I know —" The thought of her last sip of moisture being gritty, unsanitary bog water made her cringe. It was nothing like the clear, pure well water at home. Her voice caught, and she clamped down on the tears that threatened to reemerge. Just as she was about to lose her nerve, she caught Frederick's eye. He motioned for her to continue. She took a breath, unable to bring herself to make eye contact with anyone else, focusing instead on a tree root.

"I know I failed you. It's obvious now that we entered the jungle in the wrong place, and now we don't even have the journal to help us. But we need to get going. We need to find someplace to stay the night, where we won't risk getting sucked back into that bog."

"Shouldn't we try to head back? Get more supplies?" Levi asked, still sitting on the ground. Clara hesitated. They could go back the way they'd come, but by the time they left the jungle—if they could even find their way back— they'd be near desperate for water, and it was another half day to the village from there.

"We walked for a day and a half to get this far, and spent who knows how much longer trying to get out of the quicksand. We'll never make it out before nightfall," she said. "We need to rest and find water, then we can make a decision about going back."

Levi looked immediately at Desmond. "What do you think? It makes more sense to get out while we still can, doesn't it?"

Clara felt like she'd been slapped. Her face grew hot, and she looked down. She'd grown used to having her opinion respected, not dismissed or ignored as it had so often before this trip. Levi being the one to question her only made it worse.

Desmond is his friend, and he's in charge. It makes sense for Levi to ask him, she told herself, trying to soften the blow to her ego. It still stung.

"Clara is right," Desmond said. "We find someplace to stay the night, then decide where to go in the morning."

Having reached a decision, some of the company's animation returned. Some hopped up and gathered what materials were left, while others were slower than usual, the bog having taken some of the starch out of them.

Desmond reached down to clasp Vim's hand and haul him to his feet. The sailor grimaced as he put weight on a swollen ankle. Like many of them, he'd lost his shoes to the bog.

"Are you going to be okay walking on that?" Desmond asked.

Vim shrugged. "Felt it pop when I was trying to get it free of the mud. Probably messed it up inside, but I'll survive. I've had worse turns trying to cross the deck in a storm."

"Here." Marta pushed past Clara and knelt in front of the man, wrapping his foot in a strip of cloth that matched her dress. *Her sash,* Clara realized. Marta crisscrossed it around his ankle and tied it snugly, showing a level of expertise that surprised Clara.

"Thanks," Vim grunted, standing a little straighter.

Marta shrugged and got to her feet, briefly meeting Clara's curious gaze and then turning deliberately away.

They headed around the bog cautiously, staying close to the trees and feeling the ground ahead of them with sticks to make sure it was solid. It was an imperfect method, but they managed to avoid becoming stuck again. Eventually, the ground changed from sand to dirt, with enough undergrowth to make them reasonably sure they wouldn't sink into it.

The light was fading quickly, and they were all stumbling from exhaustion. Clara looked over at Desmond, and he nodded, dropping his pack.

The others followed his lead, collapsing onto the

ground and resting their heads on whatever they could find. Clara sat back against a tree. If she could just rest her eyes for a minute, then she would be able to find a more comfortable place to sleep...

Clara woke to someone gently shaking her shoulder. Soft light streamed through the green canopy of leaves and she blinked sleepily. Was it morning already?

"We need to get moving, we have to find water," Desmond told her, handing her a small piece of dried meat and smiling apologetically.

Clara took it and nodded, shifting so she could dig through her pack for a package of dried fruit. She passed it around to the others, seeing that Desmond had already split his meat with them as well. Most of the food had been in Charles and Johnny's packs, but thankfully she had thought to put something to eat in each pack, in case anyone got separated.

After sleeping and eating, the group's mood was considerably better.

"I say we head southwest," Desmond suggested, "parallel to the jungle's edge. We'll look for the stream, and if we don't find water, we can head out to the jungle's edge somewhere closer to Cape Sago."

The others agreed, and they set out. If it weren't for her dry mouth and sore muscles, the walk would have been quite pleasant. The jungle was beautiful in the morning light, but Clara viewed her surroundings with suspicion, trying to anticipate what else it may have in store for them.

The day grew warm, and then hot. As noon approached and they finished off the last of her and Desmond's food stores, Clara could feel the tensions of the previous day return to the group.

"No water yet," Frederick murmured to Clara. "I wonder if we should try to go back toward the bog and skirt it on the east, see if there is a spring on that side. The water has to come from somewhere."

"Unless the spring is underground, beneath the bog," Clara said, brow furrowed as she looked around at the jungle. *Are we just wasting our time, possibly wandering deeper into this death-trap?* Maybe Levi was right and they should have turned around yesterday, when they still knew the way out for certain.

"If that's the case, we need to figure something else out, soon. We won't last another day in this heat without water."

Old Johnny grunted as he came up beside them. "We may be thinkin' of this wrong. In my tracking days, if we couldn't find running water, we'd survive off water from plants. Eatin' berries and greens can give you a bit of what you need, help you last longer."

Clara looked over at the weathered old man. "Have you seen anything edible?"

He snorted. "Not the climate I'm used to, girl. Yella flowers and watercress don't grow in this kind of heat. Didn't you make a list that could help us?"

"I did," Clara said miserably, "It was tucked into the journal, with all the other lists I made."

"My father always told me to watch the animals. Whatever the animals are eating and drinking will likely be safe for us to eat and drink too," Frederick added.

Clara tried to remember anything the journal mentioned about the jungle's natural food chain. She knew there were descriptions of berries and animals that were similar to species back home, but that didn't necessarily make them safe. The other fruits and vegetables her grandfather had mentioned were nowhere to be seen. She searched the jungle around them for signs of life, but where there had once been the calling of birds and monkeys, now there was only silence, broken by the occasional rustle of leaves.

That's odd, Clara thought, *Maybe they're resting away from the heat.*

Up ahead, Desmond had stopped.

"What is it?" Clara asked, anxiety tinging her voice despite her attempts to keep it level.

Desmond pointed to a large purple blossom growing from a vine encircling a tree. Petals larger than serving platters nestled together and curved gracefully outward, leaving a large bowl-like area in the center.

"Is that—?" Clara began.

"Water!" Charles strode forward and dipped a finger in the clear liquid pooled in the center.

"Wait!" Desmond said, but the man had already stuck the finger in his mouth. "You don't know if that's safe!"

"Feels like water, tastes like water... I'll take my chances," Charles grunted, scooping a handful out of the blossom and slurping it noisily.

By now the others had noticed what he was doing, and were looking for more of the flowers. They clustered around the nearby trees, some using their hands, others lapping straight from the blooms, which ranged in color from pale pink to deep indigo.

Desmond sighed and looked at Clara. "Do you remember anything like this from the journal?"

Clara shook her head. "Do you think it's safe?" Her thirst suddenly intensified. She tried to swallow, but her mouth was so dry it felt like her tongue was stuck.

Desmond shrugged. He walked over to one of the blossoms and took a small sip. His eyes narrowed as he swished the liquid around his mouth and then swallowed. He smiled, motioning for her to join him and Clara's heart skipped a beat.

The water was cool and vaguely sweet. She drained the flower till its thick waxy petals held only a few beaded drops of water. Her anxiety melted away. They could survive this place. The bog had been frightening, but she shouldn't have let it scare her into fearing the jungle. This was a place of beauty. She smiled drowsily and looked up at the canopy. Green light filtered down... a handful of leaves was suddenly shoved in her mouth, the bitter taste burning her tongue. She coughed and spit them out, stumbling back and falling on her backside.

The hermit scowled down at her from the tree, where he perched on a limb level with where her face had been when she was standing.

"What'd you do that for?" Clara spluttered, trying to stand. Her feet had gotten tangled in the vines somehow. She tugged and reached to pull them away, but vines crept up her hands too, wriggling like snakes and circling her wrists. She screamed and yanked her hands away, then looked around at the others.

They all sat or stood with bemused smiles on their faces, vines creeping around their bodies. Charles was caught fast, the vines nearly to his waist, but he didn't seem aware of them.

"Stupid stupid stupid," the hermit was muttering, swinging from tree to tree and shoving fistfuls of the same dark green leaves he'd used on Clara in each person's mouth. He looked back at her, seemed to realize she wasn't untying herself, and rolled his eyes.

"Are you a sitting bird? Not moving is death! Chew the leaves, cut the vines! Don't you have a knife?"

Clara shook herself, realizing that she'd started to slip back into the lazy contentment that the nectar had induced. She shoved a few of the leaves she'd spit out back in her mouth and chewed them, grimacing. Her head cleared, and she pulled her pack off to search for a knife. It wasn't there. *Must have fallen out in the bog.*

"Here, use mine." Desmond stood, having just freed himself, and handed her a big, curved dagger. His eyes were a little wild, barely contained fear showing through. He pulled the vines away as she sawed at them, stomping on tendrils that crawled toward him, and yanked her to her feet as soon as the last vine snapped. They stumbled back, away from the dangerous plant, and fell into a tree trunk. Desmond caught her, his hand wrapping around hers over the knife handle to keep her from accidentally stabbing his leg. She looked down at his hands, noticing for the first time how strong and callused they were.

"Sorry," she gasped, pulling away and blinking, trying to clear her head. She needed more of those leaves...

The hermit stalked over, his arms folded across his chest. "Didn't I warn you about scurrytoads and nectar?" He stabbed a finger toward one of the blossoms near the base of the tree. Clara furrowed her brows, trying to make sense of his statement. A shriveled gray leaf fluttered where it had snagged on a vine near the flower... only it wasn't a leaf. Bile rose in her throat as she recognized the emaciated form of a toad, its mouth wide open with the tongue lolling, its body sucked dry till its skin resembled crinkled wafer paper.

Clara turned away from the disturbing sight. The others were working to untangle the last few of their group, shooting glances toward the hermit as they cut vines and chewed leaves.

Desmond folded his arms across his chest and glared at the hermit. "This wouldn't have happened if you'd stayed to help us."

"Helped you already," the hermit grunted, "Twice now. Can't do anything if you don't listen."

Desmond snorted. "Maybe if you didn't speak in riddles, we would!"

"Desmond," Clara said, laying a hand on his arm and shaking her head in warning. They couldn't afford to antagonize the hermit and have him leave again. Desmond clenched his jaw and closed his eyes briefly, regaining his composure. Clara smiled in relief and turned toward the hermit. "You came back. Why?"

The hermit's eyes slid away from hers, and he stared out into the jungle. "Forgot."

Levi came up beside Clara, irritation evident on his face. He opened his mouth, probably to issue a scathing retort, but Clara jabbed him with an elbow. She ignored Levi's annoyed yelp and kept her eyes on the hermit, gaze steady. "Forgot what?"

The hermit flicked his eyes back to hers and narrowed them, then pulled the journal from the dirty cloth wrapped loosely around his waist. He tossed the journal to the ground in front of her. Clara picked it up gingerly, wiping the cover on her skirt. It was a little scuffed and the pages were probably smudged from his grimy fingers, but having it back in her hands was such a relief she didn't care as much as she once would have.

"You can't read," she guessed.

The hermit grunted. "Can, just forgot."

Clara's heart panged with sadness for the man. He must have lost so much over the years, spending so much time isolated from others.

"If you forgot how to read our language, why can you still speak it?" Levi asked, stepping forward. He positioned himself so he was slightly in front of her, his shoulder blocking her view of the hermit. Whether it was intentional or not, Clara didn't know. But she didn't like it.

The hermit frowned, looking down. "Words in the mouth are different from words on the page."

"Okay," Clara said slowly, stepping out from behind Levi, trying to determine what would convince the old man to stay with them this time. He clearly wanted something from the journal, what specifically she didn't know. Maybe he was trying to find the Land of Origin too, or maybe he just sought some kind of closure regarding his first trip into the jungle.

"If you stay with us and help us find the valley my

181

grandfather saw, I'll read it to you."

The hermit met her gaze, eyes narrowing. Then his expression cleared and he gave her a lopsided grin. "Lemurs move in packs. They throw nuts at each other." He knocked a hand against his head and clucked his tongue, then turned and scampered to the group of sailors and Seekers, whacking a few in the back of the head and making them spit out the leaves they were still chewing.

"Hey!" The sailor gasped.

"Watch it!" Marta grumbled.

The hermit wagged a finger in front of their faces. "Too much chewing burns the stomach."

Clara and Desmond looked at each other, eyebrows raised.

"Are you sure he's going to be useful?" Levi said from her other side, "He seems a little..." he twirled a finger beside his head and rolled his eyes up into his skull. "And he's really old, he could have a heart attack any minute."

Clara shrugged. "He's saved us twice now, you can't argue with results."

She readjusted her pack and went to ask the hermit where to find water and food. They consulted for a few minutes, then he headed off into the jungle. The others scrambled to grab their belongings and follow.

Before long, they reached a clearing with a big leafy plant in the middle. The hermit went directly to it and pulled aside the broad green leaves, revealing a small pool of water around its roots.

The company surrounded it, most plunging their faces directly into the pool to drink, while a few cupped their hands and vigorously brought the water to their mouths. Clara let the water trickle down her chin and arms, moistening her sleeves and the collar of her dress.

Once she had her fill, she sat on the ground and tucked her heels under her. Desmond sat up straight, surveying the group and their surroundings for a moment before leaning back on his elbows and turning his face toward the setting sun. The others took his lead, letting themselves really relax for the first time since they entered the jungle. Even the hermit took a seat, digging in the foliage around him and pulling up handfuls of tube-like weeds.

Clara took the opportunity to get out the journal. She hadn't had a chance to make notes in it since they'd arrived. There were so many dangers she needed to document and potential substances for pharmaceutical use, in case Desmond's company was interested in going back to sample them.

She flipped to the first blank page, dipped her pen in the only bottle of ink they had left. Her hand hovered over the paper a moment and she bit her lip. It felt wrong to add her own writing next to her great-grandfather's. He was a real explorer! And she was just… Clara.

Slamming the book closed, she sighed, a blob of ink falling from the top of her pen onto her skirt. She frowned at it, but didn't bother trying to wipe it away or rinse it out. After the past couple days, there was nothing on earth that could get all the stains out of her clothing anyway.

Levi sat beside her and nudged her with his elbow. He smiled and nodded toward the ink stain. "Now I know why you look so cross."

Clara returned his smile, but it faded quickly. "It's not that." She adjusted her skirt to hide the stain. "I don't know how I'm supposed to help this expedition. I'm not a leader or an adventurer like my great-grandfather was. I wasn't even supposed to be here in the first place…"

Levi pursed his lips and Clara wondered what he was thinking, feeling silly for saying anything at all. She was about ready to get up and run away when Levi reached across her into her bag and pulled out the journal he had given her back on the ship.

He opened the cover and pointed to the inscription

he'd written there before handing the journal to her. "You don't have to be him. This is your voyage."

Levi stood, brushed his pants, and started toward Desmond, who had been watching the exchange. Clara stared down at the journal and opened the first page, ready to write.

CHAPTER 20

Camp

The blue sky deepened into indigo, with thin white clouds streaking across it. Clara closed her notebook and held it close to her chest, relieved to have the discoveries of the past few weeks on paper. She looked up for the first time in hours to find the rest of the company beginning to mobilize.

"We need shelter," Desmond said, addressing the group. Then he turned to the hermit. "Is this clearing a safe place to camp for the night?"

When the hermit only blinked at him, Desmond shifted his eyes to Clara. "Does he know what I'm asking?"

The hermit bounded off through the tall grass, his knees clearing the tops of the swaying blades, as if he were trying to avoid them tickling his calves. Clara watched him head toward the edge of the jungle for only a moment before gathering her skirt and trudging through the grass after him.

Desmond waved his arm and they all made their way back to the jungle where the hermit was already halfway up a ginormous palm tree, the blade of an ornate, well-polished knife between his teeth.

"Hey, that's mine!" Levi shouted from the ground, rolling up his sleeves and approaching the palm, sizing it up. Clara stifled a laugh, half hoping he would try to climb after the hermit. Before he had the chance, a frond fell from up above, knocking one of the sailors onto his backside. He lay there stunned for a moment before Frederick offered a hand, helping him up.

"A warning would have been nice!" the sailor shouted upward as another frond fell. They all watched as the hermit moved on to the next one in silence.

Clara glanced at Desmond, who was tucking in his wrinkled shirt, his own blade between his teeth.

"Are you going up there?" Clara asked him, pointing to the impossibly high tree before them.

He just crinkled his eyes in what she assumed was a smile—his mouth was rather occupied by the knife between his teeth—and wrapped his arms around the trunk to heave himself up. His climbing grew more confident the farther he went, as he learned where and how to place his hands and feet. Before long he too was cutting fronds. The hermit emerged a moment later, motioning for Desmond to keep at it, then scuttling down. He held a giant frond over his head and grinned widely. "Good for rain, eh? Get at it, need many." He pointed imperiously at the others and then up at the nearby trees. The other sailors rushed to do the same as Desmond, while the Seekers set to gathering the leaves. Levi watched, his hand twitching like he wanted to take inventory, but there didn't seem to be anything worth recording, and he'd lost his writing supplies in the bog.

The hermit motioned to the other women and set them to work cutting more of the long tube-like grass that grew nearby. Clara joined them, wondering whether the grass was springy enough to tie things together, or if the hermit had a different use in mind. It was far too wet to kindle a fire with.

Before long a rough camp had sprung up in the clearing. Palm fronds were tied together using strips of cloth torn from their clothing and lashed to existing tree trunks to create surprisingly sturdy tents. The hermit had collected stones and was making Levi create a fire pit. The scribe had a long-suffering expression on his face, and Clara could just imagine his internal objections—his delicate hands were meant for writing, not hard labor, and an activity like this should really be done wearing gloves. He looked up and narrowed his eyes as he caught her grinning at him. She looked down quickly, schooling her face to a more neutral expression.

A loud thump hit the ground beside her and she yelped, stumbling back. Desmond steadied her with a hand between her shoulder blades, his eyes twinkling. "Careful now, you'll fall and break the fronds I just cut!"

Clara swatted him with one of the tubes of grass and then yelped again as she struggled to catch the others that became unbalanced with only one arm around them. Desmond helped her steady the pile, his lips tucked in to stifle a grin. She glared up at him, but when her eyes met his, her scowl faltered. His gaze was warm and playful. Her breath caught, and her heart must not have recovered yet from the fright he'd given her, for it still pounded in her chest.

"I— I should go put these down," she murmured, looking down and shifting the pile of tube-grass into a more secure grip.

"Clara, I—"

"Good Good! Food for thought, eh?" The hermit snagged a tube from her arms and held it like a spyglass, staring down the interior at Desmond. Clara laughed and moved to put the bundle down with the others, on a frond the hermit had laid by the fire. From the corner of her eye she saw Desmond brush the tube away irritably and ask the hermit something. The old man shrugged and tucked the

187

tube under his arm like a gentleman with a walking cane, that same shrewd smile on his face.

"That man is one short step from deranged, I'd say," Levi murmured, placing the last stone and standing up.

Clara looked over at him. "He's been alone a long time, what'd you expect?"

Levi sighed. "I figured he'd be dead."

Clara flinched. Levi's words cut deeper than she thought they could. Had he lacked faith in her all along? Afterall, it was her idea to go after the hermit in the first place. If he thought going to find him was a bad plan, why hadn't he said something to her? She thought they'd been on the same page for the most part. Were there other opinions he kept hidden from her?

Clara shook her head and mustered a small smile before she walked away from him, to the other side of the fire.

"Clara," he called after her, clearly confused. She looked at him through the flames, his features illuminated in the light as the night was coming on. There was hurt there, in his expression, but she was hurt too. Perhaps she was being unfair. Maybe it was the events of the day, or that she hadn't eaten in who knew how long, but she didn't have the energy or the words to fix things with Levi now.

The hermit bumbled around the fire, placing two fresh logs and a wide flat stone over half of it. Clara stopped to watch as he placed the tube-like plants on top, shifting them with a stick every so often.

"What are those called?" Charles asked, kneeling down next to the hermit.

"Tunnel weed," the hermit grumbled and hopped a couple feet away from Charles.

"Is it only found around the clearing, or is it throughout the forest? How about the plants with the water around them?" Charles stayed where he was, but the hermit slowly inched even further away with each word.

Charles ran a hand over his beard, which had gotten out of control since they'd left home.

They needed to find a better way to communicate with the man if they were going to work with him. Clara picked up her own stick and prodded some of the tunnel weed, rolling them over to check the other side. They were starting to turn golden brown.

Using the stick, she prodded the tubes until they fell away from the fire and onto one of the blades she'd pulled from a frond. She held her make-shift plate up for the hermit to see. He nodded and did the same, crouching down with his own dinner on the outskirts of the group.

Seekers and sailors alike gathered around, intermingling with one another, which both surprised Clara and warmed her heart at the same time. Just two days ago, she couldn't imagine Frederick beckoning one of the younger sailors to sit with him around the fire or one of the Seekers serving a sailor their dinner before they'd gotten their own.

Clara looked down at her feast and grinned, picking up one of the weeds and twisting it between her fingers before taking a bite. It was surprisingly soft and easy to chew, reminding her a little of the summer squash her mother used to tend to on the farm. She might even like the tunnel weed better, because there were no mushy seeds in the middle.

"You look happy." Desmond plopped down next to Clara and nudged her knee with his own.

"You caught me at a good time, I guess," Clara said, still observing the interactions of the others and savoring the smoky flavor of the plant.

"It seems things are finally looking up."

"Maybe things wouldn't have looked so down, had I made sure we entered the jungle in the right place," Clara said, setting her makeshift plate on the ground next to her, having eaten everything on it.

"Don't dwell on the what-ifs, Clara. It won't get you anywhere you want to be." Desmond picked a few blades of grass and twirled them between his fingers. Clara watched him for a moment, his eyes focused on the dancing flames in front of them.

His dark, wavy hair fell over one eye and his tan skin glowed amber in the firelight. He looked younger, more vulnerable than when she'd first met him in the marketplace.

"Sounds like maybe you've done some dwelling yourself?" she asked.

"Not so much dwelling as waiting." Desmond laid back in the grass, his arms crossed behind his head. Clara leaned back on her elbows next to him and his voice danced up to her ears.

"The Andreyas Shipping Company is the only path I've ever known, the only future I've been allowed to explore–"

Clara raised her eyebrows.

"Before you roll your eyes and think what a spoiled, ungrateful son I am, please understand that I am extremely grateful for everything my father has given me. He's worked hard to build this empire and I plan to carry on my family's legacy. But my passion does not lie in the spice trade and it never will."

Clara glanced sideways at him, wondering if that were true, and to her surprise, wanting to know more. "Where does your true passion lie?"

"Pharmaceuticals."

"Is there more money in pharmaceuticals than spices?"

"It's too young an industry to know. But it's not about that. Think about the town that we came through on our way here, the one with vidirian fever. What if we could do something to stop that? What if we could do something to cure it? Or even just to mitigate the worst symptoms?"

Clara turned so she lay on her side facing him, her head propped up by her hand. She motioned for him to go on and Desmond's eyes lit up.

"Think of all the discoveries we've already made on this journey so far. The liquid that made us all lethargic, and the leaves that cleared our minds again. And think of the food we've been eating too." He held up one of the roasted tubes. "With the hermit's knowledge, we may be able to find nutritional avenues that haven't been explored. I've been collecting samples to send back to my family's researchers when this is over."

Clara smiled and pulled her personal journal from her bag and flipped to the page where she had been noting these things. "I had some of the same ideas myself." She handed the journal to him.

"This is brilliant, Clara!" Desmond said, running his fingers delicately over the detailed sketches she had made. "What made you think to do this?"

"My great-grandfather was a botanist, I guess it's in my blood." She shrugged, grinning when he looked up at her with an eyebrow raised. She looked away, throwing a small stick into the fire. "I was trying to hold up our end of the bargain. Frederick said you were interested in discovering useful plants. I thought I'd also include the dangerous ones, to keep people from getting hurt, but now that I know all of this, we can start looking at medicinal and nutritional components as well."

"Thank you."

Desmond closed the journal and searched Clara's eyes. She held his gaze for a moment, her heart fluttering under his intense, contemplative stare before she rolled onto her back and looked up at the night sky. She felt Desmond shift beside her, the space between them feeling too vast and too little at the same time.

"What are your plans after all this?" Desmond asked.

"I haven't asked myself that question since I left

home." Clara closed her eyes. "I can't bring myself to hope too deeply that this will all work out, that we'll actually find the Land of Origin... because if we don't..."

Desmond's hand rested on top of Clara's in the dark. She froze for a moment, her breath catching in her chest. She was sure it meant nothing, just a reassuring gesture amongst friends—no, colleagues—but even so, she spread her fingers on the grass, allowing his to intertwine with hers.

When Desmond spoke again his voice was soft, almost a whisper. "Say it doesn't work out. What would you want?"

A sudden shout from across the clearing brought Desmond to his feet before Clara could decide what to say. The hermit was rocking back and forth on his heels in distress, while Old Johnny cursed and swore at him. The Seeker's right hand was covered in bright red blood.

"What happened?" Desmond asked, crossing the clearing in a few long strides. Clara followed, stopping at her pack to dig out a small roll of bandages. The hermit had scampered into the trees. She hoped he wasn't gone for good.

"Watch out! Unless you want to lose a chunk of yerselves too!" Johnny swayed on the spot, white as a lamb's wool in spring.

Clara surveyed the area around him, noting a curiously curled thorny vine with clusters of bright purple berries. Blood dripped from one of the spirals. Desmond pulled Johnny away from it, toward the fire. A trail of red followed them.

Desmond helped Johnny sit on a large rock one of the sailors had just vacated, and Clara hurried over with the bandages. Marta had already grabbed a large frond and laid it under Johnny's fist, trying to keep more blood from splattering everything. She held out her hand for the bandages, all the while talking to Johnny in a low, firm voice, coaxing him to let go with his other hand and show them the wound. Clara passed the roll over, feeling light headed from all the blood.

Marta finally convinced Johnny to open his hand, and the sight made Clara cover her mouth and turn away. Two of his fingers had been scraped raw, skin and muscles hanging off in bloody strips. A cold hand touched her elbow. The hermit stood there, holding out a handful of feathery leaves.

"Will that help him?" Clara asked, relief flooding her.

"Keeps the wound from getting sick," the hermit grunted, then shoved the handful into his mouth and chewed them up, making a soggy clump that he spat into his hands and offered to her again.

"Keep that maniac away from me!" Old Johnny said, catching sight of the hermit.

"Warned him not to touch the berries," the hermit shrugged, dropping the green glop into the middle of the bandage Marta was about to apply and scrubbing his hands on his thighs to clean them. Marta paused, reaching to scrape away the glop, but Clara stopped her. "It's medicine."

"All blue-toned berries are edible!" Johnny argued, as Marta wrapped the cloth around his hand, "it's a tracker's rule of thumb!"

"And staying away from the flesh-eating plants is a rule of fingers." The hermit wiggled his five gnarled, but intact, digits.

Old Johnny lunged for him weakly, but Marta pushed him back and finished tying on the bandage. He swayed, eyes unfocused.

"I think that's quite enough," Desmond said sternly. "John—the hermit knows the jungle, if you don't listen to him, that's on you."

"He said they were edible!" Johnny gasped in pain and started shivering, clutching his bandaged hand to his chest.

"They are," the hermit said.

"And you!" Desmond turned to the gnarled old man, "Don't antagonize him further!"

The hermit shrugged, walking away and grabbing a long stick. He used it to prod the center of one of the spirals on the thorny plant. Faster than an eyeblink the vines closed around the stick, and cracking sounds filled the clearing. The hermit darted forward with another stick and knocked a cluster of berries to the ground. He carried the cluster over, popping one into his mouth and offering the others to them.

"Gotta be smarter than the plant." He knocked his head and clucked his tongue.

Old Johnny clenched his jaw, turning even paler.

"You need to lay down," Marta advised, "I think you're in shock, it's—"

"I know what shock is, woman!" Old Johnny stood and stumbled away. Marta rolled her eyes and followed.

"Shocking," the hermit mumbled, giggling.

Desmond sighed, shaking his head. "We'd better get settled for the night. It's going to be a long day tomorrow with two injured people to keep an eye on."

Clara nodded, then looked around for Levi. The scribe was sitting on the other side of the clearing, nearly as white as Old Johnny. Beth Ann sat with him, rubbing his back. Clara walked over to check on him, then covered her nose. It smelled like he had been puking into the bushes.

"Are you going to be okay?" she asked.

Levi nodded, still looking a little green.

"He saw a bit more of the wound than he would prefer," Beth Ann chimed in for him.

"I could say the same," Clara said, still feeling a bit queasy. She lingered awkwardly for a moment, but there was nowhere to sit, so she went to see what needed to be done in the shelters in order to sleep.

By the time everything was prepared, Clara was so

tired she felt sick again. She just needed to gather her pack and the remaining bandages from Marta before curling up in a place of her own.

She found Marta at the entrance of Old Johnny's hut, bandages in hand.

"You stay put until I come to change your bandages in the morning. I mean it."

Johnny grunted, but didn't argue. Clara imagined the man's pride was torn up as much as his hand.

Marta let the frond she was holding up fall back into place over Johnny's shelter, leaving them alone in the clearing.

"Here." Marta thrust the bandages at Clara. "Ridiculous old man doesn't know how to listen."

Clara turned the bandages over in her hands. "You were great today."

Marta shrugged. "Pa was a butcher. I've seen it all."

Clara almost smiled. "You keep these. They'll be more useful in your care, I'm sure of it."

Marta took the roll of bandages back and nodded, turning on her heel toward the shelter she shared with Beth Ann.

Clara trudged back to the middle of camp, slinging her bag over her shoulder. It weighed her down more and more with each step. When she finally reached her tent, it was all she could do to push the fronds aside that made up the entryway, kick off her shoes, and crawl onto her bed of fronds.

She rolled onto her back, her sweaty, sticky hair clinging to her cheeks and neck, and stared up at the trees that held her little home together. It only took a moment to drift off to sleep.

CHAPTER 21

Landmarks

Clara felt a presence in the tent with her. She stiffened on her pile of fronds and dared to open her eyes, letting them adjust to the darkness and shifting them until they landed on a shadowy figure only a few feet from her. She screamed, scrambling backward like one of the crabs Desmond had joked about on the beach, until a pair of dry, leathery hands clamped over her mouth.

"Didn't take you for one of them yowling lemurs," the hermit grumbled, sitting back on his heels.

Clara took a moment to catch her breath, smoothing her hair and getting a grip on her emotions before asking, "Is there a reason you're in my tent in the middle of the night?"

The hermit tossed Clara's great-grandfather's journal onto the bed next to her. He must've dug it out of her pack again. How long had he been in her tent? She picked the journal up, flipping through the first few pages.

"I know you can't read this… but I don't understand why you even need it. You know more about the jungle than any of us, probably more than my great-grandfather did."

The man snatched the journal from her and used his knuckles to roughly turn the pages until he found an entry near the end of the book and handed it back to Clara, pointing to a depiction of a campsite, one not so different from the one they were currently in.

"The last campsite..." Clara met his eyes. "You don't know where it is?"

The old man's eyes looked frightened and lost, as if he was once again the young boy on her great-grandfather's expedition. He shook his head. She wondered what he had seen there, what had happened to shake him so profoundly.

Instead of letting her curiosity get the best of her, she reached out and touched the man's forearm. "We'll help you find it."

The man jerked his arm away, but it seemed to be more out of surprise and discomfort than anger. Clara smiled at him and he squinted back at her before shuffling out of the tent.

Clara followed him out, finding that it wasn't the middle of the night, but nearly dawn. Some of the Seekers and sailors were already gathering around the firepit, stoking tiny flames in preparation for breakfast. Marta was rewrapping the foot injury Vim had acquired from the sand bog, while others seemed aimless, not sure what to do with themselves after a full night of rest, adequate water, and nourishing food.

Desmond and Frederick stood together in front of Desmond's dwelling, arms crossed and talking in low voices. Clara approached them, journal in hand, ready to tackle whatever the new day brought their way.

"Good morning, gentlemen." Clara smiled and gave a small curtsy.

"Clara." Desmond tipped his hat.

"Just the girl I was looking for," Frederick said, draping an arm around his cousin's shoulders. "I was just telling Desmond here that I think we ought to get moving as soon as possible."

"I'm not disagreeing, but we don't have a plan. We can't go traipsing through the jungle without a clear route. Even with the hermit, we can't find ourselves in situations where we lose the few supplies we have left." Desmond shoved his hands in his pockets. "We've been lucky thus far to keep everyone safe and healthy, minus a few fingers. I don't want to jeopardize that for the sake of moving quickly."

Frederick's eyes darkened. "For you and your men, the timing of it all may not be important, but for our people it is everything. Spending an entire day planning may be the difference between…"

Clara sucked in a deep breath. "Desmond has a point, Frederick." She squeezed her cousin's hand. "We can't go into this blind. Let's all sit down together this morning over breakfast and take the necessary time for safe preparations—"

"But—"

"The *necessary* time, but nothing more."

Frederick held her gaze for a moment, then snorted and shook his head in amusement. "When did you get so bossy? It feels like someone ran off with my flighty little cousin and replaced her with a tyrant." He reached out to ruffle her hair and she ducked away.

"I think the word you're looking for is 'confident leader'," Desmond said dryly, "Going through hard things can have that effect on people—they bring out the best or the worst, and I'd say Clara's just barely starting to tap her potential."

Clara's face grew warm, and she glanced up at him, then looked away, heart beating a little too fast. Did he really believe that about her?

Frederick put an arm around her shoulders. "I know that. Now let's go talk to the others. I want to get going."

Clara walked to the fire with him and sat with the other Seekers. Levi looked at her from across the fire, face haggard from a night with apparently little sleep. The jungle had not been good to him, but what had she expected? He liked everything neat and tidy and predictable, and so far the jungle had proved to be the opposite of that.

She looked down, not sure how to express her pity without seeming condescending or motherly. Desmond sat next to his friend and nudged him with his shoulder, saying something Clara couldn't hear over the crackle of the fire. Levi shot him an annoyed look, followed by an eye roll and a lopsided smile. Before long, his attitude seemed to have improved drastically, and he ate the fruit and tunnel weed mash the hermit was gleefully scooping onto leaves for everyone without a complaint.

How does he do that? Clara wondered, as Desmond turned to Old Johnny and coaxed a smile out of him too. On the ship he had been a strict master, but she realized now that it was because he cared deeply about the wellbeing of those on his ship, and the rules were there to keep them safe. The sailors all seemed to like him, and he had charisma—not the kind that came from arrogance, like she'd originally assumed, but because he was able to see how other people were struggling and adjust his responses to engage them the way *they* needed.

Desmond caught her staring at him and smiled warmly, then stood. Clara felt a flush of embarrassment and turned her attention to the mash the hermit had given her. Desmond came to put a hand on her shoulder, and she looked up in surprise, trying to pretend she hadn't just been lost in thought while gazing at his face. He wasn't looking at her anyway, but was staring around at the others instead. He cleared his throat and spoke in an authoritative voice.

"It's clear now that we're lost, but thanks to the

hermit—"

"Saanji," the old man grunted.

Desmond blinked, then ducked his head toward the man in a silent apology. "Thanks to Saanji we have a chance to get our bearings again. When we were on the ship I know Clara prepared a list of major landmarks from the journal, and we have the tentative map she compiled from them... what I need to know is, are you all still willing to move forward?"

Frederick jerked his head up sharply, and Clara grabbed his hand, giving it a squeeze. *He has to ask,* she thought at her cousin, wishing Desmond wasn't so close so she could murmur it aloud. Frederick met her gaze and sighed, seeming to understand her anyway.

"Of course we are," he replied, turning to look at the others as they nodded in agreement. Even Old Johnny grunted in assent.

Desmond's men all said they would stay with him and see it through, though Levi was conspicuously silent. When everyone else had expressed their desire to move forward, he sighed and reluctantly dipped his head toward Desmond, who accepted the short nod as good enough.

"Well then, the rest of us will start packing up camp —we'll leave the shelters here for our return journey, but make sure to bring everything else—while Clara and Saanji determine our route."

He gave Clara's shoulder a reassuring squeeze, then left to gather his own things. Clara sat with the hermit as the camp bustled with activity around them, trying to show him her map and lists. He kept turning the paper the wrong way and frowning at it, and when she showed him the list it earned a downright scowl. Finally she pulled out the journal, pointing to her great-grandfather's drawing of the place they'd entered the jungle. Saanji scratched his chin thoughtfully, then pointed to the map where she'd marked the spot they'd entered the jungle, and shook his head, sliding his finger inward, away from the edge of the trees.

"Jungle...moves. Not the same."

"So we did enter at the wrong place." Clara sighed. "You're saying the jungle looks different now?"

He nodded, then shook his head. "More trees grew. Outside is now inside."

What used to be the edge is further in now, because new trees grew, she interpreted to herself.

"Can you take us there? So we can start from the right place this time?"

The hermit furrowed his brow. "Following the whole path is long."

"Well, do you have any other suggestions?" Clara asked peevishly, instantly feeling ashamed for losing her temper. "I'm sorry. The time lost frustrates me too."

The hermit turned some pages in the journal, looking at the pictures. He grew excited when he reached the one of the archway—the picture that had first drawn her into Karrow's account.

"Read!" he said, stabbing the page with one gnarled finger. Clara did, describing the plant they'd found as well as reading the next day's entry.

The hermit jumped up, looking around the clearing, then bounded to the edge and motioned for her to follow.

"Okay okay, we're coming. Don't take off without us!" Clara called, climbing to her feet. Desmond handed her her pack and she stowed the journal with the rest of her things. Then they all headed into the jungle after the hermit.

At first the walk was lively, they trusted he knew where he was taking them, and his excitement had been a bit infectious. But after an hour or two, it became clear that the landmark he had recognized wasn't just a short jaunt away. The ground was uneven, and going was slow. Levi walked an arm's length behind the hermit and winced each time the man shuffled across a tree root or loose rock.

It reminded Clara of a mother hovering over her toddler while they took their first steps, though the scene in front of her was much less touching.

"The old coot is going to break a hip and I'll be darned if I have to carry him on my back until we reach the valley," Levi grumbled.

"Levi," Clara snapped, eying the back of the hermit's head.

Levi spoke louder, "What? He can't hear a darned thing anyway. I've been trying to tell him all morning that I can mend the broken strap on his sandal and all he does is mutter something about frog legs."

Clara cracked a smile. Even though Levi didn't feel comfortable with the hermit's abilities, she was glad to have the old man with them. She felt like they were safer with him there. It's true that Old Johnny had gotten hurt on his watch... but Saanji had tried to warn him. And without his knowledge, who knows if they would have ever found the pools of water, discovered that tunnel weed was edible, or figured out how to safely harvest the churnberries. His contributions were essential if they were ever going to find the Land of Origin.

The trees parted up ahead, revealing a stone archway nearly swallowed entirely by twisting vines, and Clara felt some of the tension of the last few days melt away. She pulled out the journal and compared the drawing to the arch. The stone was more crumbled, the vines larger, but there was no doubt in her mind that this was the same place.

Levi smiled and prodded her forward, while the others sat with their backs against the trees for a quick breather. The hermit hovered around her as she approached the archway and laid a hand on a tiny bit of exposed stone.

Desmond came up beside her. "This is different from the buildings the natives construct. In fact the way the stones interlock is similar to old buildings I've seen in Aldonia. If you needed proof that your people used to live here, this could be it."

Clara looked at him in surprise. "Are you an expert in architecture?"

"I dabble," Desmond said coyly, then smiled, the corners of his eyes crinkling. "My education was extensive. My parents saw to that. You never know what piece of information is going to give you the upper hand during a negotiation."

"That seems..." Clara searched for the right word, not wanting to offend him.

"Exploitative? Unscrupulous? Underhanded?" Desmond filled in for her. She cringed, and he laughed at her mortified expression. "Believe me, I've heard it all. Merchants... aren't always well-liked, sometimes for good reason. Some can be manipulative and do anything for a deal, but my family tries to do things differently. We find a need and try to fill it. You get the best deals that way. My father wanted me to learn everything I could, not as leverage or something to use to trick people, but to give me the best chance of understanding people's needs." He placed his hand on the archway next to hers, and a tingle of warmth went through her.

"You're good at that," Clara said, "understanding people's needs, I mean." She blushed, then turned away and buried her face in the journal before he could see her embarrassment.

"Which way from here?" Levi asked from behind her. She looked up, startled. She'd forgotten he was there. Had he been listening to their conversation? Her eyes flickered back to Desmond, and she thought she saw him and Levi exchange a look, but maybe that was all in her head.

Focus Clara! she berated herself, looking back down at the journal and skimming for where Karrow's expedition had gone from here.

"That way." She pointed between two trees, toward a mountain rising in the distance.

CHAPTER 22

❖

Monkeys

They followed the journal south for a few days, building camps in the same places her great-grandfather had described. They even found occasional traces of the expedition—a ring of stones for a fire, now covered in moss, an old tin cup lost out of someone's pack, initials carved into a tree. The jungle had swallowed most signs of human passing, but even it couldn't eliminate everything.

The deeper they traipsed through the jungle, the more aware Clara became of its sounds. Some had become familiar to her, while others were still a mystery. Insects hummed and whirred all around them and flashes of color streaked through the canopy as birds flitted overhead. Clara's heart lifted with them as they flew through the trees. They were finally *truly* on their way to the Land of Origin.

One sound in particular started to become the most dominant, echoing in the tapestry of leaves above their heads. The eerie chants sounded almost otherworldly, reminding her of the distinct song of loons on the water back home. Though sometimes she felt as if the jungle was another world, she supposed she would need to get used to its sounds, considering if the expedition succeeded, this would be her home.

With that thought in mind, she tried to familiarize herself with the sound that was growing louder. It sounded more mammalian than fowl. She racked her brain thinking of all of the animal encounters her great-grandfather had cited in his journal. It only took her a moment to remember the monkeys that had caused the first expedition so much trouble, though what kind of trouble he hadn't specified.

Saanji stopped abruptly, his head whipping up toward the trees. Levi bumped into the old man's back, an annoyed grimace spreading across his face, but Saanji hardly seemed to notice. He turned in a slow circle, holding a finger to his lips. The rest of the company stilled and Clara's breath caught in her throat.

The eerie howling was now deafening and several people covered their ears. Clara clenched her teeth together and watched the trees. All at once, the motion up above ceased and all was silent. Clara's eyes snapped to Saanji, who met her gaze.

"Run," he whispered.

The deafening noise began again and Saanji took off, weaving a haphazard trail through the wide tree trunks. Clara hiked up her skirts and took off after Saanji. Her feet pounded hard against the ground and her heart followed suit. She snuck a glance over her shoulder and through the frightened, confused faces of those behind her, she could see huge, brown masses of fur.

She screamed and ran faster, keeping on the heels of the men in front of her. She looked from side to side trying to catch glimpses of Frederick or Desmond or Levi. She knew Levi had been in front of her at the start, but now she wasn't sure which trail he'd taken. She tried to remember where Desmond and Frederick had been with no luck, just hoping that they were ahead of her now.

Clara chanced one more look behind her and saw Marta and Beth Ann on either side of the sailor that had hurt his ankle. They were dangerously close to being overtaken by the beasts behind them. Clara stopped in her tracks, turning around. She'd only taken a few steps before a strong, determined hand gripped her elbow, pulling her the other way once again.

"Let go!" She clawed at Desmond's arm, trying to break free of his now painful grip. He was unrelenting, pulling her forward toward some unknown location. "We have to help!"

When she glanced behind her this time, one of the monsters was close enough that she could see the whites of its eyes. They were rimmed with a solid patch of bright red fur against its dark brown coat, making it look demon-like. Its heart-stopping cry came from a fang-filled mouth, unlike the flat, human-like teeth she was used to seeing on such animals. The beast ran on all fours, its hands like a bear's paws, but thinner and with the addition of an opposable thumb, complete with thick, long claws at the end of its fingers.

Clara's arm ached where she pulled against Desmond, but she didn't stop even when one of the monkeys, if they could even be called that, sunk its teeth into the wounded sailor's leg. She watched helplessly as Marta dropped Vim and kept running. Beth Ann dove to the ground, grabbing both of the man's hands, trying to pull him from the monster's grasp. Marta spun back, pulling Beth Ann's shoulders, pleading with her to let go.

It wasn't until Marta stood and stomped on one of Beth Ann's wrists that she involuntarily released Vim's hands. The man was dragged away, screaming helplessly as the beast carried him up into a tree, the others following after it.

Clara sobbed in horror and disbelief, wishing she could erase the scene from her memory. Instead, it replayed over and over as they continued to run. The howling stopped and turned into a flurry of rustling and chittering in the canopy. Clara's stomach churned. She let Desmond pull her along until they reached a shallow cave, its entrance covered in overgrown thistles.

Desmond pulled her through the entrance, the thistles cutting the skin on her arms and neck and face, and once Beth Ann, Marta, and a few others toppled in, the vines were strategically pushed into place, blocking the entrance once again. Clara's sobs hadn't stopped, and she didn't try to make them. Desmond wrapped his arms around her shoulders and she sobbed into his chest. He stroked her hair with one hand and she lifted her face to look at him.

"Why didn't you let me help? Vim... he..." Clara's face crumpled and tears streamed down her face.

Desmond searched her eyes. "I couldn't let you go. I —"

Frederick stumbled over to Clara in the dark, pushing himself between her and Desmond. "You're alive." He rested his head on her shoulder and let out a shaky sigh of relief before facing her again. "I couldn't find you, Clara! I couldn't find you and I didn't know if I'd ever see you again and I didn't know what I'd tell Uncle Warren and Aunt Kate if anything had happened to you."

"I'm okay," Clara whispered, wiping away her tears. Now that she knew Frederick was safe, she just needed to find Levi. "Levi... is he?"

Frederick motioned to one corner of the cave, keeping one hand in hers. There was a dark silhouette sitting on a large rock, knees pulled to his chest, head shaking back and forth. Clara fell back against the wall of the cave in relief. There was Saanji, and Old Johnny and Charles with the sailors, and then Marta and Beth Ann.

Oh, Beth Ann.

Clara's throat burned as she tried to hold back fresh

tears. She broke free of Frederick's hold and offered her hand to Beth Ann, who refused it.

"No one helped me." She stared blankly, cradling her wrist against her chest.

"You couldn't have saved him, Beth Ann," Marta said, her voice as gentle as Clara had ever heard it, reaching for her sister's shoulder.

Beth Ann pulled away and a fire lit in her eyes. "You killed him!" She spat at her sister.

"You think I wanted to leave him behind? I've spent the better part of a week tending that man's wound," Marta straightened. "I didn't kill him. But I did save you. It may take you some time to see that, but I will not, even for one second, regret what I did."

The fight seemed to leave Beth Ann and she sunk to the ground with a whimper. Marta sat beside her and moved her sister's head to her shoulder, where she quickly quieted.

The men had huddled together and were talking in hushed tones, save Saanji who fidgeted on the outskirts of the group.

"—here till morning. Just to be safe."

"What if those monsters sniff us out and we're sitting ducks in here?"

"Do you want to take your chances outrunning them again? We have no supplies, no weapons—"

The men talked over one another, no singular answer seemed to satisfy the group and Clara began to fear that the progress of the past few days would be lost when Saanji piped up. "Morning," he said matter-of-factly, taking a seat on a small boulder as if to seal the decision.

Clara found a pile of rocks and took a seat. Her mind swirled with thoughts and images and she had a hard time making sense of them. She caught glimpses of red-rimmed eyes and blurry tree roots and tanned hands. She looked down at her arm, which she was now painfully aware of, and could see the black and purple bruising even in the dark.

The last image she saw before being taken by sleep, was Desmond's warm, dark, worried eyes.

I couldn't let you go.

CHAPTER 23

Discussions

Clara woke to the sound of grumbling and opened her eyes to find Saanji using a long stick to not-so-gently nudge the men awake. Before he could reach her, she lifted her head from the ground and groaned, her neck stiff and eyes puffy.

It was still dark in the cave, only a few soft strands of light made their way through the tangle of thorns into the crowded space. It took Clara a moment to remember where she was and what had happened only the day before.

Images flooded her mind once again. Ginormous paws, fluttering green leaves, a hat falling to the ground...

Sucking in a sharp breath, she stood up, moving toward the entrance, suddenly needing to be anywhere else. She reached out to move the thorns away only to be whacked on the back of her hand by Saanji's stick.

"Ouch!" Clara rubbed her hand where it was stinging and turning an angry red. She was about to ask the hermit why he wouldn't let her leave the cave when Desmond slapped his hands on his knees, pushing himself to a standing position.

His clothing was rumpled and his dark hair flopped

into his eyes for a moment before he ran his hands through it, slicking it back to its usual position so he could put on his hat. He smiled wanly when he saw Clara and her heart fluttered.

She smiled back, unable to keep her eyes from him. How was it that he could look equally at home on the deck of a ship, in the home of a village chief, or in a grimy cave? How was it that he could make her feel instantly more at home as well?

"Saanji," Desmond clapped a hand on the old man's shoulder, making him grimace though he didn't move away, "was just telling me that it would be best if we moved together in a tight group until we're out of the monkeys' territory. We were too spread out yesterday. It made it easier for them to... target... individuals."

Clara flinched, hearing the sailor's screams ringing in her ears as he was carried into the canopy. Desmond's face was apologetic. His hand twitched at his side, as if he was holding it back from reaching out to her.

She stepped away from the entrance of the cave, turning so Desmond wouldn't see how much it hurt that he had held back. She would wake Beth Ann and Marta—a gentle shake on the shoulder would be a better awakening than the sharp stab of Saanji's stick.

"Beth Ann," Clara whispered, nudging the woman's shoulder. Beth Ann woke with a start, her sudden movement jostling Marta awake. Marta's eyes were wild and searching until they adjusted and recognized Clara.

"What?" Marta snapped. Clara raised an eyebrow, wishing she had let Saanji use his stick after all, or better yet, that she'd used it herself.

"We're getting ready to move," Clara grumbled. She was startled by a strong grip to her elbow and wheeled around to find Saanji on her heels. "Oh, hello."

He blinked at her and then tugged at her bag. Instead of fighting him, she slid the bag off and handed it to him, watching as he rummaged around for the journal. Once he found it, he tossed the bag behind him, her belongings skittering across the flor.

Clara's face scrunched in agitation, wondering if the rest of the day would continue this way. As if the rest of the people in the cave could perceive her thoughts, an argument whether to retreat back to camp or press forward toward the next landmark broke out.

Instead of paying them any mind, Clara looked over Saanji's hunched shoulders and asked, "what do you think?"

The man pointed ahead to the next landmark, using his finger to trace a new route to it, a less straightforward route than they'd originally planned.

"We can't keep going the way we were?" Clara's anxiety increased. It seemed nothing could go as planned.

Saanji shook his head, tapped his knuckles twice against her forehead, and simply said, "Monkeys."

Clara gritted her teeth. At least now that there was a plan she could get out of the cave. She didn't care if half the group would disagree with Saanji's decision.

The hermit pushed aside the thorny vines just enough so he could see out, then he motioned once for them to follow and slipped through. The men glanced up as a sliver of light came into the cave as Saanji exited, then rushed to follow him. Clara sighed, gathered her scattered things, and was the last one out of the cave.

Once out in the open, Clara didn't feel the relief she'd expected. Fear wormed its way up inside of her instead, snaking through the pit of her stomach and tightening around her heart till she could barely breathe. Fear that something would drop from the trees, fear that this time it would take someone she cared for more deeply. She looked around the group that was now slowly moving away from the cave.

Those who had traveled from Aldonia with her were

people she'd seen her parents care for and minister to for her entire life. Frederick was family by blood, but the others were family by choice, through shared beliefs. She may not have known them well individually, but their faces were a familiar part of her childhood. They'd brought treats on holidays, meals when they were sick, and Clara had played with or helped watch over their children and younger relatives. They'd edified and strengthened her faith in her youth. She couldn't imagine telling their families that something had happened to them, any of them.

Her eyes flashed to Frederick and she felt a stirring of shame. Maybe she shouldn't have turned back for the sailor. Marta was right that there was nothing Beth Ann could have done to save him... Why had Clara thought she could do anything different? All she would have done is put the burden of her horrific death on Frederick's shoulders, to carry all the way back to her family across the sea.

If he could even find them.

She pushed bleak thoughts about her parents out of her head and ran her fingers through her hair. She didn't recognize the texture anymore. The humidity had made it puffy, even though it was weighed down with dirt and grime and who knew what else. She moved on to her bag, brushing off debris from the cave floor as she walked along, and tossing out handfuls of leaves and twigs that had made their way in over the past few days. Then she worked on retying her skirts, higher above her knees this time, so it would be easier to run if necessary. It was difficult to do on the move, but she didn't want to get too far behind the others, not after yesterday.

Finally, she tore a scrap of fabric from an under layer of her skirts and fastened it into a tie for her hair. She was surprised she hadn't thought of it sooner, and for all the comfort it brought, she wished she had. It was almost enough to make the fear subside and something almost like contentment take its place.

"You look nice."

Clara was relieved it was already so warm this morning, or her blush would have been unmistakable. "Thanks, Levi."

He nodded, clasping his hands behind his back as he'd often done on the ship when he was thinking through something. Clara was glad he'd come to speak with her. He'd looked so lost last night in the cave and she hadn't had it in her to comfort him at the time. Their friendship had been so strained lately, maybe now was her chance to reach out.

"How are you doing?" she asked, her voice low so those around them wouldn't easily overhear.

"Better." His eyes were bright and his cheeks were flushed, making him look more vibrant and healthy than he had in a while. He looked into Clara's eyes for a moment and then took a deep breath and faced ahead once more. "The past couple days have been... hard. This whole experience—being here in the jungle, I mean—has been hard. It's not an experience I can say I've much enjoyed, if I'm being entirely honest."

Clara muffled an inadvertent snort. "I've noticed." She noted his hair sticking up from sleeping on the ground the night before, and the mud stains on his trousers. The Levi she'd known on the ship wouldn't have stood for any of it, and she knew it was killing him to let those things go now.

Levi stopped walking and turned to face her. Clara stopped too, looking at him in confusion. She felt a little self conscious as others passed them, their curious glances occasionally visible in her peripheral vision, but they moved on without a word.

"I'm glad you said something," Clara started. She glanced after the group, not wanting to lag too far behind. "I wanted to talk with you last night but I wasn't...

I couldn't... Anyway, I'm glad you're doing better this morning."

He smiled down at her, taking a step closer. "As awful as yesterday was, it got me thinking. There are things I wish I would have done differently, things I regret. I don't want to have any more regrets."

Clara squinted up at him. "What do you mean—?"

His thoughts came out in a rush. "Like I said, I haven't enjoyed the jungle. Not any of it. But I don't regret stepping off that ship, because what I have enjoyed, Clara, is you."

Clara's eyes widened. She'd misunderstood something, surely. "Me?"

"Yes. You possess qualities that I admire and wish to emulate. You are open and honest with your feelings, you try to do what you think is right, you speak up."

"Those are all of the things that get me into trouble." Clara furrowed her brow. Where was he going with this?

Levi looked down at his feet, then took a deep breath and looked back up at her, determined. "They're just a few of the reasons why... I love you."

Clara brought a hand to her mouth, searching his eyes. *He loves me?*

"I know there's a world of difference between us, but I saw my parents work through so many things that were meant to keep them apart. My father is Estanyan and my mother is Aldonian. She gave up her family, her country, everything, to be with my father. You remind me so much of her."

Clara lowered her hand and wrung the strap of her bag. "I admire her strength, but—"

Levi cut her off with a light-hearted laugh. "I wouldn't ask you to do that. Our life—if you'll have me —could look however you imagine it. I'd follow you to the ends of the earth, Clara Bowman. I already have." He gestured to the jungle around them and grinned, taking her hands in his.

Clara opened her mouth but no words came out, so she snapped it shut again. She had no idea how long he'd been harboring these feelings and she didn't know what made him speak them aloud now. And she certainly didn't know how to untangle the knot in her stomach that had formed as he spoke.

"Yesterday when I saw you turn around and run toward those beasts," Levi squeezed her hands tighter. "I couldn't bear the thought that something almost hurt you." He noticed the bruises on her arm and moved his hand up, gently running a thumb over them.

"You saw what happened?" Clara whispered.

"Some of it. I saw you turn around and when Desmond ran after you I knew he'd bring you back, but Saanji was disappearing, so I followed him to make sure you both would be able to find your way to safety by following me. I know it wasn't very brave, but I'm not brave, Clara, I'm practical. I make lists and I plan ahead… and you make me want to be impulsive and throw caution to the wind. I think we could both learn a lot from each other, if you'll give me a chance."

Clara pursed her lips. His explanation made sense, it was logical, she liked him a great deal, and maybe she *could* learn a lot from him… but did she love him? Better yet, did he actually love her? Or did he just like how being with her forced him to be more spontaneous?

She looked down at the ground and slipped her arms out from his hold. "You've given me a lot to think about. If you'll excuse me." She hurried after the group, her mind spinning.

Levi followed, seeming a bit deflated by her response, but she couldn't answer him the way he wanted when her insides were still a tangled mess from yesterday's events.

Desmond had stopped the group up ahead until they

caught up, and the look of concern he gave her made the knots in her stomach tangle even tighter. Was he worried about her physical safety because they'd dropped behind? Or did he suspect Levi's feelings for her and he worried she felt the same way? Was that just wishful thinking? Was she reading him all wrong? Maybe he didn't care about her other than as a member of the expedition, and she was foolish to consider rejecting Levi in the hope that maybe...

"Are you all right?" Frederick interrupted her thoughts with a hand on her arm.

"I'm fine." Tears welled in her eyes, and Clara dashed them away. There was too much at stake for her to be worried about something so frivolous. What did it matter who loved her if they all died in the jungle anyway?

Frederick put his arm around her shoulders and pulled her along with the group as they stumbled through the jungle after Saanji. *Solid, steady Frederick.* She wiped her eyes and gave him a wan smile.

"Thanks," she whispered.

He nodded. "It's been a terrifying few days—few months if I'm being honest. Ever since we heard that proclamation I've been so afraid for the future. I don't blame you for crying, might shed some tears myself later."

Clara snorted, trying to hold in a laugh. She probably seemed a bit hysterical, but it was all just too much.

"Shhh!" Saanji turned to stare at her accusingly, and she sobered. They were still in danger here. Extra noise was a bad idea.

They walked the rest of the day, not pausing for lunch, and finally reached a grove of trees that resembled the one described in the journal. The sun would set soon, and they got to work building their camp with what was now a practiced efficiency. This time, though, there was an undercurrent of fear to everything they did.

Work quickly, their movements seemed to say, *the jungle isn't safe.*

CHAPTER 24

Altercation

The fire was built, and Saanji had left to gather more food. The tension Clara had felt all day seemed to intensify as the sailors and Seekers performed tasks to ready the camp, or found seats near the fire. Charles grabbed a stick to poke the tunnel weed Marta had added to the fire earlier, and accidentally stepped on a sailor's hand.

"Watch it!" the man growled, pulling his hand away forcefully enough to make Charles stumble and nearly fall into the fire. Charles whirled on him, dropping the stick and clenching his fists. "Maybe you should be helping instead of lounging by the fire! No reason to push me in for not seeing your hand where it had no right to be!"

"No right?" The sailor leapt to his feet and stabbed a finger accusingly at Charles, "I've trekked through this godforsaken place for weeks in search of your imaginary paradise, and now one of my closest friends is dead. I've every right to do whatever I choose!"

Desmond put down the wood he'd been gathering and held out his hands placatingly. "Let's just take a breath —"

Charles swiped the man's finger away. "Watch where

you're pointing that. You didn't have to come. I heard your boss give you all a choice."

"Charles..." Frederick said warningly as the two men stood toe to toe.

"A choice I'd take back if I could—Vim is dead! And none of you zealots care. Well, I'm not losing any more friends chasing after this, this poppycock!"

"Zealots? At least we believe in something, which is more than I can say for you sorry lot of pagans!"

Charles spit at the sailor's feet as Frederick tried to pull him away. Desmond stepped between the men to separate them just as the sailor threw a punch.

Clara cried out as Desmond reeled back and fell to the ground. She rushed to his side and placed her hands on either side of his face. He blinked up at her and groaned, left eye watering and the skin around it beginning to swell. She gingerly prodded his cheekbone, checking for a break. He winced, but Clara couldn't feel anything unusual. He seemed all right other than a budding black eye and being a little dazed.

She stood and glared at the sailor with an expression she hoped was reminiscent of her mother's sternest, soul-piercing gaze. "Are you happy now? We've already lost one man and half of us are injured in one way or another. Do we need anyone else hurt because you can't keep your temper?"

The sailor looked down, arms going limp by his sides. Charles still struggled against Frederick somewhere behind her. She turned the same expression on him. "This 'sorry lot of pagans' has helped us at great personal risk, when even our own countrymen turned their backs on us —"

"He called our beliefs poppycock," Charles muttered, shrugging off Frederick and trying to meet Clara's gaze. His eyes dipped to the ground, unable to withstand her glare of disappointment.

"Yet he is still here, helping us. You don't know what he believes, but belittling it in the face of a minor insult is beneath you, Charles. They've all lost a friend and are just as terrified as the rest of us of losing someone else! How about you give him a little grace?"

Charles grunted and stalked off to one of the shelters. Clara sighed and turned back to the others.

Desmond climbed slowly to his feet, using Clara's shoulder for support. He faced the sailor. "If we were on the ship that would've earned you a night in the brig, Gerrault."

"Yes sir, sorry sir. It won't happen again." The sailor murmured, clasping his hands behind his back. His eyes flicked up to meet Desmond before turning downward again, ashamed.

Desmond sighed and touched the spot under his left eye gently, wincing in pain. It was already swollen nearly shut and turning mottled purple and blue. Clara bit her lip. She hoped he could still see out of it. Having a limited field of vision would be dangerous out here.

"See that it doesn't." Desmond turned to the others. "I know we're all shaken up by the loss of Vim, but we can't turn on each other or none of us are going to make it out of here. From now on any fighting will earn the perpetrators a night spent tied to a tree together, understood?"

The sailors murmured their agreement, and the Seekers all nodded, looking troubled.

"Now, it's just a little further to the last camp. A few more days and we should be able to rest and restock our food supplies in the place locals call the Valley of Paradise. I know you're all tired and scared, but turning back would mean going through all of that—" he motioned to the dark jungle behind him, "—again. Our only choice is to press forward."

The others seemed to accept this. The hermit, who'd returned sometime during the scuffle and calmly continued cooking dinner, handed Desmond a leaf with some blackened tunnel weed and rubbery looking pieces of what Clara suspected was snake meat. When Desmond took it the old man scuttled off into the jungle, muttering to himself.

Desmond sat beside the fire and patted the ground nearby for Clara to join him. He handed her a piece of the meat and some of the tunnel weed and they ate, listening to the quiet bustling of the camp's activities until their shared meal was gone.

"Are you okay?" Desmond asked. His good eye was full of concern.

Clara laughed out loud. "What do you mean, am I okay? You're the one that just got punched in the face."

"Oh, that was nothing." He smiled and the motion made him wince. His smile faded and he looked into the fire in front of them, which had been built large and hot and crackled loudly. "I'm sorry about what Gerrault said."

"Are you?" Clara whispered. She wanted to believe that he meant it, but this was still the same man that had suggested she hide her amulet in the marketplace. *But he's also the same man that risked his own life to save mine.*

Desmond cocked his head to the side. "I've spent my life traveling, spending time among cultures with beliefs far stranger than yours. And they've all dealt with—and dished out—prejudice of one kind or another. Comments like that... they often come from ignorance, not true malice."

Clara smiled to herself. "My Pa always told me that too. He said to pay them no mind, though I'm not sure how good I've been at heeding his advice."

"Wise man," Desmond said. "You may have trouble paying them no mind, but you haven't seemed to let comments like that hurt your faith—at least not enough to keep you from seeking the Land of Origin."

Clara thought about that for a moment. Her parents had tried to instill a sense of steadfastness in her, but the truth was that until she had met Desmond at the market, her faith had never really been tried. She thought back to the bog and still felt ashamed of how she'd reacted. The doubt she'd felt in that moment still gnawed at her, not because it remained, but because she worried it would return.

"To be honest, comments like that do bother me. It's one thing for someone to disagree with what I believe. That I can understand. But to belittle something that means so much to someone else, something that defines so much of who they are…"

"He was harsh." Desmond rubbed a hand across the back of his neck. "I've been harsh too." Clara turned to look at him and he met her eyes. "My parents are practical people who follow the state religion of Estanya. They're consistent, but not particularly devout. I seem to be even less so."

Clara furrowed her brow. *Why is he telling me this?* "What do you mean?"

"All I'm saying is that I've seen things, out on the ocean." Desmond looked past her into the darkness. "I've been through things I shouldn't have come out of alive. I do believe there's a higher power, someone or something out there that's aware of us, and I do find comfort in that. It gives me hope and makes me feel like there's a reason I'm still here." He shifted his gaze back toward her. "If I feel that way without searching something out, I can only imagine how you feel, having grown up the way you have."

Clara nodded. Desmond smiled softly, prevented from anything more by the swelling of his cheek.

"I can't say I understand all of what you stand for, or why it means so much to you, but I'm willing to learn."

They were only inches from each other and Clara couldn't remember when or how they'd gotten that close.

The hermit returned with a bunch of tiny yellow flowers that he crumpled and squeezed a greenish liquid out of directly onto Desmond's face. Clara jumped up to avoid the ooze and stifled a giggle at the long-suffering look Desmond gave her. They were all getting used to the Hermit's way of infringing on personal boundaries— something Clara found ironic since Saanji seemed to hate when people did the same to him.

"You'd better get some rest," she told Desmond as he stood, fighting the urge to reach out and brush his hair back from his forehead. "Thanks for... everything."

She turned to leave, but Desmond caught her hand. "Goodnight Clara." He pressed his lips against the back of her hand before releasing it. "Thank you."

Clara nodded and turned away, speechless.

CHAPTER 25

Rain

Night hadn't brought Clara any respite from the confusion of the day before. As she trudged through the jungle once again, her feet felt heavy and so did her eyelids. Still, she carried on with the hope that they'd soon reach their destination. The last camp was only a day or two away, according to the journal.

She stuck close to Frederick's side and was grateful for his steady, predictable presence. She could still feel Desmond's lips pressed to the back of her hand and could hear Levi's words ringing in her ears. Part of her wondered if she ignored it all, maybe it would go away. The trouble was, the other part of her didn't want it to. She had grown close to Levi during their voyage, she valued his friendship, even if it had been strained lately. And Desmond... she still felt a little ashamed of how badly she'd misjudged him. If she'd known at the beginning of their journey that she would come to crave his approval, she would've laughed at herself.

Clara huffed and brushed a few loose strands of hair from her forehead. Her eyes ventured from the ground in front of her and found that Levi was watching her. She quickly moved her gaze back to the ground and grabbed a fistful of her skirt.

Levi didn't strike her as one to offer up his affections again after she'd asked for time to think. He was too pragmatic for that. But that didn't mean he didn't deserve an answer, even if she couldn't give one right away.

Clara frowned. If she'd met Levi in Aldonia, under normal circumstances, she was sure he would have eventually caught her eye. Levi was someone her parents, especially her father, would approve of, other than his lack of religious convictions. He was hardworking, diligent, bright, and clearly cared about her. He was stable. She would have felt like the luckiest girl if he'd tossed his attention her way. But they weren't in Aldonia and she wasn't the same girl that had stepped onto the ship at port.

"You've been melancholy this morning," Frederick interrupted her thoughts as he held a branch out of the way for her.

She ducked under it and flashed him a quick thank-you smile. "Just thoughtful is all."

He narrowed his eyes skeptically and quirked his mouth to the side. "The Clara I used to know pretty much said whatever was on her mind."

She rolled her eyes and nudged him with her elbow, but didn't give him the explanation he was clearly digging for.

Even though Frederick had been exaggerating, he wasn't completely off the mark. She was turning into someone she didn't recognize, but was excited to get to know better. She was less impulsive in many ways, but somehow also less inhibited. Even though there were things she feared, it didn't stop her from acting. When she had decided to run into danger to help Beth Ann and the sailor, Levi had turned the other way. He said all the right things, that he admired her ability to do what she thought was right, and she didn't doubt that he wanted to change, but ultimately he had let her go.

And then there was Desmond, who had consistently done the exact opposite. He'd put himself in danger to make sure she was safe. He wanted to know the parts of her that he couldn't yet understand. He hadn't confessed his love for her, but didn't his actions show that he cared about her? True, sometimes he teased her and drove her crazy, but he was also there when she really needed him.

Clara shook her head. She was probably reading too much into his actions. He'd made it clear on the ship that he felt a deep responsibility for the safety of the people under his charge. He would have turned back for anyone. That's the kind of man Desmond was.

Clara's thoughts continued to trouble her through their short lunch, during which Desmond barely glanced her way, busy conversing with Levi and some of the sailors. When they moved on, the jungle grew thinner for a time, with more brush and fewer trees. The sun beat down on them, and Clara let her troubles fade to the back of her mind as she struggled to keep putting one foot in front of the other when all her body wanted to do was melt into a puddle in the shade of one of the trees.

The rain came out of nowhere.

Initially Clara sighed in relief as the first drops slipped from the foliage high above and trickled onto her head. She held her open canteen under a leaf to catch the water that streamed down it, and turned her face upward to enjoy the cooling effect of the rain. The sensation lasted a mere two seconds before the drops began to hit with more force, stinging her cheeks with their angry barrage. She yelped and looked back down, then held her pack over her head as she ran to catch up with the others. It didn't do much good, in seconds she was soaked clear through.

Saanji had broken into a run, presumably to find shelter, and they all scrambled after him. Desmond waited till Clara drew abreast of the others, then held his hat above her so she could clutch her pack to her chest and as they ran together through the jungle. The sound of rain was deafening. The downpour was strong enough to pelt the leaves and branches above them so powerfully the sound drowned out the shouts of the others. Desmond abandoned trying to shield her and instead gripped her hand tightly with one of his own while he held the other above his eyes in an attempt to see through the sheets of rain.

Clara wasn't sure where the others were, but she clung to Desmond's hand and focused on the ground in front of her, which was quickly becoming slippery with mud. A branch crashed to the ground just ahead of them, and Clara screamed. They were forced to slow their pace to a more reasonable speed, and Clara managed to catch a glimpse of Marta and Beth Ann off to the right.

The women swerved to avoid another falling branch, and Marta slipped and fell, cracking her head against something. The sound was loud enough to be heard over the rain. Clara's stomach sank, and she changed direction, pulling Desmond with her. They stumbled to a stop beside Beth Ann, who was screaming and crying for her sister to get back up again. Marta lay with her head at an impossible angle, eyes staring sightlessly at the canopy above them.

Clara looked away, letting go of Desmond and grabbing Beth Ann's arm. "We have to go!" she shouted, her voice barely audible over the downpour.

Beth Ann jerked away and knelt next to her sister, weeping and shaking her by the shoulders as though she could wake her up. Desmond bent and lifted the body, tugging it out of her grasp. He hoisted Marta over his shoulder and then pulled Beth Ann up with his free hand. He nodded to Clara and she led the way back toward where she thought the others may have gone.

The rain let up slightly, turning from an uncontrolled deluge of water to a steady drumming that allowed Clara to hear the others shouting for them. She turned toward the sound, and found them beneath a fallen tree with a massive trunk wide enough to create a bit of shelter.

Desmond laid Marta against the tree that supported the fallen trunk, resting his hand on Beth Ann's shoulder in silent apology and turning to the others.

"Who are we missing?" he asked, doing a quick headcount. Clara turned to Beth Ann, who had sunk to the ground weeping. She sat next to the woman, unsure how to comfort her when her own heart sat heavy in her chest. She'd struggled to get along with Marta, but she'd never wished her gone in such a permanent way.

"I shouted at her for saving me," Beth Ann's voice was choked with emotion. "She was just looking out for me, and I accused her of killing—" she broke off and covered her face, shuddering with sobs.

Clara rubbed circles on Beth Ann's back, staring out into the rain. Was it lessening? The drumming of water still filled her ears, but it had faded to a background murmur rather than an insistent beat.

Clara searched for the words she would want to hear, if she was in the same position. "Your sister knew you loved her. And she saved you because she loved you. We may not have seen eye to eye about everything, but I don't think she'd want you to blame yourself for having a human reaction in a moment of stress. She did what she thought was right, and your accusations didn't change that."

Beth Ann wiped her eyes and nodded, hugging her legs to her chest and staring at the tree trunk with puffy eyes. Levi came up behind them.

"Sorry to interrupt, but they need you Clara."

Clara sighed and patted Beth Ann on the shoulder before accepting Levi's proffered hand and pulling herself back up.

"Stay with her please? I don't think she should

be alone right now," Clara murmured, and Levi nodded, squeezing her hand slightly before letting go and settling himself awkwardly next to the grieving woman.

"I was told you needed me?" Clara asked when she reached Desmond and the others.

"Saanji," Desmond said, nodding toward the hermit.

The old man was pacing back and forth frantically at the edge of their shelter, muttering and ranting to himself in a disturbing manner. The rain was slowing to a drizzle, and he didn't seem to notice that he was only half under the tree trunk and getting soaked. Clara felt a surge of irritation. Couldn't they deal with Saanji? She had enough on her plate trying to comfort Beth Ann while dealing with her own feelings of guilt and loss. She took a deep breath and let it out, then turned to Desmond. "It looks like things are letting up, we need to take care of Marta's body before we move on, could you...?"

Desmond nodded curtly and turned to some of the others. They immediately started looking for a spot free of tree roots and other obstructions, where they could use sticks and rocks to dig a hole.

Clara walked over to Saanji and rested her hand on his arm. The hermit stopped pacing, and turned toward her with eyes wide. Then he shook off her hand and continued pacing.

"The rain is clearing up," Clara said, "we can head back out soon."

"Cursed, cursed," the hermit muttered. Sunlight broke through the clouds, and he seemed to break out of whatever mental loop he'd been stuck in. He stopped and looked directly at her. "Have to find them, but the curse doesn't like it. Have to help them rest." He tried to dart out into the jungle, but Clara anticipated this and stepped in his way.

"Hey," she said calmly, trying to catch his eye, "we need you to wait. We have to take care of our dead first."

Saanji glanced at the body lying against the tree, and his face sobered.

"Quickly, quickly, before the curse sends something else," he muttered, hurrying over and using a rock to help dig.

An uneasy feeling settled in the pit of Clara's stomach, joining the other negative emotions that roiled there. Saana and her grandfather had mentioned a curse too. The natives believed that the valley was protected by some supernatural force, and after all they'd encountered in the jungle, she couldn't blame them. She clasped her amulet in one hand, seeking comfort. Desmond had said he was impressed by her faith. She wasn't sure it was anything special. She'd come on this journey more to keep from feeling useless than out of faith. She had doubted in the bog. And even now she wondered if maybe the natives were right and there really was a curse. Tears dripped down her cheeks mingling with the rain water. It was her fault that Marta had come in the first place. Didn't that also make her responsible for Marta's death?

Beth Ann touched her elbow, and Clara started.

"We're going to say a few words, do you want to come?" Beth Ann's eyes were puffy and the tip of her nose was red, but she seemed more calm than she had been when Clara left.

Clara followed her to a spot on the other side of the tree, where the others stood in a circle around a shallow grave. The men were splattered with mud, and the edges of the grave were already sliding in.

"Let's make this quick," Johnny said gruffly. Desmond nodded to Frederick, who stepped forward.

"Marta was a valuable addition to this expedition. We don't have the time or resources to give her a proper burial, but we can at least recite a prayer to dedicate her place of rest. Before I do, does anyone want to say anything?"

"Marta wasn't always the easiest to get along with," Charles said, tossing a handful of dirt on the grave, "but she took care of those around her, and she always said what she meant. I'll miss that."

"She looked after my friend when he was hurt. If he was still here with us, he'd have said he was grateful." Gerrault stepped forward and threw some dirt down as well.

"She didn't want to come," Clara whispered, "But she did anyway. I don't know if it was to help her sister or because she was trying to do what she thought was right, but she gave up her own desires in order to help others. I wish I'd known her better."

Beth Ann put a hand on her arm, tears flowing freely down her face. Her voice, though shaky at first, grew stronger as she went. "She struggled with her faith, as we all do sometimes. She often felt unloved, unneeded, and forgotten. But this expedition gave her purpose. It gave her a sense of community she didn't feel back home. She told me—" Her voice broke, and she blinked back the tears as she continued. "She told me a few days ago that until now she'd never felt like the Land of Origin was a real place, at least not a place she'd ever see. But seeing the faith of this group, seeing the sacrifices you all were willing to make... it bolstered her. Seeing your belief gave her back her own."

She threw in a handful of dirt, then nodded to Frederick.

"All things begin, and all things end," he said, reciting the words Clara had heard her father say at funerals. She repeated them after him in a murmur, along with the other Seekers. "Your journey here is done, your path has turned back to the place where it all began. May the Divine One bless you with rest, and those you have left behind with the strength to go on. Amen."

Clara looked around at the faces of the sailors. Some looked uncomfortable with the ritual, but most looked contemplative, reverent. When the final "amen" was spoken, the men got to work filling in the grave. Beth Ann turned away, arms wrapped around herself as though she could somehow hold in the pain of loss.

Their group was quiet as they made their way through the damp undergrowth toward the final campground detailed in the journal. Clara pondered Beth Ann's words as they walked, recognizing that Marta must've been referring, at least in part, to her. And she was struck with a realization so simple, she marveled that she hadn't seen it before: in all her moments of doubt in herself, her fears of failure, and her struggle over whether to hide her beliefs from others, she had never once doubted the beliefs themselves. The Land of Origin existed. It might not be the valley her great-grandfather had found, but it was out there somewhere. A place for her people, prepared for them by a Divine being who loved them and wanted to guide them home.

Tears sprang to her eyes, and Clara reached a hand up to grasp her amulet. *Thank you,* she thought, closing her eyes for the briefest of moments. She'd been wrong. It wasn't that she lacked faith, but that her faith was so ingrained in who she was that at times she couldn't see it.

That thought sent a flood of warmth through her, and she could feel herself standing a little straighter as she walked.

CHAPTER 26

Dead Ends

They made camp a little before dark, the group working together with a degree of civility Clara hadn't seen from them before. While Vim's death had frightened and divided them, somehow Marta's had done the opposite.

Clara helped Saanji gather food while the others made the best fire they could from the wet kindling. By the time she was ready to eat, she discovered that Beth Ann had already gone to bed, and Desmond was deep in conversation with Frederick. Since she wasn't ready to talk to Levi yet, and he was sitting with a large group of the others, that left her essentially by herself on the other side of the fire.

Clara watched him for a moment, noting the stains and wrinkles on his once perfectly-pressed clothing, and feeling a surge of guilt for how much she'd put him through. She also had to acknowledge what it said about his feelings for her, that he was willing to go through such an uncomfortable experience to be with her. He pulled at the edge of his sleeve, almost subconsciously trying to straighten it, and she smiled, a sudden rush of fondness for the scribe flowing through her. Immediately on its tail came a wave of remorse. She was fond of Levi. She enjoyed working with him. But she did not love him.

She looked away swiftly, afraid he'd see her looking and presume too much from her gaze. Her belly grumbled, but suddenly she couldn't eat. She got up and walked to her shelter, handing her leftovers to Saanji, who perched on a log at the edge of the firelight. With only Beth Ann inside, it felt empty.

Clara curled up on her pile of fronds and tried to sleep. She'd had an emotional day, and she wanted to approach the conversation with Levi feeling well-rested and in full control of her faculties.

Sleep eluded her.

She turned toward the wall, then shifted back, staring at Beth Ann's curled form just a few feet away. Beth Ann, who'd left things unresolved with her sister, and now would never be able to tell her how she really felt. It had only taken an instant for the rain to come, Marta to fall... Who knew what tomorrow would bring, or if she'd have a chance to talk to Levi before they got underway?

Clara sat up, groaning to herself and shaking her head. There was no use waiting. She took a deep breath and went back out into the darkness. The fire was dying down, its light a soft glow that guided her steps. Most of the others had retired as well, but she was in luck, Levi was helping Desmond package up the remaining food and hang it between two trees on the far edge of camp, away from their shelters.

"Clara, I thought you'd turned in already? Is everything all right?" Desmond asked, his mouth turning up in a smile but his eyes holding concern.

"I'm fine," she said, "but I need to talk to Levi... do you mind?"

"We were just finishing up anyway."

Levi handed Desmond the rope and walked to the

other side of the clearing with her. She gripped her skirts with both hands, not sure how to start. Was Desmond watching them?

"Have you... thought about things?" Levi asked, standing stiffly. Clara nodded, looking up at him.

"What happened to Marta was so sudden and it made me realize..."

Levi's eyes brightened and Clara's dropped to her feet. He tilted his head trying to recapture her gaze. Clara swallowed hard before looking up at him again, his countenance more questioning now, but still full of hope. She took a deep breath.

"It made me realize that I didn't want to leave things unresolved with you." Her words started to come out in a rush. "You told me that this journey has made you want to change and be a better man. I wholeheartedly believe you can do that. I've seen what you've willingly endured on this expedition and I know the Levi I met on that ship would be proud of the man standing in front of me now. I know I am."

"Thank you," Levi whispered, a shy smile gracing his lips.

"But..."

Levi drew in a sharp breath as if he was bracing himself for the sting of a cold cloth on an open wound. Clara looked past him into the darkness, afraid to see the hurt she knew her words would cause.

"Who I am... and who you are becoming... Those people aren't meant to be together." She forced herself to look back at him, steeling herself for his reaction.

Levi's brow furrowed and he searched Clara's face. "I don't understand. I'm willing to be whoever you want me to be."

"I know you are." Clara's voice broke. "That's the problem. You told me our life together could look however I wanted it to look, but I don't think you would be happy with the life I envision."

"I'm sure I could manage."

"Of course you could." Clara smiled sadly and took Levi's hands in hers. "I don't want you to have to settle for a life you don't want. I know what it's like to spend your days feeling trapped in someone else's idea of what your life should look like. You need to be free to discover who you want to be, not who someone else wants you to be."

Levi took a step closer to her. "What if who I want to be, is yours?"

Clara felt his even breathing against her cheek and the warmth of his hands in hers. She closed her eyes for a moment, strengthening her resolve. She wished she didn't have to see this conversation through to the end, to spell things out so resolutely, and hoped above all else this wouldn't end the friendship they shared.

"There's something else too…"

"Your faith."

Clara nodded.

"I don't have anything against it—"

"I know. And it's okay that you don't believe the same things I do, but it's not enough that you're just okay with me having beliefs. I need someone who is willing to stand up for me and bolster my faith when needed, not cast doubt on it."

Clara finally let herself meet his gaze, watching sadness overtake his features.

Levi nodded once. "I don't know if I can do that…" he trailed off, his eyes flicking to the other side of the clearing. He sighed, seeming to come to a decision. "But I know someone who can." He squeezed Clara's hand a little tighter. "I've known Desmond our whole adult lives and I've rarely seen him worried, and I have never, not once, seen him scared. Until he thought he might lose you."

"You don't have to—"

"Yes, I do. I didn't run after you, I didn't stand up for

you, and I may well regret those decisions for the rest of my life. I don't want that for you. You said you didn't want to leave things unresolved. If you feel for Desmond the way I suspect he feels for you... the way I feel for you... don't hold back."

Clara let out a shaky breath. "Thank you."

"You're welcome." Levi gently pressed his lips to Clara's forehead before walking away.

When Clara finally turned toward the camp, expecting to see Desmond at the edge of the clearing, he was gone. All that was left was the dim flicker of the dying firelight.

The next morning an air of excitement permeated the camp. Despite their physical and emotional exhaustion, the promise of finding the last camp and being that much closer to their goal was an intoxicating elixir that lent energy to every movement and put a spring in their steps. Despite missing her chance to talk to Desmond alone, Clara felt lighter than she had in days—weeks really. Having settled things with Levi left her with a future full of unending possibilities, and though that meant there was a lot of uncertainty as well, it filled her with hope.

They set off into the jungle and made good time through the undergrowth, their excitement propelling them forward at a faster pace than they'd gone in days prior. Clara walked up front with the hermit this time, wanting to be absolutely certain of their direction. Desmond lagged a few paces behind the rest of the group, seeming immune to the eagerness that had infected the rest of them.

The jungle around them grew denser again, and Clara had to scramble to keep up with Saanji's deft navigation of the trees, bushes, and rocks that crowded their way. She had just fought her way free of a tangling vine and emerged from around a tree trunk so wide it could have fit their entire group inside it, when she stumbled to a halt.

Saanji stood on the edge of a steep embankment, hands loose at his sides, eyes wide with despair.

"Did we go the wrong way?" Clara asked, as the rest of the group rounded the trunk and joined them. She went as close to the edge as she dared, the soft ground beneath her feet shifting more than it ought to. Down below where there should have been trees and underbrush, there was only dark, barren earth.

"Mudslide," Gerrault said matter-of-factly, shaking his head. "Must've happened during the rain yesterday. The whole side of the hill just collapsed."

Saanji muttered under his breath, then scrambled up a tree and hung out over the ravine, presumably searching for a way around or over. He made his way down, much slower than usual, and Clara's heart sank. She let her pack slip off her back and hit the ground with a thud, suddenly too weary to carry the added weight.

"Anything?" she asked, when he rejoined her near the edge. "Did you at least see the camp? Even if we have to take more time going around..." she trailed off as Saanji shook his head, scowling.

"Gone. Gone. Gone! Gone! Gone!" With each word he became more agitated, stomping in a circle and pulling at his hair.

"Whoa! Easy now!" Desmond put one hand on the old man's chest to stop him and rested the other on his shoulder. "The way to the camp may be gone, but if we can —"

"Here!" Saanji shrieked, grabbing Desmond's arm and pointing it down at the edge of the embankment. "Here here here! Gone gone gone!"

Clara walked over to him, trying to catch his eyes, but the old man was shaking his head and twitching as though he couldn't hold still with so much frustration inside him.

"Okay, so the camp is gone," she said gently, "but we can still get to the Land of Origin, we just need your help going around, we can—"

"No!" Saanji stilled for a moment, glaring at her, eyes wild. Then he ducked his head and began to pace in small circles again, muttering, "Cursed, it's cursed. Can't find them, never find them, won't leave, can't leave, cursed, it's cursed..."

Clara stared at him, despair welling up inside her, consuming the hope and anticipation from earlier in the day. They would never be able to find their way safely around the mudslide without Saanji. And without the precise location of the last camp to start from, how would they locate the direction her grandfather had gone? He'd been following hiliblooms, counting the different colors. She'd been banking on finding the flowers near the campground and doing as he'd done, then finding the tallest tree in the area to look south.

Without the camp, they couldn't do that, without the camp...

"No," Clara set her jaw and forced away the despair. She stared over the ravine. "This can't be the end. We can find a way around, or down—"

"Clara." Desmond's voice was gentle, but firm. She rounded on him, hearing all the things he was going to tell her just from his tone.

"What?" she snapped, "We came this far, we can't just—"

"Without Saanji we could get lost trying to go around, and we don't have the equipment to go down. Maybe we can come back again—"

"Come back?" Clara cried, "While more of my people are imprisoned, or worse? Come back so more people can die on our way out and back through, so we can get to this same spot only to discover it's overrun with panthers, or—or giant spiders, or some other cursed thing that the jungle wants to throw at us until we give up and have to leave again only to find out that while we took our time, my people died of starvation trying to make their way through countries where they aren't welcome because no one believes this place exists!"

"It won't do your people any good if we break our necks trying to climb down unsteady ground!" Desmond raised his voice to match hers. The others stayed back, quiet. "We need to think rationally—"

"Think rationally? I am thinking rationally. After all we went through to get here, giving up would be the irrational thing to do!" Clara turned to the others, hoping they would back her up. "We came here to find the Land of Origin, do you really want to leave before—"

"It's not worth your life!" Desmond grabbed her arm and yanked her around to face him.

"Not worth my life?" Clara said, her voice deathly cold, "Maybe it's not worth it to you, all you have on the line is money."

Desmond let her go, looking like she had struck him, but she kept going, stabbing her finger at him for emphasis.

"You don't care if we actually make it to the Land of Origin, you've already found enough to make this expedition profitable. But me? This is my people's future, our ability to live without being stifled by laws that tell us we can't believe the things we know to be true! It's not worth it to you, but it's everything to me."

Clara knew she was being unfair, but she could feel their goal slipping away again—she couldn't let their hard work and sacrifices to get here be for nothing. Gripped in equal parts by terror and determination, she stomped to the edge of the ravine and peered over, looking for a way down.

The ground shifted. Clara turned back as Desmond

lunged to grab her, and the dirt dropped away from beneath her feet.

CHAPTER 27

Falling

Dirt stung Clara's eyes and filled her nose and mouth. Rocks and roots bruised her shoulders, her back, her legs, as she tumbled down the steep incline. She fell for what seemed an eternity, desperately trying to grab onto something, anything to stop herself. But the ground was falling with her, and anything she grabbed just came free in her hands.

Then, blessedly, she stopped.

Clara coughed, spitting out the bitter soil, and groaned. She tried to move, but every part of her ached. All she could see was the dust that filled the air.

"Clara!" Frederick's voice was faint, somewhere far above her. She tried to call back, but her throat was raw. She didn't remember screaming, but her body seemed to.

A groan came from somewhere to her right, and her heart skipped a beat. *Desmond... He tried to catch me!*

She scrambled across the loose dirt and made her way toward the faint sound, tripping over something soft and skinning her palms.

"Ow!"

"Desmond!" Clara turned and felt around, finding

Desmond's arm. She helped him sit up, a torrent of loose dirt coming off his shoulders and chest. She waved the dust away from in front of her face, and did a cursory check to see if he was hurt. His eye was still healing from its encounter with Gerrault's fist, but other than that and a few minor scrapes, he seemed fine.

"I'll live," he said, waving her away and wincing as he stood and brushed off more dirt. He stopped suddenly. "You're bleeding!"

Desmond lightly touched the back of her head, and Clara sucked in a pained breath. His fingers came back covered in blood. "We'll have to clean it somewhere else, the dust in the air is just going to get in my canteen if I open it here."

"What about the others?" Clara looked up in the direction of the ridge, straining to hear if they were still shouting. "Shouldn't we try to communicate with them, let them know we're alive?"

"How? We can't climb up the bank, it'll just collapse again. We can't throw anything that far, and we can barely hear them, so I doubt they'd be able to hear us. Our best bet is to get out of this dust cloud and try to signal them from somewhere higher up."

Desmond's tone was dull, his eyes focused past her to the other side of the ravine. Clara bit her lip. He was right to be angry with her. She never should have yelled at him like that, accusing him of not caring.

She felt a lump form in her throat. He deserved an apology, but she couldn't find the words. They were separated from the others, without any of their supplies except Desmond's canteen, which somehow had stayed looped across his chest as he fell. If this part of the jungle was anything like the rest of it, they were in very real danger on their own, and it was all her fault.

"Okay," she said, holding back tears, "which should we go?"

Desmond stumbled across the uneven piles of dirt and rock, boots squelching when they hit a particularly wet bit of ground. It wasn't long before they heard the rushing of water, and Clara hurried toward the sound.

A narrow river, swollen from the rain, blocked their path forward, winding its way to the east. Clara sighed, sinking down on the rocky shoreline and staring at the water. She barely recognized her reflection. Besides being covered in dirt, her face was slimmer, any trace of childhood roundness gone. She had expected as much after weeks of hardship, but what surprised her was the feeling that she was looking at someone who possessed more depth and wisdom than before.

Desmond walked past her and pulled a crumpled and filthy handkerchief from his pocket, then rinsed it in the river before coming over and crouching next to her.

"May I?" he said, looking at the back of her head. She nodded and turned so he could see her injury better. He squeezed some of the water onto her hair and gently dabbed the cloth on the area. Clara winced, biting her lip.

Desmond worked silently, an invisible barrier thickening the air between them, despite their proximity. By the time he had rinsed the cloth a third time, she had tears in her eyes, and—mortifyingly—had to sniff to keep her nose from dripping. His dabbing stopped, and Clara sensed him stiffen behind her.

"Are you all right? Does that hurt too much?" There was genuine concern in his tone, and Clara felt even more miserable. Even though he was angry at her he was still worried about her comfort. How could she ever have thought he was selfish or only cared about profits?

She shook her head and hunched her shoulders, wrapping her arms around her knees and pulling them close to her chest.

Desmond put the rag down and sat next to her, keeping a little distance between them. The inches felt like miles to Clara, and all she wanted to do was lay her head against his arm and feel his warmth.

"I'm sorry for what I yelled at you," Clara mumbled, sniffing again and wiping tears from her eyes with her sleeve.

Desmond shifted toward her, and she peeked up at him. His eyebrows were raised in surprise, head tilted to the side. "Did you think I was still mad at you about that?"

"Aren't you?" Clara tried to interpret his tone. Was he laughing at her? She felt a flood of irritation replace the guilt. Couldn't he just accept her apology and be done with it?

He reached out a hand to her arm and she jerked away, scrambling to her feet and then swaying a bit from the sudden change.

"Careful!" Desmond said, jumping up and putting a hand on her back to steady her. "You hit your head pretty hard, you should sit and rest."

"We need to find a way back to the others," Clara said, "They'll be worried."

Desmond's hand dropped, and he stood there for a moment before bending to pick up his handkerchief. He turned the wadded ball over and over in his hands a few times, and then looked up at her.

"Do you miss him that much already?"

"What?" Clara struggled to adjust to the rapid change in topic. "Miss who? My father? Of course I—"

"No, Levi." Desmond gave her a strange look.

Clara raised an eyebrow. "It's been like, an hour, maybe two. Why would I miss him already?"

"Some couples—" He stopped abruptly and shook his head. "Not my place. I'm sorry."

He turned and started back the way they'd come, then stopped and turned to face her again. "I told myself I'd stay out of it, if Levi makes you happy then who am I to get in your way? He's a good man and as his friend I should be happy for him, but Clara, I can't just sit back and not—"

"Levi and I aren't a couple."

"—tell you how I feel. Clara you—huh?" Desmond looked like he'd been the one to hit his head.

Then the rest of his words began to sink in. Clara's heart sped up, and she felt a glimmer of hope work its way to the surface.

"Levi and I aren't a couple," she repeated, "I turned him down."

"Oh," Desmond just stood there for a moment, then he walked back toward her and took her hand, looking directly into her eyes for the first time since they'd fallen.

She sucked in a breath, the touch of his hand sending tingles up her arm and warmth flooding through her body.

"Clara, from the first moment I saw you I knew there was something special about you—"

"As I remember you said something condescending and—"

Desmond cupped her cheek with his hand and ran his thumb gently over her lips, silencing her. His eyes crinkled, and Clara's mouth twitched into a grin.

Desmond's gaze suddenly turned serious. She looked up at him, heart hammering in her chest, eyes flicking down to look at his lips and then back up to his warm, brown eyes.

"You are everything Clara. You're determined, and intelligent, and incessantly optimistic... You care deeply for people you barely know, and make me want to be a better man... I don't want this to be the end of our time together, regardless of whether we can find the Land of Origin or not."

"You drive me crazy sometimes, you know," she said, smiling, "but you also encourage me to do the things no one else thinks I can, and you're there to help pull me back when I go too far. I think you bring out the best in me too, and I don't want this to end either."

"Would you consider staying then? With me. On the ship I mean." He stumbled over the words, sounding like a schoolboy trying to explain why he'd broken a rule. "You could keep helping as a scribe and travel the world with me and help with my research and... we could be together."

A thrill jolted through Clara, starting in her chest and spreading outward, but she wasn't sure how to respond. Being with him, knowing he cared for her, felt better than anything. And she loved the thought of traveling, seeing new places. Making a difference. But what of her people? If they didn't find the Land of Origin, she couldn't just abandon the other Seekers to whatever fate the government decided for them.

"I know it's a lot, and there are things to consider," Desmond said, "But think about it, please?"

Clara nodded, then pulled back and searched his eyes for understanding. "Being with you—" something colorful over his shoulder caught her attention, "hiliblooms!"

"What?" Desmond tried to catch her hand as she darted away to examine the flower. Delicate, teardrop-shaped petals of varying sizes surrounded a fuzzy brown center, drooping asymmetrically. They were exactly like the drawings in her great-grandfather's journal.

"These are hiliblooms!" Clara looked up at Desmond. "My great-grandfather was following them when he saw the valley!"

Clara looked around and saw more of the flowers upriver.

"Come on!" She grabbed Desmond's hand and pulled him along to the next patch.

They followed the trail of flowers until they saw another patch across the river, then they followed the river's edge till they found a shallow place to cross and continued following the trail of flowers uphill.

"Did your grandfather actually follow these flowers this far from the camp?" Desmond gasped, bending to put his hands on his knees as he tried to catch his breath after a particularly steep part of the hill.

"He got far enough away to be lost," Clara replied, breathless as well. She looked around. "He had to climb a tree to find his way back, that's the only reason he even saw the valley..." Her eyes lit on a nearby tree, one of the massive ones with a trunk ten feet wide. Desmond smiled and shook his head, walking over to give her a leg up. She stepped on his bent leg and then hauled herself up using a vine that twisted its way up the wide trunk.

Once he had made sure she was stable, Desmond selected a spot nearby and pulled himself into the tree as well. They climbed together, every once in a while Clara pointed out possible routes when Desmond got stuck, and Desmond reached down to give her a hand up when the next handhold was too high for her. Eventually they found a wide branch thick enough to support them both, and stood on it near the trunk, peering between the branches to see the jungle around them.

The sight was breathtaking. Trees spread out in every direction beneath them, some with vine-covered branches, others with fronds like the ones they used for their shelters. Few were as tall as this one, and Clara could clearly see the path the river cut through the mountains, which were much nearer than she'd expected. There, in the gap the water created, she could see a lush green valley carpeted with flowers. Trees lined the river as it flowed from a waterfall high on the other side. It was exactly as the journal described.

"It's beautiful," Desmond said, taking her hand. She nodded, still staring, tears pricking her eyes. She clasped her compass in her fist and said a silent prayer of thanks.

The Land of Origin. The place her ancestors had come from, the place her people were destined to return to.

Home... for them. But not for her. Not yet.

She turned and flung her arms around Desmond,

who grabbed a trailing vine to steady himself and wrapped his other arm around her.

"Careful, we're up really high," he murmured into her ear, his breath tickling her neck.

"Yes," Clara said breathlessly. "Yes, I will go with you. After we get my people settled, that is. If you'll help me bring them here."

Desmond grinned and lifted her with one arm, spinning them until her back was safely against the trunk. He pressed his lips to hers, his arm still wrapped around her, his hand a gentle pressure on the small of her back. The other still gripped the vine, stabilizing them. She melted into him, arms tightening around his neck. After a long moment, he pulled back, and she looked up at him, smiling.

"Of course I'll help you." He frowned suddenly, brow furrowing. "Bringing them through the jungle will be dangerous. The children, the elderly..."

"I've been thinking about that," Clara said, "ever since we crossed the river." She turned to look the opposite direction from the valley, one hand on the trunk for balance. "Rivers all flow to the sea eventually. Don't they?"

"They do." Desmond took her free hand and followed her gaze.

"Then can't we sail along the shoreline till we find the river, and follow it up?"

"If there's not a reef, or with a shallow enough draft...maybe. How do you plan on getting upriver?"

"Sailing?" Clara looked over at him, and he shook his head, an amused smile playing on his lips.

"Rowing against the current for that long would be near impossible, even in the smaller boat we'd need for navigating the rocks and shallows of the river."

"Well, we'll figure it out...look!" She pointed back the way they'd come. A little group of people was coming up the hill beneath them.

They scrambled down the tree as fast as they dared,

jumping down just as Frederick crested the hill.

"How'd you find us?" Clara asked, flinging her arms around her cousin. Frederick grinned and extricated himself from her embrace, then pointed to a picture of a hilibloom in the journal. "I knew you'd keep looking, even after nearly falling to your death. So I just followed the flowers, like I knew you would." He handed her the book, and Clara took it, cradling the precious artifact to her chest protectively. It felt good to have it back.

"I meant how did you get down the mudslide?" Clara crinkled her nose at him.

Frederick shrugged. "If you could roll down a slope, we figured we could too." He indicated his mud-streaked clothes, and Clara could see that this was in fact what they must've done. Even Levi, though he was rubbing at the stains and still trying to brush dirt from his hair.

"And Saanji?" she asked, looking around for the hermit.

Frederick's smile faded. "He came down with us... but he stayed at the base of the hill, digging through the mud. He was muttering something about his father... we eventually gave up trying to talk sense into him and came to find you."

Desmond squeezed her hand, and she rested her head against his arm, thankful for the comfort. Out of the corner of her eye she saw Levi and Desmond exchange a brief nod. Levi's expression was guarded, but not hostile or devastated. She exhaled a sigh of relief.

"Well, what now? Do we continue on or try to head back?" one of the sailors asked. Clara realized with a start that she hadn't told them yet.

"We found it Frederick, the Land of Origin! It's just upriver!"

The Seekers stared at her in surprise, then their weary faces suddenly brightened. Charles clapped Old Johnny on the back and broke out in a huge grin. Beth Ann

251

looked like she might cry from relief.

Levi looked at Desmond, who nodded once and motioned to the tree. "Climb up and have a look if you want."

"We'll take your word for it," Levi said, looking up at the height of the branches.

"Come on," Clara said, taking Desmond's hand.

The little group followed the river, camping when dark set in before they made it to the valley. This side of the jungle didn't seem bent on killing them like the other had, though they continued to use the precautions Saanji had taught them.

When they reached the pass early the next day, after a harrowing uphill hike, Clara stood with Frederick looking out at the green pastures and distant, massive waterfall that poured from between a crack in the mountains opposite them.

"Do you really think this is their mythical paradise?" Gerrault asked Desmond behind them, his voice low but still easily overheard.

"Does it matter?" Desmond replied, "It's a place for their people to live, outside of the oppression of any government, and beyond the reach of most who would try to harm them. It's fertile, it's beautiful, and if I'm not mistaken, it's free for the taking. If that's not a paradise, I don't know what is."

Clara smiled. Desmond might not share her beliefs, but he'd shown time and again that he was willing to defend them.

"Go ahead," she told Frederick, "I'll meet you on the valley floor."

Frederick nodded and followed the rest of the Seekers down the steep, ancient-looking path that wound down the side of the mountain.

Clara waited for the other sailors to pass her, then greeted Desmond with a smile and took his hand. "Thank you," she said, "for believing in me when it would've been easier not to."

Desmond cocked an eyebrow. "Easier? Clara Bowman you make it downright difficult to do anything but believe in you. Haven't I told you already that you're stubborn, brilliant, and infernally optimistic?"

Clara fixed him with a playful glare. "It's 'infernally' now is it? I believe last time you used the word 'incessantly'... they're not exactly the same."

Desmond shrugged, leaning toward her. "Close enough," he murmured against her ear, then kissed her gently on the mouth before she could come up with a retort. He grinned and stepped quickly out of reach when she tried to smack his arm teasingly, heading down the path.

Clara looked back one more time, her eyes following the curve of the river and wondering if the glint she saw as it disappeared into the distance was the ocean. She tilted her head back, closing her eyes to soak in the sun's warmth, and a cool breeze brushed her face. She thought it carried with it the faint tang of salt.

"Are you coming?" Desmond's familiar, melodic voice floated back up the path.

Smiling, Clara opened her eyes and turned to face her future.

Epilogue

Port of Orescal, Estanya, Day 1

It's been a year since I've opened the cover of this journal and read its contents, and even longer since I've made an entry. I think I felt like if I wrote more, if I finally documented what's happened since we reached the valley a year and a half ago, I'd be closing a chapter of my life that I thought I'd never want to leave (it was my first real adventure, after all!). But I realize now that not only does it deserve to be written, but it needs to be. If not for my own sake, then for the sake of my people and our posterity.

Once we finally reached the Land of Origin, we spent hours swimming in the crystal clear water and laying in the soft, tall grasses. We gathered every variety of fruit, root, vegetable, and herb we could find, but resolved not to eat anything we couldn't easily identify using grandfather's journal. The afternoon sun started sinking lower and lower in the sky, and with it our enthusiasm began to cool. We had been through enough to know that nightfall could bring new challenges that we were likely unprepared for.

There were too many questions and too few answers. We needed Saanji, especially if Desmond, Levi, Frederick and I were going to make it back through the jungle with the other sailors so we could cross the ocean once more to find everyone we'd left behind. It was decided that we would hunker down beneath the wide canopy of a tree until morning, keeping vigilant watch until it was safe to go back to the ravine.

When we found Saanji the next day, he was knee deep in mud, frantically shoveling it over his shoulder with his bare hands. He looked smaller and weaker than I'd ever seen him and my heart broke for him. He had taken us all that way, saved us from starvation, thirst, and certain death (numerous times) only to be just out of reach of his own goal.

We could only assume he was searching for the last camp, though we still didn't know why. It wasn't until Frederick, Desmond, and the other men (even Levi) rolled up their sleeves and started digging too, that Saanji muttered enough for us to put everything together.

I knew from my great-grandfather's journal that his company had all perished from disease... all except him, their guide, and Saanji. What we failed to put together was that Saanji was still mourning the loss of his father who had died along with the rest of the company at the last camp. All those years, Saanji had been living on the outskirts of the jungle, unable to put his father to rest.

Once we knew, a party was arranged to help excavate the campsite and recover the remains of the first expedition and give them all a proper burial (an undertaking that ultimately took months, and was completed long after Desmond and I left). To my surprise, Levi volunteered to spearhead the excavation project and help settle the valley. He claimed there was no way he was going back through that jungle again so soon, this side of the river seemed safe enough. (He also told Desmond that he wanted to prove to himself that he was made for more than keeping tidy notations on perfectly bound pages, but I didn't find that out till later.)

Once the arrangements were made and we had ferried the remainder of our original expedition from the village to the valley (I was right, the river did join the sea, and the hike along its banks was much safer than the trek through the jungle) the crew set sail. It was risky business, sailing back to that part of the world, with Draunland divided in civil war and Aldonia persecuting Seekers.

At our first chance to restock, we learned that shortly after the expedition set sail, the Aldonian government closed all borders to neighboring countries, barring Separatists from leaving the country. At first, my parents believed this to be a blessing in disguise, considering Draunland fell into civil war shortly after. They were determined to keep their heads down, follow the law, and make it through until the expedition returned with news of the Land of Origin.

But it didn't seem to matter how quiet they made themselves. Seekers began disappearing from their homes and Sunday meetings were disbanded after an attack on the church building. Markets stopped accepting their goods for trade and sale. Soon they were isolated with no one to rely on but themselves, and winter was already upon them.

I don't have space to describe in detail how we snuck them out of the country, that will have to be a story for another time. But through the kindness of a great many people, and Frederick's ingenuity, we were able to evacuate my family and most of the others, first to Estanya, where they blended in amongst the workers in the Andreyas' herb fields, and later in a single voyage to the valley.

Upon our return we found things much changed. Levi had designed a clever pulley system utilizing the trees along the riverbank, so when we reached the mouth of the river, Saanji was waiting there for us with a raft attached to ropes and a crank he could use to pull us upriver. It was much faster and allowed us to move many more supplies and people at once.

The settlement, which they had named Laaikka or "place of refuge" in the local dialect, was thriving. It was small, but they'd constructed sturdy homes and developed systems for gathering food, rules for the community, and a way to air grievances. Beth Ann had trained one of the abnormally large local insects and had begun the process of creating a domesticated herd of the creatures (I shall not dwell on them here, the things give me nightmares!) Levi, of course, had a list of supplies for us to obtain for them, so they could improve upon what they'd already built.

Desmond's family has been fully supportive of our work assisting the settlement. Of course it helped that the samples he sent them of the various plants we gathered have apparently yielded incredible results. They've been effective for curing a number of ailments and seem likely to turn a decent profit. As for Desmond and I, so much of our time and energies have been spent helping the settlement that we have not yet had a chance to visit Estanya together, until now. As we draw closer, Desmond has been hinting at a surprise of some kind. He had a long, private conversation with my father before we left Laaikka, and I'm dearly hoping this means he intends to ask me to marry him already, so he can present me to his parents as more than just his scribe.

This last year and a half has shown me he is so much more than the man I believed he was when we first met in the marketplace so long ago. Even if he does not intend to propose just yet, I'm excited to see the place he calls home and learn more about his childhood—I'm sure he was a mischievous little boy! This time with him has been everything I hoped it would be. I look forward to a future where we can enjoy the freedom of pursuing our dreams together.

Clara Bowman

Acknowledgements

Writing a book is hard. Publishing it is even harder. There are bumps and roadblocks and so many obstacles along the way—which is why it's wonderful to have a teammate! We (Makayla and Trenna) wrote and published this book together, and we couldn't have done it without each other or without the help of a lot of other people. With that in mind, we'd like to thank the following for their help bringing this book to publication:

Cadence McMullin and Elizabeth Nielson, for beta reading with all the enthusiasm and passion we could have hoped for, even if things didn't always turn out how they might have wanted.

Our other beta readers: Chris and Sylvia Brown, Kayli Gill, and Braden Mace. We appreciate the time and effort you took to read our story in its less than perfect form, and to give us your opinions on it. Violet Nielson for her unending excitement and interest in all things involving our writing endeavors.

Katrina Conrad for her entertaining reactions while beta reading, and for bringing Clara's world to life through her beautiful stickers and the gorgeous cover art (see more of her work on instagram as @artistfae). Calista Foley

(@artby_cali_) for the amazing maps in the front of this book, and for the stunning artwork used in our social media posts. Jane Nielson for her fantastic and unique sketches of Clara, also used in our social media posts.

Last, but definitely not least—our families (and extended families) for being supportive of our writing and being our cheerleaders every step of the way.

Makayla Nielson
Trenna McMullin
November 2025

About the Authors

Makayla Nielson

Makayla Nielson is a fantasy, science-fiction, and short story writer. In addition to The Voyage of Clara Bowman, she has written short stories for Manawaker Studio's Flash Fiction Podcast, Twisted Tales, Tall Tale TV, Flash Fiction Magazine, Balloons Lit. Journal, Inkpot Literary Magazine, Stance: Studies on the Family, and Collective Tales Publishing.

Keep an eye out for her dystopian novel, Chimera's Blood, co-authored with Alexandra Ely, at the beginning of 2026 with Jumpmaster Press.

Makayla was raised in Normal, Illinois and currently resides in Lehi, Utah with her husband and three (almost four!) children. She earned a bachelor's degree from Brigham Young University with a major in Family Studies emphasizing Human Development and a minor in Gerontology. She also earned a master's degree in Gerontology from the University of Utah.

Find her at: makaylanielson.com ; @authormakaylanielson

Trenna McMullin

Trenna McMullin was raised in the beautiful Flathead Valley of Montana and spent her childhood enjoying the outdoors near Glacier National Park, where the stunning vistas and ancient trees fed her imagination. She graduated from BYU-Idaho with a bachelor's degree in University Studies, including a minor in Elementary Education and clusters in European History and French Language. After moving around the Pacific Northwest she has settled back home in Montana with her husband and seven children, where she bakes, reads, and writes as often as possible.

Find her at: trennamcmullin.com or @trennamcmullin on socials

Together, Trenna and Makayla strive to create stories featuring strong-willed young women who grow and change in positive ways.

Coming Soon

Look for "The Proving of Levi Perez"
coming Fall 2026